"What's the problem, Perry?" asked Paul Drake.

Perry Mason said, "I don't know, Paul. All I have is the sound of a woman's voice. She's in a jam. She's a woman who wouldn't get stampeded easily, but she's half-hysterical now."

"Oh-oh," Drake said. "One of those things where everything went black, then she felt something jerking in her hand and heard loud banging noises. She looked down and found she was holding a gun, and there was John lying on the floor. She has no idea how he got there. She ran to him and said, 'John, John, speak to me. Oh, John, speak to me.' So then she calls her lawyer."

"Don't kid about it," Mason said. "You may be a lot nearer the truth than you know."

THE CASE OF THE NERVOUS ACCOMPLICE
was originally published by
William Morrow and Company, Inc.

ERLE STANLEY

GARDNER

THE CASE OF THE
NERVOUS ACCOMPLICE

PUBLISHED BY POCKET BOOKS NEW YORK

THE CASE OF THE NERVOUS ACCOMPLICE

William Morrow edition published 1955

POCKET BOOK edition published July, 1958

6th printing .... June, 1974

L

This POCKET BOOK edition includes every word contained in the original, higher-priced edition. It is printed from brand-new plates made from completely reset, clear, easy-to-read type. POCKET BOOK editions are published by POCKET BOOKS, a division of Simon & Schuster, Inc., 630 Fifth Avenue, New York, N.Y. 10020. Trademarks registered in the United States and other countries.

FOREWORD

DR. JOSEPH W. SPELMAN, THE STATE PATHOLOGIST OF Vermont and an associate professor in pathology at the University of Vermont, is a shrewd, cautious, level-headed investigator. He is a member of a group which, unfortunately, is all too small, a group made up of men who by training, aptitude and temperament are qualified to investigate homicides in a scientific manner, determining the cause and the time of death. What these men can discover by examining a dead body is startling to those who haven't realized the strides made by science in the field of forensic medicine.

Dr. Spelman, like Dr. Richard Ford, head of the Harvard School of Legal Medicine and medical examiner in Boston, has spent a great deal of time preparing a collection of colored slides showing various aspects of deaths due to violence.

These men have amassed thousands of such slides, covering unusual gunshot wounds, the typical pattern of powder tattooing, wounds of exit and wounds of entrance, cases where murder was perpetrated under such circumstances that it appeared to be suicide, cases where suicides would almost certainly have been branded the victims of murder by less well-trained investigators.

These colored slides form a constantly increasing reference file which is of inestimable value in the detection of crime, although it may take years before prosecutors generally realize the extent to which their work can be aided by reference to such photographs.

Not only is Dr. Spelman interested in forensic pathology and in the detection of crime, but he has gone further and has devoted a lot of thought to the problem of penology, of punishment, of rehabilitation, of probation and parole.

Those who know Dr. Spelman best have high regard for his unusual abilities in correlating those legislative conflicts which inevitably arise when the modern medical-examiner system supplants the older coroner system.

The thing that particularly impresses me about Dr. Spelman, however, is his objective, intellectual perspective. It is hard to tell just what makes for a well-balanced mind. Some men who are experts in one line, whose judgment is perfectly sound in dealing with the highly technical problems with which they are familiar, are likely to have a warped perspective when dealing with problems arising in fields which are strange to them.

This is not the case with Dr. Spelman. He has an alert mind which is remarkably well balanced and he has, what I can only define for want of a better term, intellectual perspective.

A short time ago, a rather remarkable group of men gathered at my ranch in Southern California. These men collectively knew more about murder than all of the fictional detectives in history put together. They were Dr. Richard Ford of Harvard, Dr. Russell Fisher of Baltimore, Dr. Samuel Gerber of Cleveland, Dr. LeMoyne Snyder of Lansing, Michigan, and Dr. Joseph Spelman of Vermont.

We sat up until the small hours of the morning discussing some of the off-the-record facts and the behind-the-scenes backgrounds of some of the famous cases in which these men had participated. (Each one of them had, at one time or another, been connected with cases which made newspaper headlines from coast to coast.)

For some years now, I have been trying, through

these forewords and dedications, to make the reading public aware of the importance of forensic medicine and the necessity for greater public appreciation of this branch of medicine. The public should have a better understanding of what can be done by these expert forensic pathologists, who approach the detection of crime armed with well-developed powers of observation and a background of technical knowledge. Some of these men have even gone so far as to become attorneys at law after having secured their degrees as doctors of medicine. All of them have encyclopedic knowledge of the technique of crime detection.

As it happened, four out of the five men who were gathered at my ranch that night had been the subjects of forewords and dedications.

I had from time to time heard a great deal about Dr. Spelman and had followed his career with interest. What I saw of him that evening interested me even more. I was particularly impressed with his astute appraisals, his sound, sane judgment. He is a quiet man, shy to the point of diffidence, and it is necessary to look beneath the surface in order to recognize his true character. He is competent, forceful, and his thinking is always logical.

So it gives me great pleasure to dedicate this book to my friend:

JOSEPH WORCESTER SPELMAN, M.D.

—Erle Stanley Gardner

Cast of Characters

THE CASE OF THE
NERVOUS ACCOMPLICE

1

DELLA STREET, PERRY MASON'S CONFIDENTIAL SECRE-
tary, said, "We have a Mrs. Enright A. Harlan in the office who seems to be having domestic troubles."

Mason jokingly jerked his thumb toward the corridor.

"I know," Della Street said. "I told her that you didn't
handle divorce cases and she said this wasn't a divorce
case. It was simply a case of domestic difficulties."

"Not a divorce?" Mason asked.

"That's what she says."

"And not an action for separate maintenance?"

"She says not."

"Then why does she want a lawyer?"

"She said she'd have to explain that in detail. She
says she has a scheme she wants to talk to you about."

"And it's about a domestic difficulty?"

"That's right."

"Did she tell you what kind of domestic difficulty?"

"It seems her husband is cheating."

"I take it there's something unusual about this woman, Della, or you wouldn't have adopted this attitude."

"What attitude?"

"Wanting me to see her."

Della Street nodded.

"Why?"

"Perhaps I'd like to know what scheme she has in
mind. It might come in handy some day. I can tell you
one thing—she's most unusual."

"In what way?"

1

"It's hard to describe—the way she dresses, the way she carries herself, the swing of her shoulders, the tilt of her chin."

"How old?"

"Twenty-six or -seven."

"Good-looking?"

"Not what you'd call beautiful, but she has character, individuality, fire, fight, quickness of perception, and personality plus. And if that doesn't arouse your curiosity, Mr. Perry Mason, you're not human."

"That does it. Send her in," Mason said. "Let's see how to handle a cheating husband without divorce, without separate maintenance and by using a scheme which requires the advice of a lawyer to keep it within the limits of law."

Della Street nodded approvingly. "I'm glad you'll see her. As I mentioned before *I* might learn something that would stand *me* in good stead in the future."

She went to the outer office and returned in a few moments with the prospective client, who glanced swiftly around the office, in a quick appraisal.

She didn't wait for introductions but came forward, her hand extended. "Good morning, Mr. Mason. It's nice of you to see me. Where do I sit?"

Mason indicated the big, overstuffed chair reserved for clients.

"I told your secretary my troubles. I presume you know all the preliminaries. I'm Sybil Harlan—Mrs. Enright A. Harlan."

Mason nodded.

She seated herself, put her purse on the floor, crossed her legs. "My husband's stepping out on me and I want to do something about it."

"How long have you been married?" Mason asked.

"Five years. Today is my fifth wedding anniversary, if that helps."

"Is this the first time he has strayed from the fold?"

"I don't think so."

"What did you do the other times?"

"Not times. It was one time. I simply waited for him to come back home, gave him something interesting to think about, and beat the other girl's time."

"This is different?" Mason asked.

"This time it's different."

Mason said tentatively, "I don't know what you have in mind, but I don't handle divorce cases. I don't care for them."

"Neither do I."

"I believe you told my secretary you didn't want separate maintenance?"

"That's right."

"Is there any community property?"

"Lots of it. There's also quite a bit of my own separate property."

"So you don't want alimony?"

"All I want is Enny."

Mason raised his eyebrows.

"Enright," she explained. "Everybody calls him Enny."

"You think his infidelity may lead to a permanent attachment?"

"Don't make any mistake, Mr. Mason. The little minx who has her claws in him this time has them way in, and she doesn't intend to let go."

"And how does *he* feel?"

"Completely infatuated, gone, in a swoon. Within the next two or three days he's going to come to me and make a clean breast of the whole thing. He's going to tell me that he's fallen in love, passionately, violently, wildly, that he knows I'm too good a scout to stand in his way. He'll tell me he's willing to do the square thing on a property settlement, that he's perfectly willing to let me save face by going to Reno and getting a Nevada decree. He'll tell me that if I'll get my lawyer to meet with his lawyer, they can iron out the property settlement."

"Then you want me to represent you in that property settlement?" Mason asked.

"Don't be silly! I want my husband. The minute he comes to me and starts talking about property settlement, I get cast in the role of giving him financial headaches while she gets cast in the role of glamor girl. Then I'm finished. I want to head off that situation."

"Nip it in the bud?"

"Not the bud. It's blossomed."

"Then what *do* you want me to do?"

"Cut the stem."

"I take it you have some plan?" Mason said.

"I have a plan."

"What is it?"

"My husband is in the real estate business."

"How old is he?"

"About five years older than I am."

"You say he's amassed a lot of property?"

"He's a gambler, a smart operator, a quick thinker, and ingenious as the devil. You're going to have to match your wits with him, Mr. Mason, and that's going to keep even you hustling. If you aren't very, very careful, he'll outwit you and leave us holding an empty bag."

"Assuming," Mason said, "that I am willing to accept your case."

"I think you will. I think it will appeal to you."

"Just what did you have in mind?" Mason asked.

She said, "I want you to buy some stock as an investment."

"What kind of stock?"

"A real estate development company."

"And then what?"

"Then," she said, "I want you to attend the directors' meeting this afternoon and fail to co-operate."

"Co-operate with whom?"

"With anybody, with everybody. I want you to be a thorn in the flesh, a monkey wrench in the machinery.

I want you to be the nastiest, most technical, most conservative old fuddyduddy in the world."

"That part hardly fits my character," Mason said, smiling. "At least I hope it doesn't."

"I know," she said, "but you can start the ball rolling and later on you can get some lawyer to work with you. You know the type I want. One of these fellows who is afraid to make a move in any direction for fear that it may be the wrong direction. He won't move himself and he gets in a panic if anyone else tries to move."

"And what do we do after you have achieved that objective?" Mason asked.

"Then we let go."

"And just how is this going to help you?"

"Right at the moment," she said, "my husband, Enny, is completely infatuated with this little Roxy girl. Whenever he's with her he looks into her eyes and talks about sweet nothings. He's entranced by the color of her hair, the smooth contour of her skin, and he simply loves those great big soulful brown eyes. Fortunately he met Roxy through a business deal. I want that business deal to go sour. Then Roxy's selfish character will come to the fore. *She'll* be the one who is talking about money. She'll be the one who is talking about business. Every time my husband gets with her she'll hurry through the affectionate embrace in order to ask him embarrassing questions about business matters."

"How do you know the questions will be embarrassing?" Mason asked.

"That's what I'm paying you for."

"And where will all that leave you?" Mason asked.

"Then," she said, "I will become the body beautiful while Roxy will be the woman who is giving him financial headaches. I'll reverse the field on her. Whenever a man starts straying from his home and fireside, there comes a time when he's more or less equally balanced. He has a sense of obligation to his marriage, the memory of years of companionship on the one hand, and he has the thrill of infatuation and a new conquest on the other. Then the wife throws a tearful scene. She talks about having given him the best years of her life. He sees her tearful, swollen-eyed and wronged. She tries to enmesh him in legal ties. His sense of guilt puts him on the defensive. This is, of course, the very worst thing a wife could possibly do. Instead of emphasizing her feminine charms, she emphasizes his wrongdoing and his legal obligations."

"Go on," Mason said, regarding her thoughtfully.

"Then she goes to a lawyer. The lawyer talks about property settlements, about alimony. That completes the alienation. Every time the husband hears his wife's name, he associates it with financial worries, injunctions, court hearings, *alimony pendente lite,* and all of that. The other girl furnishes the fun. By that time the man wants his freedom badly enough to pay through the nose. His wife has come to signify a legal headache, impeding his true love for the 'most wonderful girl in the world' who is filled with 'sympathy and understanding.' "

"I see," Mason said.

"So," she told him, "as I said before, I want to reverse the field on this woman. Whenever he comes home to me, I'm going to furnish the loving attention, the companionship, the laughter and the play. Whenever he turns to the other girl, he's going to find himself talking about financial and legal complications. Whenever he thinks of me, the thought will be associated with soft lights and seduction. Whenever he thinks of her, the thought will be associated with liabilities and litigation."

Mason smiled. "Now that *should* prove an interesting experiment."

"Then you'll help me?"

"Yes."

"We'll have to work fast."

"How fast?"

"Terribly fast, even for you. You see, he's getting ready to come to me and face the situation, and today is our fifth wedding anniversary, although the thought hasn't as yet occurred to him."

"And you don't want him to confess his infidelties?" Mason asked.

"Of course not. A woman should never forgive a man for infidelties. She should remain in complete ignorance."

"Exactly what am I supposed to do?" Mason asked.

She said, "Just pick up that phone. Call Mr. George C. Lutts at the office of the Sylvan Glade Development Company. Give Mr. Lutts your name. Ask him what he will take for the two thousand shares of stock he has in the Sylvan Glade Development Company."

"And then?" Mason asked.

"Then," she said, "you accept his offer, whatever it is. Tell him that you will come over immediately, give him a certified check, and pick up the stock. You tell him you want to be present at the directors' meeting at one-thirty. You ask him to wait in his office until you can get there."

"That's hardly the way to buy stock," Mason said. "His first price will probably be about fifty to seventy-five per cent higher than what he would actually take."

She shook her head impatiently. "I'm not buying stock. I'm buying a husband."

2

GEORGE C. LUTTS WAS APPARENTLY A BADLY FLUSTERED individual. Not only was he curious as to why Perry Mason should be interested in the Sylvan Glade Development Company, but he was anxious to make certain that he receive the excessive price which he had quoted over the telephone. His anxiety was tempered by a very evident fear that some secret development concerning which he knew nothing was making the stock worth far more than he had dared to ask.

Mason put the certified check on Lutts's desk.

"There you are, Mr. Lutts. A check payable to George C. Lutts, dated today, duly certified, in an amount of thirty-two thousand seven hundred and fifty dollars. You note that I have written on the back of it that this check is payment in full for your two thousand shares of stock in the Sylvan Glade Development Company, that you agree to arrange for me to attend the directors' meeting this afternoon. You will there announce that you have sold your stock to me, and give me an opportunity to address the meeting."

George Lutts was a man in his fifties, with heavy, bushy eyebrows under which suspicious gray eyes peered with the intensity of a man trying to look through a thick fog. He pushed his head forward, as if by so doing he could see Perry Mason's face to better advantage, and he studied the lawyer's features. Blinking his eyes rapidly, he seemed almost to be sniffing the air.

"You have the stock?" Mason asked impatiently.

"Yes, yes."

"All endorsed?"

"I'm prepared to endorse it."

"There are five directors?"

"That's right."

"Will you," Mason asked, "tell me something about the temperaments and personalities of the various directors?"

"The directors are very harmonious, very broad-minded, and for the most part, our meetings are entirely without friction," Lutts said. "I am quite sure, Mr. Mason, that you will find no serious objection on the part of any director to carrying out any legitimate business proposition which is for the best interest of the company."

Mason looked at him steadily for a few moments, then grinned.

"Well, of course," Lutts said, hastily averting his eyes, "we occasionally *do* have differences of opinion, but I think that's only normal. I think there are always differences of opinion whenever people get together. After all, Mr. Mason, this is a democracy, and we progress through the consideration of different opinions."

"And who will furnish the difference of opinion this afternoon?" Mason asked.

"Ezekiel Elkins sometimes requires a little more explanation than some of the others. He's intensely practical."

"You mean hardheaded?"

"You might call it that."

"And who is opposed to Elkins?"

"No one. No one at all."

"But Elkins does occasionally express himself as having what you have just referred to as a difference of opinion?"

"Well . . . yes."

"And with whom does he usually differ?"

"Well, of course," Lutts said, "wherever there are strong personalities there is an inescapable tendency for different viewpoints to clash."

Mason nodded.

Lutts said, "Cleve Rector is, in many ways, temperamentally opposed to Ezekiel Elkins, and they are the two largest stockholders."

"Who else is on the board?"

"Herbert Doxey."

"Who's he?"

"He's my son-in-law. His holdings are very small."

"Who's the other director?" Mason asked.

"Regerson B. Neffs. Now understand, Mr. Mason, my stock doesn't represent a controlling interest in the corporation, not by any manner of means. While I am the president, these other people have much larger holdings."

"I understand," Mason said. "But isn't it a fact that if you vote with one of the other large blocks of stock, it does make a controlling interest?"

"Well," Lutts said, hesitating, "yes and no."

"What do you mean?" Mason asked.

"Well, it's rather difficult to work out a combination of that sort because the situation varies from time to time and person to person. Of course, Mr. Mason, there are essentially no differences of opinion except on minor matters. We are engaged in a constructive real estate development, and, quite naturally, everyone is interested in promoting that development so that it will work out to the best interest of all concerned."

"I just wanted to know," Mason said cryptically.

"Mr. Mason, you aren't buying this stock with the idea of making some sort of a combination and getting control, are you?"

"What makes you think that?"

"Well, the questions you are asking and . . . the fact that there were no bargaining negotiations."

"What's the matter?" Mason asked, making his voice sharp with suspicion. "Isn't the stock worth the money?"

"Oh, yes, of course, Mr. Mason! *Of course!* It's *well* worth the money. In fact, I may say you're getting a bargain, Mr. Mason."

"Then why should I have engaged in what you refer to as bargaining negotiations?"

Lutts frowned. "I hadn't been aware that you were taking an interest in the property owned by the corporation."

"I don't usually precede my negotiations for property by a formal announcement that I'm interested," Mason said.

"No, no, of course not. But you didn't make any investigation—that is, we weren't aware of it if you did."

"Exactly."

"Exactly what?"

"You weren't aware of it if I did."

Lutts cleared his throat and tried another tack.

"This isn't entirely unexpected, Mr. Mason."

"No?"

"No. I want to show you an anonymous letter I received this morning."

"Why should I be interested?"

"Take a look," Lutts invited, and handed Mason a sheet of typewritten paper which read:

> Your Sylvan Glade Development stock may be worth a lot more than you think. Better get out there and prowl around the old house for a while. You might be surprised at what you'll find—if you're lucky.

Mason regarded the letter with a skeptical eye. "Anonymous letters aren't worth their postage."

"Nevertheless, it is significant that your offer comes right on the heels of this letter."

Mason yawned.

"You don't think much of the letter?"

"No."

"Am I to understand that you're familiar with the assets of the company?"

"Familiar enough to accept the offer that you made."

"That was my first offer," Lutts said speculatively.

"Do you usually make more than one?"

"No, no, no, but . . . well, it's rather a peculiar way to do business in a deal of this magnitude. I . . . I really feel, Mr. Mason, that if I am going to go ahead with this deal, you should tell me exactly what it is you have in mind, exactly why you have become interested in this stock."

"Why should I?" Mason asked.

"I think it's only fair."

Mason studied the man's face carefully, then pushed back his chair, picked up the certified check and started for the door.

"Wait a minute . . . wait!" Lutts called in a panic. "What are you doing, Mr. Mason? Where are you going?"

"I thought," Mason said, "you had changed your mind about selling the stock. You said 'if' you were to go ahead with the deal. I had thought the deal was made, and——"

"Now, Mr. Mason, don't misunderstand me. I was only trying to get matters straight in my own mind."

Mason stood by the desk. He was still holding the certified check he had picked up.

Lutts hastily opened a drawer and brought out two certificates of stock.

"You will, of course, be in accord with leveling the hilltop property, Mr. Mason?"

"I'm not certain as to my future plans," Mason announced coldly.

"But that particular property won't be worth anything unless it is leveled."

"I am not anxious to buy valueless property. In your opinion, is the stock overpriced at the figure you've quoted me, Mr. Lutts?"

"No, no, of course not. Now don't misunderstand me, Mr. Mason. Don't misunderstand me. That property, when the Sylvan Glade Development Company purchased it, was just a run-down, second-rate suburban residential district. It had been high class at one time, but the city had moved on and left it high and dry. Then the buildings were filled with little businesses. The carline was abandoned, the rails torn up, and then even the businesses moved away. The property was up on a hill and . . . well, I'll be frank, Mr. Mason, we bought it for a song.

"Our preliminary estimate showed that by cutting away the hill we could make a small fortune. It was a splendid business stroke, Mr. Mason. Then we found that the freeway was going to go through. That freeway will be needing dirt for a fill. We'll be able to level the property, sell the dirt, and——"

"Have any agreements been made to sell the dirt for highway construction?" Mason asked.

"Nothing has been signed, yet. The owner of the adjoining property has sold dirt. She sneaked in on the thing . . . found out what we were intending to do and leveled off the back end of her property so that she beat us to it. We had to tear down houses, you know. This woman, Mrs. Roxy Claffin, has a smart real estate man, Enright Harlan. Of course, we're cooperating now, but he certainly beat us to the punch. He knew about the freeway before we did."

"The houses are now all torn down?"

"Don't you know?" Lutts asked.

Mason looked at him steadily. "No."

"All except one," Lutts said. "A former old mansion that had been taken over by small businesses. Mr. Mason, if you don't know what houses have been torn down, how can you fix a value on the stock?"

"*I* didn't fix it," Mason said. "*You* did."

"*I* fixed the price. *You* fixed a value."

"Was your price excessive?"

"Now wait a minute," Lutts said in a panic. "I'm not sure of the value. In fact, I'm having an auditor go over my books next week. I'm selling this stock so I can take a capital gains profit. I make no representations as to its value. Perhaps I am selling too cheap. There's no way of telling until the books are audited."

Mason said, "I am in a hurry. I have here a certified check for thirty-two thousand seven hundred and fifty dollars as the purchase price of your stock. In precisely fifteen seconds I'm going to walk out of this office. If I should renew my offer tomorrow morning, it will be for twenty thousand. If that is not accepted I will offer you twelve thousand tomorrow afternoon. The day after tomorrow the price will be ten thousand. The following day I won't want it at any price."

"But why?" Lutts asked. "What's going on that I don't know about?"

Mason indicated the two certificates of stock. "Either use that fountain pen now or I'll tear up the check. Which do you want?"

"Wait, wait! I'm signing, I'm signing!" George Lutts said. "Give a man time, can't you? My heavens, don't be so impatient. I've never seen such a man."

Lutts signed the endorsements on the certificates of stock and pushed them across to Mason.

Mason handed him the check.

"Who is the secretary of the company?" Mason asked.

"Herbert Doxey."

"Where will I find him?"

"Right in that back office."

"Is he expecting me?"

"Well . . . yes and no."

Mason grinned. "You mean that he felt that at the last minute I'd back out of paying any such price for your two thousand shares of stock?"

"That wasn't what I said."

"That's what you had in mind," Mason told him. "I'll step back and meet Mr. Doxey."

Mason moved around the desk, smiled at the perplexed and exasperated Lutts, walked back to a second office, the door of which was lettered "Herbert Doxey, Secretary" and pushed the door open.

Doxey, attired in shirt sleeves, was pushing papers around with the overhurried activity of an idle man who has slid his racing sheet in the desk drawer promptly upon seeing a shadow fall on the frosted glass of the entrance door.

Mason stood watching him.

Doxey tried the pretense of being so busy that he had neither seen nor heard Mason enter. Under the steady impact of Mason's eyes he could no longer stand the strain. He glanced up and made a farcical failure of registering surprise.

"My name's Mason," the lawyer told him. "I want two thousand shares of stock transferred on the books of the Sylvan Glade Development Company."

"Yes, yes," Doxey said. "I understood that you were making a deal with Daddy Lutts."

Mason extended the shares of stock.

Doxey opened a drawer in the desk, took out a stock book and the seal of the corporation.

"I want these stock certificates turned in," Mason said, "and new stock certificates issued in my name—Perry Mason."

"Is there a middle initial?" Doxey asked.

"No."

Doxey filled out the certificates, then, unable to restrain himself, asked, "Mr. Mason, would you mind telling me just what you think that stock is worth?"

"A very great deal," Mason said. "Do you expect any trouble at the directors' meeting this afternoon?"

It was Doxey's turn to be cryptic. "I don't. You might."

"Thank you," Mason said and walked out.

3

■

MASON UNLOCKED THE DOOR OF HIS PRIVATE OFFICE.

"Mrs. Harlan is here," Della Street said, and smiled. "You arrived in the nick of time. She just came in."

"Show her in," Mason said, tossing his hat in the direction of the bust of Gladstone where it landed at a rakish angle.

Della ushered Mrs. Harlan into the office. "Did you get it?" Sybil Harlan asked anxiously.

"I got it," Mason said. "I could probably have saved you better than ten thousand dollars."

She gestured impatiently. "I was afraid you might try something like that. I told you to pay the price he put on it."

"I paid it."

She added by way of explanation, "If anything had happened, and he'd stopped to think it over, he might have called my husband, and if he had . . . well, you can't tell *what* would have happened. This is the last chance I have, Mr. Mason. At least, it's the only thing I could think of. If that hadn't gone through we'd have had to start from scratch."

"All right," Mason said, "what do we do now?"

"Now," she said, "as a stockholder of the Sylvan Glade Development Company, Mr. Mason, it will give me great pleasure to show you what you have purchased. My car is downstairs and we can go out right now. I want to show you the layout because this is probably the last time we dare be seen together. By this time tomorrow, they'll have detectives shadowing your office, trying to find out who your client is. They'll be smart enough to realize that you didn't buy this for yourself."

"I hope so," Mason said, reaching for his hat. He motioned Sybil Harlan to precede him.

She flashed him a glance from the doorway. "Why?"

Mason said, "I don't want people to get the impression that I go around buying property at the asking price. You should have seen Lutts. He was afraid we'd found uranium on the property. He didn't want to sell, but he was afraid to let me get out of that door for fear I'd get away and wouldn't come back. All in all, he was in quite a predicament."

Mason told Della where he would be and followed Mrs. Harlan to the car.

"Tell me some more about the property," he said as they eased into traffic.

"It was out at the end of a carline. At one time it had been a rather exclusive suburb. Then it was sold, subdivided into lots, went through a fashionable period, then became a real estate white elephant. Around 1933 or 1934 a fire wiped out many of the old mansions. Then for a period of five or ten years, the place started filling up with shacks. It was a strange combination. A couple of the old mansions, standing in utter disrepair, surrounded by squalid hovels.

"Then the carline was discontinued. New roads were cut through and Lutts was shrewd enough to realize that if he could buy the property, tear it down, move away the buildings, and level the hill, the place would make a wonderful close-in site for a gold course or good subdivision property. He tried to tie up all the adjoining property, and that's when my husband got in on the deal. Enny is a pretty shrewd real estate operator. He realized what Lutts was trying to do.

"About that time, Enny became infatuated with Roxy. At first, the interest was legitimate. Roxy was a young divorcee with money to invest. She wanted Enny to recommend good real estate investments.

"Enny found out that the new freeway was going to come very close to this property, that they would need a lot of dirt for a fill. So, while Lutts was picking up options at a more or less leisurely pace, Enny, representing Roxy, swooped in and got hold of all the property to the north. Then he made the first deal with the contractor who was constructing the freeway and sold him dirt for the fill."

"How much dirt?" Mason asked.

"All they had. You'll see for yourself when we get out there. Roxy's property has been leveled right up to the line. In fact, after the last rain our property caved and started to slide. The road contractor needs more dirt right away, and he's negotiating with Lutts. That's really what the directors' meeting is about this afternoon."

"To consider the contractor's offer?" Mason asked.

"To accept it. After all, they can't do anything else. He's willing to pay for all the dirt and pay for tearing down the house and pave a roadway along the side of the property and along Roxy's property. That's why Enny will be at the meeting this afternoon."

"To see that the offer is accepted?"

"Yes, he's very anxious. He's sold *his* dirt and got Roxy's property leveled, so naturally he's anxious to see that construction is speeded up and that Roxy gets the benefit of the paved road. The contractor is willing to build along the property lines so he can haul the dirt to the second fill. Dirt from Roxy's property went into the first fill."

"Suppose the corporation doesn't accept the contractor's offer?"

"Then they'd be stuck with moving the dirt and they'd have to find a place to put it."

"Where would that leave the road contractor?"

"Well, he'd get dirt from somewhere. There has to be a fill. Of course, the deal is a natural, Mr. Mason. The contractor needs the dirt, and the Sylvan Glade Development Company wants the hill leveled."

"And what am I supposed to do?"

"Try to make Roxy pay for her roadway through the nose."

"But it's all one deal with the contractor?"

"Yes. Actually, the Sylvan Glade wants the roadway paved and dedicated because they'll be using it. Roxy is willing to dedicate the roadway provided she gets it paved for nothing. The contractor is willing to pave for nothing provided he gets the dirt from the Sylvan Glade Development Company."

"That's the deal?" Mason asked.

"That's the deal."

"And what do you want me to do?"

"Throw enough wrenches in the machinery so that Roxy knows she's in for trouble. Do everything you can to embarrass her."

"That might be in conflict with your best interests as a stockholder."

"I told you before, Mr. Mason, I'm not buying stock. I'm buying a husband."

Mason nodded, lit a cigarette, settled back in the car, and surreptitiously studied Mrs. Harlan's profile.

She kept her eyes on the road, said, "I can feel that you're putting me in a test tube, Mr. Mason. I suppose pure cussedness is the analysis."

"Not exactly," Mason said. "You interest me."

"Thank you. Do you think I can interest my husband —again?"

"You did it once," Mason said.

She nodded. "That was five years ago. Now I'm having to give my opponent a six-year handicap."

"You can do it," Mason said. "Where did this Claffin woman get all the money—insurance, an estate, or——?"

"Or gold digging," she interrupted.

Mason looked at her in quick surprise. "I thought she was well fixed, the way you were talking."

"She's supposed to be, but where did she get it . . . or rather, where is she getting it?"

"No alimony?"

"Not a cent. She was on the losing end."

"Investments?"

"Now she has investments, but the original cash came from somewhere. She's a plunger and she's hit a potential jackpot now."

"You think your husband may have contributed?"

"No. He might be imposed upon now, but when the relationship started, it was on a business basis. It didn't stay that way long. Trust Roxy for that."

Mason studied her angry profile.

She turned the car off the highway, drove over half a mile of pavement which had been sadly neglected and was full of broken irregularities, then negotiated a sharp turn and climbed a steep grade up a hill.

"Here we are," she said, indicating a three-story house

which had at one time evidently been quite a mansion but which was now standing in solitary isolation. "That's the house which is to be torn down. Those piles of lumber represent salvage from some of the shacks that were pulled down. Most of that lumber isn't good for anything except to be sawed up as kindling. The company's been selling it for what it can get. It's been running ads in the classified section, offering second-hand lumber for sale—as is."

Sybil Harlan stopped the car. Mason got out.

"Want to go in the house?" she asked.

Mason nodded. "Let's take a look."

She opened the glove compartment of the car, took out a leather key-container and a leather binocular case.

"What's that in the back?" Mason asked sharply.

She snapped the door of the glove compartment closed. "A gun," she said casually.

"What's it for?"

"For protection."

"Whose protection?"

"Mine. It's one of Enny's."

"*One* of Enny's?"

"Yes, he has quite a collection. He's quite an outdoor man . . . used to do a lot of hunting."

"And why the need for protection?" Mason asked.

"Because," she said, avoiding his eyes, "I come up here every once in a while, and it's lonely. I always put this gun in my handbag when I go inside the house. You read too many stories of women being attacked for me to take chances up here."

They left the car and walked to the door. Mrs. Harlan opened the leather container, fitted a key to the lock, and slid the bolt back.

"Works smoothly," Mason said.

"I oiled it."

"May I see the keys?"

She hesitated. Mason held out his hand with steady insistence.

"Oh, all right," she said, and gave him the leather key-container.

Mason looked through the keys. "These are all skeleton keys."

"Yes."

"How did you get them?"

"My goodness, Mr. Mason, don't be naïve. Every good real estate man has a collection of skeleton keys. I filched these from Enny's car."

"Didn't he miss them?"

"Yes, but he didn't know who had taken them. He has others."

"Exactly what's the idea?" Mason asked.

"I *was* going to show you," she said, "but now I'll tell you. From up here on the third floor you can look directly down on the house which is on Roxy's property—you can look into the patio and right into the swimming pool. Now, does *that* answer your question, Mr. Mason?"

"You've been keeping tabs on your husband?"

"Exactly."

"Have you seen anything?" Mason asked.

"Lots."

Mason said, "If you wanted to get evidence, why didn't you employ a detective?"

"I told you, Mr. Mason, I don't want to get evidence. I don't want a divorce. I don't want a separation. I want my husband."

"How many times have you been up here?"

"Enough to find out what's going on."

"All right," Mason said, "let's go."

She opened the door. "I'll lead the way," she said.

The interior of the house was musty; the air was stale and had a faint smell of mildew.

Partitions had been ripped out and rearranged on the lower floor to provide places for small businesses. These businesses had, in turn, moved out and left a helter-skelter of junk—old newspapers, broken chairs, a few pieces of old clothing, wrecked counters, and partitions. Over all, was a coating of dark, heavy dust.

"Dispiriting, isn't it," she said.

Mason nodded.

"I'll lead the way," she said. "You'll pardon me, Mr. Mason. This is dirty and my skirt is white."

She raised her skirt, drew it tightly around the upper part of her legs, holding it with one hand while she climbed a steep flight of stairs.

Mason regarded the white shoes, the long length of nylon stockings. "You're hardly dressed for a tour of inspection here," he said.

"I know. I have an appointment at the beauty shop right after we leave here, and I dressed for that appointment instead of for this. I hope you don't mind my making a spectacle of myself, but I don't want to get dirty."

"Lead on," Mason told her.

The second floor had been given over to bedrooms. Here, again, there was a litter of rubbish where people had moved out, leaving behind old mattresses, broken bed sets, cheap furniture which in the course of years had become unglued at the joints and was not worth repairing.

Mrs. Harlan, still holding her skirt high and tight so that it would not brush against anything, climbed to the third floor, led the way to a room with a northern exposure. Here it was cleaner and less cluttered. The room's only chair was covered with a newspaper and placed in such a position that one could sit in it and look out through the thin lace curtains of a window.

Mrs. Harlan's white skirt dropped back into place; she looked down at her shoes to see if she was carrying any dirt on them, stamped them on the floor in order to get rid of the dust. "Here we are, Mr. Mason," she said.

Mason looked down the steep excavated slope to a red-tiled, white stucco house. "Gives you a feeling of insecurity," Mason said. "I can't get over the feeling that this house may start sliding down the hill any minute."

"I know how you feel," she said. "The rains have washed gullies. Within thirty days this will all be torn down and the hill will be leveled. Look down there now, Mr. Mason. Do you see what I mean? Those two figures."

She stepped to the window, released the catch and raised the sash. The lace curtains billowed in a faint breeze. She slipped a cord over the curtains, holding them back.

Then, stepping away from the window, she opened the leather binocular case and brought out a pair of expensive binoculars. "Just sit in that chair. You can look right out through the window."

She handed Mason the binoculars, and Mason, curious, moved the newspaper, seated himself in the chair, adjusted the binoculars and looked down on the red-tiled roof of the patio and the swimming pool.

A man and a woman were at the pool. The man wore a business suit, the woman wore virtually nothing. She was lying on a foam rubber mattress.

"Sun-bathing," Sybil Harlan explained. "She does that a lot, particularly when Enny is calling on business."

"I take it that's your husband."

"That will be Enny," she said. "Probably talking about the directors' meeting, getting last minute instructions."

As Mason watched, the man leaned forward and extended his hand; the woman took it, and with a light, swift motion bounded to her feet. For a moment she stood facing the man and then grabbed up a robe and hung it around her.

Mrs. Harlan, who had been watching over Mason's shoulders without the aid of binoculars, said, "That gives you a good idea of what's going on, Mr. Mason."

"Want the binoculars?" Mason asked.

"I wouldn't think of depriving you of the treat," she said. "Now, she'll get the robe and be very modest, very demure—after having given Enny a complete eyeful. A neat figure, don't you think, Mr. Mason?"

"Very."

"Otherwise," Mrs. Harlan said dryly, "I wouldn't have had to invest thirty-two thousand seven hundred and fifty dollars in stock that I didn't want. Now she'll invite him into the house for a drink or a cup of tea and——"

Harlan had been standing by the woman, who was smiling up at him. Mason could see her lips move as she said something, then, with her face near to the man's, she paused for a moment, her chin elevated at just the right angle.

Abruptly, the man swept her into his arms in a crushing embrace.

Mason lowered the binoculars to glance at Mrs. Harlan.

She had turned her back to the window and was standing with her fists clenched.

"All right," Mason said, "I've seen the property."

"Ready to go?"

"I think I'd better. That directors' meeting is for one-thirty. I want to be there when it opens."

"Enny will be leaving any minute now," she said.

"Was that house built after the property was——"

"No, the house has been there for some time. That's on the level part of the property. The hill commenced just back of where the swimming pool is now. That's new. Enny likes to swim. That wall around the patio, enclosing the swimming pool, gives them privacy. That unpainted boxlike shack just below here is the contractor's shack."

"Hasn't it occurred to her to look up here?" Mason asked. "Can't she see you at that window?"

"I have been very careful. They never even bother to look up here. They take this old empty house for granted, the way a wife takes her husband for granted—until she suddenly finds it's too late to salvage her marriage."

"You're wearing white today," Mason said. "When you raised that window, you could have been rather conspicuous and——"

"I don't wear white when I come up here. I wear something dark. I just wanted you to see the property, Mr. Mason. You'll have to understand the setup. Do you want to go down and look at the boundary line?"

"Can we see it from here?"

"We can see it from here, but, as you pointed out, I'm too conspicuous. Let's go."

Mason put the binoculars back into the case. She held out her hand.

"I'll carry them," Mason said.

Mrs. Harlan again carefully raised and folded her skirts. "I feel as much of an exhibitionist as that minx down there at the swimming pool, but the dirt in this house just jumps at you if you give it a chance—and I take it you've seen legs before, Mr. Mason."

"Not that good-looking," Mason said.

She laughed. "Thank you. I think I needed that to build my morale—otherwise, I wouldn't have fished for it. They are good. I know my good points, Mr. Mason, but sometimes I'm afraid I don't know my bad points."

"What do you mean by that?"

"I'm a creature of emotions. In my case, sophistication is a thin veneer. At times I have the most savage, ruthless impulses. Sometimes I— Well, Mr. Mason, there are depths in my emotions I'm afraid to look into. I'm not a well-controlled person. Sometimes I'm afraid I could become a vicious, clawing savage.

"You know, some women would have become friendly with the mistress, trying to size up her technique to see what she had that the wife didn't have. I've seen them do that, cooing at each other, sparring for position in a cold war that was all sweetness on the outside. I couldn't do that. I'd have been at her throat.

"I know I can't trust myself. I'll just have to stay away from that woman, that's all."

"That might be a good idea," Mason said.

"What idea?"

"To keep away from her."

"You're right. Let's quit talking about her, shall we?"

She led the way down the stairs. Mason followed her to the ground floor. She opened the outer door, released her skirts, fluffed them into place, and stood a moment in the doorway, the bright sunlight showing the silhouette of her figure through the light, white skirt. She stretched her arms above her head, with the tips of her fingers she smoothed her hair back around her ears, glanced over her shoulder at Perry Mason. "Think I stand a chance?"

"I would say you stood a very good chance."

She stepped out into the sunlight, holding the door open for Perry Mason, and he followed her through the door. She closed and locked it.

"The boundary line comes right along here to the northeast," she said. "You can see where they stopped the excavation. Then our property caved down after it rained."

"It'll cave some more if there are further rains," Mason said.

"I suppose so. But after all, what difference does it make. The house is going to be torn down.

"Think of the stories this house could tell, Mr. Mason. At one time it was a mansion out in the exclusive suburbs. Those were the days when you traveled by horse and buggy and went back and forth to town on an interurban streetcar. Beautiful women climbed up and down those stairs. There were marriages . . . births . . . deaths . . . and then there were people who moved in, common, ordinary people, then another class of people. Can you imagine persons moving out of a house and leaving all of that nasty litter behind them? It's awful when something outlives its usefulness, Mr. Mason."

She stood in the sunlight, facing the lawyer, her face

hard and bitter. "Six years," she said, and spat the words out.

Mason said, "I thought it was your *fifth* anniversary."

"My fifth anniversary," she said, "but I'm talking about that beautiful brown body down there. She's six years younger than I. That's the handicap I have to give. That's what I'm fighting against. And as I get older, I'll have to give more and more of a handicap. There's always a young crop coming along with curves and . . . oh, hell, Mr. Mason, I think I'm going to bawl."

"Wait a minute," Mason said sharply. "This is your fifth wedding anniversary, remember? You're going to the beauty shop. You're going to gild the lily and paint the rose, and then you're going to turn on your personality and make that woman in the red-tiled house down there look pale by comparison."

"She isn't pale. She's beautiful. She has a wonderful brown body. Her skin has beautiful golden tints. I've watched her, I've studied every inch of her—and she's six years younger than I am."

"And," Mason said, "she's going to start asking your husband why he didn't protect her property rights and what is meant by the doctrine of lateral support?"

"What *is* the doctrine of lateral support?" Mrs. Harlan asked, suddenly curious.

"That," Mason said, grinning, "is what the directors of the Sylvan Glade Development Company are going to be asking in just about forty-five minutes. And if you don't mind accepting the appraisal of an expert, Mrs. Harlan, that girl down there doesn't have anything on you. You can spot her curve for curve, and she can't touch you on personality."

"Thanks for trying to boost my morale, Mr. Mason. You don't know how I need it. I'm getting pretty desperate. I——" She suddenly jumped into the car, unlocked the glove compartment, started to put in the binoculars which Mason held out to her, hesitated, then took the gun out and put it into her handbag.

"What's that for?" Mason said.

Her laugh seemed cheerful. "I'll put it back among my husband's other guns. I'm not going to need it after all—now that I am beginning to understand the way *you* have things planned."

4

GEORGE C. LUTTS, SITTING AT THE HEAD OF THE MA-hogany table, tapped gently with the gavel and said in his dry, rasping voice, "This meeting will please come to order."

The men seated at the table straightened expectantly.

Lutts said, "This is a regular directors' meeting, at which time we are to consider the offer of the Aurora Paving and Excavating Company for tearing down the house remaining on our holdings, moving away the hill, and paving the road which will give us access to the new freeway.

"Before we start in on this business of the meeting, however, I have an announcement to make." He paused, cleared his throat, said, "I have as of this day disposed of my entire interest in the corporation. My stock has been purchased by Mr. Perry Mason. I wish to intro-duce Mr. Mason, the lawyer, and then announce my resignation as president of the board.

"I am going to ask Mr. Mason to say a few words. I also wish the minutes to show that Mr. Enright Harlan is attending the meeting by special invitation. Mr. Harlan represents Mrs. Roxy Claffin, who owns property on the north. Now then, I'm going to ask Mr. Mason——"

"Just a moment. I rise to a point of order," Ezekiel Elkins rasped.

"All right, what's the point?" Lutts asked impatiently.

Elkins scraped back his chair and got to his feet, a dogged, lantern-jawed individual in his early fifties, with sharp, suspicious eyes, sparse hair, a florid face, and the habit of shoving his hands down deep in his trousers pockets whenever he talked.

"How much did you get for your stock?"

"None of your business," Lutts snapped.

"I thought we had a gentlemen's agreement that if any offer was made for our stock we'd each give the other directors the first refusal."

"I didn't sign any such contract."

"I'm not talking about a contract. I'm talking about a gentlemen's agreement."

"I didn't make any such agreement."

The others murmured protest.

"It was agreed right here around this very table. We talked it over when we organized the company."

"Someone suggested that it would be a good idea," Lutts said, "but there wasn't any definite agreement."

"There was an agreement," Elkins said doggedly.

"Well, my stock's been sold," Lutts snapped angrily.

"And you won't tell us what you got for it?"

"No."

Elkins turned to the other members of the board. "Move we accept Lutts's resignation as president and director," he said, "on the ground that he is no longer qualified to sit as director on account of his not being a stockholder on the records of the company."

"Second the motion," Regerson Neffs snapped.

"I haven't given my resignation, yet," Lutts said.

"You can't sit on the board. You aren't qualified. You have to be a stockholder to be a member of the board of directors," Elkins said.

"I might get a share from Herb Doxey, just to qualify me," Lutts went on. "I'm still interested in——"

"It has been moved and seconded to accept the resignation of George C. Lutts," Elkins said. "All those in favor signify by saying aye."

Four voices said, "Aye."

"So ordered," Elkins said. "Who's going to be president of the company?"

"I move Mr. Cleve Rector be elected president," Regerson Neffs said.

"I move Ezekiel Elkins be president," Herbert Doxey said.

"That leaves us two and two," Neffs said. "That isn't going to——"

"I'm voting for Elkins," Rector interrupted.

"You are?" Neffs said.

"That's right."

Doxey said, "Under the bylaws we can only elect a chairman to act as presiding officer until the next meeting of the stockholders. The stockholders elect the president."

"We'll have a stockholders' meeting right after this," Elkins said. "Now, let's hear from Perry Mason. All right, Mr. Mason, do you have something to say to us?"

"I just wanted to announce that I am a stockholder in the corporation," Mason said, "and as such I am interested in anything that is done by you directors."

"Whom are you representing?" Elkins demanded.

"The stock is in my name."

"You're representing somebody," Elkins said. "You didn't drop down out of a clear sky and buy stock in this company without any previous negotiations and at such a price Lutts didn't dare let the deal slip through his fingers by giving us first chance at the stock, the way we promised each other we would."

Cleve Rector said, "He's representing that Claffin woman, of course. If you ask me, she's taking altogether too much of an interest in the affairs of this corporation. She sneaked in and purchased her property right out from under us. She——"

"Now, just a minute," Enright Harlan interrupted, getting to his feet. "*I'm* representing Mrs. Claffin. I resent having things like that said about her, and I happen to know that she is not Mr. Mason's client."

"What makes you think I have a client?" Mason asked.

"Don't be silly," Harlan said.

"Of course, he'd deny it anyway," Rector said. "I think this man, Mason, is a Trojan horse. I think anything he says should be viewed with suspicion. I think he's simply trying to manipulate the affairs of this corporation for the benefit of Roxy Claffin. I don't think he's a bona fide stockholder. I don't want him on the board of directors."

Mason said impatiently, "I don't want to go on the board of directors. I want to address the directors on a matter of business."

"Well, I guess you've got a right to do that," Elkins said.

Mason said, "You gentlemen seem to be obsessed with the idea that you're going to grade down that hill and level the property."

"Well, why not," Elkins said. "That was the idea of getting the property in the first place."

"All right," Mason said. "When you get done, what do you have? You have a flat property. You are going to have drainage problems. Now, I believe that hill can be terraced and turned into attractive residential property. I think the house that's on the hill can be renovated, that a big outdoor balcony can be put on it and glassed in, that the place will make an attractive restaurant and night club."

Mason paused. The directors looked at him in openmouthed astonishment.

"You're crazy," Lutts said finally.

"In which event," Mason went on as though he had not been interrupted, "we would, of course, be in a position to sue Mrs. Claffin, who owns the property on the north, for having invaded our right of lateral support."

"Lateral support? What's that?" Lutts asked.

"That is the right of all property to have the natural, normal support of the adjoining property. I notice that Mrs. Claffin has gone ahead with excavations which have not only gone right up to the boundary line of the property, but have even passed the boundary line of the property and have undermined the foundations of the house on the hill. This has caused the Sylvan Glade Development Company great and irreparable damages. I personally feel that before this corporation makes any agreement relating to leveling that hill, it should first investigate the possibilities of turning the property into an attractive, exclusive hillside residential property, and file suit against Mrs. Claffin for the unlawful violation of our lateral support.

"I wish to call to the attention of the directors that there have been a series of dry years, that this level propery is immediately adjacent to a natural drainage, which, in view of developments to the north and west, can well become a raging torrent in the event of an unusually wet year. The water would then sweep down across our property, if it were leveled, cutting great channels and causing enormous damage. As it is now, this hill is attractive, artistic, and, above all, even in the wettest years it will be dry. There was a time when the steepness of the hill detracted from the value of the property. In view of the fact that it is now possible to come in on the freeway, take the turn-off on the edge of the Claffin property, follow that around to our property, and terrace the hill, we could make a very fine residential property."

"I think you've got something," Cleve Rector said. "I want it investigated."

"Now, wait a minute, wait a minute," Enright Harlan shouted. "This is simply blackmail. You see now why Mr. Mason got in here. He's trying to drum up a lawsuit. In the first place, if you people don't make some agreement with Mrs. Claffin, you can't even use the roadway across her property. She's only willing to dedicate that for a highway in the event your property is leveled and in the event she receives a reasonable contribution toward the cost of the dedication."

"You mean she wants money from us?" Lutts asked.

"You want a road from her, don't you?" Harlan asked.

Ezekiel Elkins turned to Mason. "What's this doctrine of lateral support you're talking about?"

Harlan said, "Just a minute, gentlemen. If there's going to be any dissertation on your legal rights, I want to have an opportunity to get a lawyer here and——"

"Shut up," Elkins said. "You're not a stockholder here, you're not a director. You're here by sufferance. Your interests are opposed to ours and always have been. Go ahead, Mr. Mason. What do you mean by lateral support?"

"Under the original common law," Mason said, "property was absolutely entitled to lateral support. That doctrine has now been changed somewhat by Section 832 of the civil code, but under that section, before any person can make an excavation which will in any way damage the lateral support of the adjoining property, it is necessary that a written notice be given to the adjoining property owner. Did Mrs. Claffin ever give this corporation any notice?"

"She did not," Rector said.

"Now, wait a minute," Harlan interposed. "Don't get stampeded."

"Let's see a lawyer," Regerson Neffs interrupted.

"We've got one here," Rector said. "I move we adjourn."

"Second the motion," Herbert Doxey said.

"Now, wait a minute," Harlan insisted. "We've all got a problem to consider. We——"

"Rise to a point of order," Regerson Neffs interrupted.

"The motion to adjourn is always in order. It's been duly seconded. Put it to a vote."

"All those in favor of adjournment signify by saying aye," Elkins snapped.

"Aye," four voices said.

Chairs scraped back. "We're adjourned," Elkins said. "I want to talk with you, Mr. Mason."

Enright Harlan pushed Elkins aside, confronted Mason. He was, Mason saw, a handsome man despite the fact that he was flushed and angry. He was tall, square-shouldered, slender hipped, athletic. His gray eyes were sharp with anger. "Are you," he shouted, "trying to turn an asset into a lawsuit?"

Mason grinned at him. "I'm turning a lawsuit into an asset," he said, and walked away.

5

∎

MASON FINISHED THE AFTERNOON'S DICTATION, PUSHED A file of mail away from him, said, "I can't keep up with it, Della."

"You've done fine this afternoon," she said. "Two more hours tomorrow and you'll be completely finished with the important matters."

Mason regarded the bulging mail file with disgust. "Well, it's twenty minutes to six, long past closing time."

"You're leaving?" she asked.

"No, I have some law points I want to look up. I'll put in an hour or two in the library. You go on home, Della. I'm sorry I kept you so late."

Knuckles tapped on the door, and Gertie, the receptionist, pushed her head in through the doorway. "You didn't leave instructions about Mrs. Harlan," she said, and then added parenthetically, "the woman who saw you this morning."

"What about her?" Mason asked. "And what are you doing here this late? I thought you'd closed up the outer office long ago."

"She's on the telephone. She says she simply has to talk with you right now. I told her I didn't know whether you were in, that I thought you had left for the day but that I'd try to find out. I went out, but came back to wait for my boy friend, and when the phone rang I answered it."

"I'll talk with her, Gertie," Mason said.

Gertie nodded, returned to the other office, and Mason picked up his extension phone. A moment later he heard the click of the connection. "Hello," he said cautiously.

"Mr. Mason, Mr. Mason, is that you?"

"Yes."

"This is Sybil . . . Sybil Harlan."

"Yes."

"Mr. Mason, something . . . I must see you at once! Something very unforeseen has happened."

"Now, wait a minute," Mason said. "Get yourself together. You sound half-hysterical."

"I am . . . I'll be all right. I'm just nervous."

"Where are you now?" Mason asked.

"I'm down at the Union Station. I took a cab there because I thought it would be less conspicuous and——"

Mason, his voice sharp, said, "Don't try to tell me over the phone. Grab a cab and get up here as fast as you can. Don't go to the outer office. Come down the corridor to the side-exit door marked 'Private.' Tap on it and I'll let you in."

"Thank you, thank you. I was so afraid I couldn't reach you."

"Never mind," Mason said. "Get up here."

Mason hung up the phone, nodded to Della, said, "Get Paul Drake at the Drake Detective Agency for me, Della."

Della Street started for the outer office.

"No, no. The private unlisted telephone," Mason said. "I want to be sure I catch him."

Della Street's fingers flew over the dial and a moment later she nodded and handed the receiver to Mason.

Mason said hello and heard Drake's voice on the line. "Yes, Perry, what is it?"

Mason said, "Can you wait there for another hour or so?"

"Yes."

"I think I have an emergency matter coming up. Got any operatives on tap?"

"There are a couple of good men making out reports here in the office. I can hold them if you want."

"Hold them," Mason said.

"What is it?" Drake asked.

Mason said, "I don't know, Paul. All I have is the sound of a woman's voice. She's a woman who wouldn't get stampeded easily, but she's half-hysterical now. Stick around, Paul."

"What's your connection with her?" Drake asked.

Mason said, "She's in danger of losing her husband. She doesn't intend to sit back and let that happen. She had schemes. Now she's in a jam."

"Oh-oh," Drake said. "One of those things where everything went black, then she felt something jerking in her hand and heard loud banging noises. She looked down and found she was holding a gun, and there was John lying on the floor. She has no idea how he got there. She ran to him and said, 'John, John, speak to me. Oh, John, speak to me.' So then she calls her lawyer."

"Don't kid about it," Mason said. "You may be a lot nearer the truth than you know. Stay in your office, Paul, and be ready to come down here the minute I give you a buzz."

Mason hung up, looked at his wrist watch, said to Della, "Well, you'd better stay on, too. I'll buy you a dinner."

"Sold. Let's tackle that mail file again."

"No mail," Mason told her. "I want to review the situation in my mind, so I'll have the various factors at my finger tips. We may have to work fast."

The lawyer started pacing the floor, head thrust forward, thumbs pushed into the armholes of his vest. Della Street watched him solicitously.

During the next ten minutes, Mason looked at his watch at least ten times. Then Della heard the tapping of quick steps in the corridor and impatient knuckles on the door of Mason's private office.

Della Street threw the door open.

Sybil Harlan stood in the doorway. Her face was a frozen mask.

"All right," Mason said, "come in and sit down. Now tell me, what is it?"

"George Lutts," she said as Della Street closed the door.

"What about him?"

"He's dead."

"How did he die?"

"Someone shot him."

"Where?"

"In the chest. I——"

"No, no," Mason said. "Where was he when he was shot?"

"Up in the house on the hill."

"Who was with him?"

"I was."

Mason stepped in front of her. His voice was like a slap. "Cut out the dramatic stuff. Get yourself together. Who else was with him?"

"Only one person."

"Who?"

"I don't know."

"What do you mean you don't know?"

"Someone who was hiding in the house. Someone who had a key."

"Go on," Mason said, "let's have it."

She said, "George Lutts is a smooth operator. He felt that if his two thousand shares of stock were worth thirty-two thousand seven hundred and fifty dollars to you, the stock would be going up in value. No one else knew what he had been paid for the stock. Apparently, after the directors' meeting, Regerson Neffs complained about the fact that Lutts had sold out. Lutts told Neffs he'd buy his stock at whatever price Neffs wanted to put on it."

"So what?"

"So Neffs, who had three thousand shares of stock, put a price of eight dollars a share on it, and Lutts wrote him a check for twenty-four thousand dollars."

Mason said, "That left Lutts holding three thousand shares of stock instead ot the two thousand he'd had earlier in the day, and left him with eight thousand seven hundred and fifty dollars in clear profit."

Mrs. Harlan nodded.

"Go on," Mason said.

She said, "Lutts was waiting for me when I came out of the beauty parlor."

"What time was that?"

"Shortly before four o'clock."

"How did he know where you were?"

"He phoned my house. When I called home for messages, the girl who comes in three times a week to do cleaning told me a Mr. Lutts had phoned about half-past three and told her it was very important he get in touch with me at once, and she told him he could reach me at the beauty parlor."

"What did he want?"

"Blackmail."

Mason's eyes narrowed. "Go ahead, tell me all the details. Don't hold back anything."

"He was clever—greedy and diabolically clever."

"Never mind all that now. Tell me what happened."

"He told me to get in the car with him. He said he wanted to show me something. There was something in his manner . . . well . . . I was suspicious."

"Go on," Mason told her.

"In some way, Mr. Mason, he had found out that I was the person who had told you to get the stock for me."

"How did he find that out?"

"I don't know. I've thought and thought. I haven't the faintest idea. But he knew. He was certain of his ground."

"Go on," Mason said, "tell me what happened."

"Lutts tried . . . a sort of blackmail. He had me where I had to . . . to do what he said."

"Why?"

"I didn't dare quarrel with him, Mr. Mason. If Enny had found out that I was the one who had commissioned you to purchase that stock, if he realized that I was trying to make trouble for him in the business deal with Roxy Claffin . . . well, that would have been the last straw. He would have walked out on me cold. And Lutts threatened to go to Enny and tell him."

"Go on," Mason said.

"Of course, George Lutts didn't realize what I was trying to do. He thought that I had some inside information. He also thought I was trying to throw a terrific scare into Roxy and make her let her holdings go cheap. Lutts knew Enny would never have an interest adverse to one of his clients, so Lutts decided I was making a fast play and that I'd do almost anything to keep Enny from finding out.

"So he told me I had to tell him, otherwise he'd go to Enny. You can see what a spot I was in and the reason motivating his actions. If he could purchase stock at eight dollars a share, and I had inside information that made the stock worth over sixteen a share, he naturally wanted to load up with stock. But he didn't want to sink any more money in unless he knew the reason for my interest."

"It never occurred to him what it was?"

"No, he just thought there was some inside information. He thought my motives were purely financial."

"So what did he do?"

"He told me to get in the car with him. He drove up toward the property, trying to make me tell him what it was I knew, and finally, he drove all the way up to the place on the hill."

"Parked his car?"

She nodded.

"You went in the house?"

"Not then."

"Who opened the door?"

"He did. He had a key."

"What happened?"

"I was in something of a panic. I knew that once he went in that house and got up to the third floor, if he went up that far, he'd find where I'd been watching. Once he found that, he'd put two and two together and then he'd be in a position *really* to blackmail me."

"Did you try to keep him from going in?"

"Of course I did."

"And it didn't work?"

"I thought if I sat in the car and didn't make a move to get out, he'd change his mind."

"But he didn't?"

"He almost did, Mr. Mason. He sat there and talked for a minute or two, but he kept thinking that there was something in the house which accounted for my interest in the stock. I saw that he was determined to go in."

"So he went in."

"Yes."

"And you sat in the car?"

"Yes."

"Doing what?"

"Pretending to be just as completely unconcerned as possible. I sat there with the radio going, listening to some jazz music."

"All right, what happened?"

"Well, after three or four or five minutes, it suddenly occurred to me that if I went in there, I just *might* be able to distract his attention so that he wouldn't find where I had fixed up that room upstairs, where I did my watching. You see, if he'd ever told Enny that I'd been up there spying . . . well, Enny would have resented it terribly. I just *couldn't* let him find that room."

"So what did you do?"

"So I shut off the radio, jumped out of the car, ran to the door and called him. I thought I could cook up some sort of a story to get him back down."

"You called, and what happened?"

"He didn't answer."

"So what did you do?"

"I started up the stairs."

"Then what?"

"I kept calling his name."

"Anyone who was in there could hear you coming?"

"Yes, of course."

"And what did you do?"

"I got to the second floor. He wasn't there. I started up the steps to the third floor, and there he was, lying head down with blood coming out of his chest and . . . oh, it was the most ghastly thing you've ever seen."

"Did you hear any shots?"

"No."

"How many holes in his chest?"

"I don't know. I didn't look."

"But you know he was dead?"

"I reached down and felt his wrist. There wasn't any pulse at all."

"Then what?"

"And then I heard this person on the floor above me."

"Where?"

"Up on the third floor, sneaking along on tiptoes. First, I heard a board creak. Then another board creaked. And then I saw this gun and a hand holding it and a part of an arm."

"Man or woman?" Mason asked.

"Good heavens, Mr. Mason, don't ask me. When I heard those boards creak, my knees just turned to water, and when I saw that gun, I guess I let out the loudest scream I ever let out in my life and I went down those stairs so fast I don't think I even touched the stairs. I went out through that door—I must have all but taken it off the hinges."

"Did you scream after that?"

"I screamed two or three times going down the hill. Then I saved my breath for running."

"No one came after you?"

"No one. I looked back and no one was coming. Believe me, Mr. Mason, I sure was running."

"All right, then what?"

"I ran until I was out of breath, and I was so frightened and my heart just seemed to quit beating. I had to slow down to get my breath, and then, as soon as I got a little wind, I ran some more and . . . well. I just went plunging down the hill, until I hit the road near the bottom."

"Why didn't you take Lutts's car?"

"He had locked the ignition and had taken the keys in with him when he went in. Believe me, he wasn't taking any chances on having me take his car and drive off and leave him out there. He was after information. He wanted to know what I knew about that stock that he didn't know, and minutes were precious to him. He was planning on making some more stock purchases this evening if he could."

"And you don't think he had any idea of the real reason you wanted to buy in?"

"Well," she said thoughtfully, "he didn't when he started in that house. But if he got up to the top of the stairs and saw the way I'd cleaned up that room, with the newspaper on the chair and things, he might have known."

"You don't know how many shots were fired?"

"No, that's because I had the radio going in the car."

"All right, go on, what happened?"

"Well, I thought I was going to have to hitchhike, but as it turned out, I didn't."

"How come?"

"When I hit the main county highway, I was really in a panic. I would have gone in any direction, taking the first car that came along. But as it happened, I was in luck. A taxicab was coming toward town. Evidently, it had been out to the country club and was running back empty. I saw it coming when I was still a little way from the road and I started waving. The driver saw me and pulled right off to the side of the road, and then he came down and picked me up."

"He could see you'd been running?"

"I guess so. I guess I looked a mess."

"What did he say?"

"Well, of course, he . . . he was curious. He wanted to know if I was all right, if anything had happened, if anyone had attacked me or anything of that sort."

"What did you tell him?"

"I told him everything was quite all right, that I was just in a hurry to catch a train."

"To catch a train?"

"Yes, I wanted him to take me to the depot. I felt that if he took me there, I could pick up another cab from the depot and——"

"You didn't have any baggage?"

"No, I told him my husband had gone on ahead with the baggage and I was supposed to have joined him, but I'd been detained."

"Did he ask you anything other than that?"

"He tried to get me into a conversation, but I clammed up on him and became dignified. I'll say one thing, he sure made a fast run, getting me to the depot."

"In other words, you think you convinced him?"

"I think I did. He asked me a few questions at first, and then he seemed to take my story for granted."

Mason said, "Good Lord, why didn't you notify the police?"

"I was afraid to. My story would have sounded crazy, and the minute I told it, Enny would have found out everything. I've invested thirty-two thousand seven hundred and fifty dollars in trying to save my marriage, and I'm not going to back out now."

"Now, wait a minute," Mason said. "Let's get something straight."

"What?"

"You invested thirty-two thousand seven hundred and fifty dollars in trying to save your marriage," Mason told her. "That was this morning. A lot of things have happened since then."

"I'm still fighting to save my marriage."

"You *may* be fighting to save your life," Mason warned. "You've been mixed up in a murder. You told me a story that isn't going to sound very convincing to the police."

"Don't you believe me?"

"I'm inclined to believe you," Mason said, "because you came to me earlier in the day, and I think I understand something of the impulsive nature of your character. You're a daring gambler. You'll hatch out some original scheme and then put a stack of blue chips right on the line, backing up that scheme. By the same token, you'd gamble your life and your liberty trying to save your marriage."

"Without my husband," she admitted, "life wouldn't be worth living. I love him—too much."

Mason regarded her thoughtfully. "As an attorney, there's only one piece of advice I can give you."

"What's that?"

"Let me pick up the phone and report what you have told me to the police."

"I can't, Mr. Mason."

"Why not?"

"You know why. The minute Enny knew that I was out there with George Lutts, he'd know right then and there that I was the one who had brought you into the company. The money that I invested, trying to save my marriage, would prove to be the thing that hopelessly wrecked it."

"I'm still advising you that, *under the law,* you have to report this to the police."

"Suppose I don't do it. Are you going to betray me?"

Mason said, "I'm your lawyer."

"How about Miss Street?" Sybil Harlan asked, looking at Della Street with hard, appraising eyes.

"She's my secretary," Mason said. "Anything she learns in the course of the business is a privileged communication. You can count on her."

"Fair enough," she said.

"What do you mean by that?"

"If I've made a gamble, I won't whimper if I lose. You don't need to worry about that, Mr. Mason. I'll take my medicine. I'll march into that gas chamber with a smile on my lips and a song in my heart. If I can't have my husband, if I can't salvage my marriage, I don't want to live."

Mason frowned. "That's what frightens me about you. You play a peculiar game all your own, and when you bet, you don't have any limit."

"If I'm going to bet, I may as well bet every chip in my stack."

"Well, you've done it now," he told her. "Are you going to notify the police?"

"No."

Mason said, "Technically, I should."

"Never mind the technical end of it. Let's be practical. Are you *going* to?"

"Probably not," Mason told her, "if you tell me not to; but I still think it would be better to do it that way."

"Why?"

"Because they may find that you were up there with Lutts, and if you don't notify the police——"

"Isn't it too late now to notify the police?"

"It's pretty late, all right," Mason admitted.

She pressed her advantage. "Look at it from the standpoint of the police—and the newspapers. I go up there with Lutts. He's trying to blackmail me. Something happens and he's killed by a gunshot wound. I run away. I don't try to call the police. I take a cab. I go to the Union Station, so the cab driver can't trace me. Then I consult my lawyer. The lawyer tells me I should call the police. When you put those facts together, what does it mean?"

"It means you'll be the number one suspect."

"All right," she said. "Then there's nothing to do now, except to try to cover up. Besides no one can ever prove I was out there with Lutts."

Mason regarded her thoughtfully. "Where's that gun you had?"

"In the glove compartment of my car."

"You had it in your purse."

"I know, but I put it back in the glove compartment of the car when I went to the beauty shop."

"It's there now?"

"Heavens, I hope so. I locked the glove compartment and put the car in the parking lot. Of course, I suppose sometimes thieves *do* get at locked glove compartments."

Mason pursed his lips in thought.

"So, Mr. Attorney," she said, "I'm in your hands. What do we do now?"

"First, we'll go look at that gun in the glove compartment of your car."

"And then?"

Mason said, "Wait a minute." He stood by the desk, his eyes narrowed.

She started to say something, and Mason impatiently motioned her to silence.

"The cab driver noticed you particularly?" Mason asked.

"I feel certain he did."

"You had on that white outfit?"

"Yes. I was dressed just the way I am now."

Mason said, "That's a hell of a way to be walking along a road that far out in the country."

"I know."

"The cab driver will remember you."

"Of course."

"What kind of a cab was it?"

"The Red Line."

"You don't know the number?"

"Heavens, no."

"And you stayed with that same cab until you got to the Union Station?"

"Yes."

Mason shrugged his shoulders. "Well, there's nothing we can—wait a minute. What happened when you paid the meter?"

"The meter was two dollars and ninety-five cents. I gave him three and a half."

"He rang up the meter?"

"Yes."

"A slip of paper came out?"

"Oh, yes, that's right. The receipt."

"And I suppose you threw that away?" Mason asked.

"No. I have it."

Mason said, "That's fine. Let me take a look at it."

"What does it show?"

"It shows the number of the cab, it shows the number of the trip, and the amount that was paid," Mason said, unfolding the crumpled piece of paper.

Abruptly, he put the paper in his wallet, turned to Della Street and said, "Della, get Paul Drake busy. The cab number is seven-sixty-one. It's a Red Line cab. Find out where that cab is now. Have Drake put a man in a car and trail that cab. I want to know where it is every minute of the day and night until that driver goes off duty."

"I don't see what good that's going to do," Mrs. Harlan said. "What are you trying to accomplish, Mr. Mason?"

Mason brushed the question aside, said to Mrs. Harlan, "Let's go. You wait here, Della."

Della Street nodded. "I'll get your hat, Chief."

She walked to the closet, handed him his hat. "Be sure about the paper in the band," she said. "That's the hat which was too tight, you know."

Mason looked at her, nodded absently, his mind on the problem before him.

"The band," Della Street said.

Mason ran his fingers around the hat band, found the note Della Street had placed there. "Yes, yes. Thank you, Della."

Mason held the hat in his hand, pressing the note against the interior of the crown. In the elevator he had a chance to read the note:

Chief, those aren't the same shoes and stockings she was wearing this morning. Watch out.

Mason crumpled the note in his pocket, escorted his client from the elevator.

He picked up his car at the parking lot. "Tell me which way to go."

"Straight out Seventh Street, then turn left and go two blocks."

"Your car's in a parking lot out there?"

"Yes."

"You have the ticket?"

"Yes."

Mason said, "I'm going to drive you on by the entrance to the parking lot. I'll stop. You walk back, get the car, drive around the block and meet me."

"Anything else?"

"Follow me," Mason said, "until I find a place where we can both pull in to the curb and— Let me see your bag."

She opened her bag.

Mason found a place by a fireplug and pulled in to the curb. He looked through the contents of the opened handbag.

"You don't believe me, do you, Mr. Mason?"

"I'm making sure," Mason said. "Now, look. You won't like this, but you've got to give me some assurance against a double cross."

"How?"

"I have to make certain you haven't got a gun," Mason told her. "I'm not going to let you get in the car, pull a gun out of your clothes somewhere, put it in the glove compartment, and then——"

"But you can go in there with me, if you don't trust me."

"We can't afford to do that, neither of us. Later on, someone will recall seeing me there with you. I'm not entirely unknown, you know. My picture gets in the paper a lot. The parking attendant may recognize me."

"How much of a search would you have to make?"

"Just enough to find out that you haven't got a gun on you."

She clenched her fists. "Go ahead."

Mason felt along the lines of her rigid body.

"Satisfied?"

Mason nodded.

"I'm telling you the truth. I wouldn't lie to my lawyer."

"It's a hell of a story," Mason said, and eased the car away from the curb.

They drove in silence until Mason came to the parking lot.

"This is it."

Mason said, "I'll run down here a half a block and let you out. You walk back. I'll double-park if I can get away with it. There doesn't seem to be any place where I can park here. Get your car, drive out and follow me."

She nodded.

Mason slid the car to a stop. She jerked open the door and jumped out. Mason sat there waiting, watching in the rearview mirror.

A car some thirty yards ahead pulled out from its place at the curb, and Mason moved on, making an awkward attempt to park his car. In that way he was able to keep it pointed out in traffic, yet couldn't have been ticketed for double-parking.

Sybil Harlan drove her car out of the parking lot, came speeding down the street.

Mason gunned his car out into traffic, waved her a signal, then slowed, drove down the boulevard, turned to the right on a cross-street, then finally found a place where there was room for two cars.

Mason pulled his car to a stop, and Sybil pulled in behind him. The lawyer got out of his car and walked back to her car.

"Mr. Mason, look," she said, indicating the door of the glove compartment.

The door was warped back. The catch on the lock had been broken out of its seat.

Mason's voice was hard. "I'm looking."

"Someone broke in here."

"I see," the lawyer said coldly. "I suppose the only thing missing is the gun?"

She nodded. "It must have happened just minutes ago. It must have been the police."

Mason's voice was level. "You didn't say anything to the parking attendant?"

"Heavens no."

"Where did you get the screw driver?"

"What screw driver?"

"The one you used to pry open the door?"

"I didn't do it, Mr. Mason. Honestly, I didn't do it. Look, if I'd done it I'd have the gun, wouldn't I? Or I'd . . . well, anyway, I'd have the screw driver. Search me. Go ahead, search me."

Mason shook his head. "The time's past for that. You're a client. I'm your lawyer. If you want to lie to me, go ahead. I can tell you one thing, lying to your lawyer or your doctor is an expensive and sometimes a fatal pastime."

There were tears in her eyes. "Mr. Mason, what can I do to convince you of my good faith?"

"Nothing, now."

"You've closed your mind against me, haven't you?"

"No. You're my client. I'm going to see that your rights are protected. I'm going to see that any evidence presented against you is the truth. I'm going to cross-examine any witness who takes the stand and testifies against you."

"You don't believe me, but you'll represent me?"

"I'm keeping my opinions in abeyance. I'm going to do what I can. Did you kill Lutts?"

"No."

"All right. I want you to do exactly as I say. Do you have some woman whom you can trust?"

"You mean to tell what happened?"

"No, no," Mason said impatiently. "I mean trust, with ordinary confidence. Someone who's levelheaded, calm, and sufficiently prominent to——"

"Yes, there's Ruth Marvel."

"Who is she?"

"She's the president of our Current Topics club. She's remarkably well informed."

"And a good friend?"

"A very good friend."

Mason said, "Do exactly as I tell you. Take your car, drive home, go in and change your clothes, put on an entirely different type of outfit—get something dark and somber. Then ask Ruth Marvel if she'll go out to look over some property with you, some property that you intend to buy. Tell her that it's very important, that you'd like to have her opinion on it, but don't tell her where the property is."

Sybil Harlan nodded.

"Tell her that you'll be by for her," Mason said. "Then grab the paper and open it to property that's listed for sale in the classified ads. Find a place that's not too far away but a place that's on the outskirts somewhere."

Again Mrs. Harlan nodded.

"Are you getting this?" Mason asked.

"Yes, it's simple."

"It's simple," Mason said, "but it's tricky as hell. You have to do exactly what I tell you to do."

"All right. I get Ruth Marvel. I get her to go with me. I get the listings of property that's not too far out."

"That's right. Now then, we come to the tricky part. After you have Ruth Marvel ready to go with you, you get in your car and start out. Then you tell your friend that the trouble with looking at property in your own machine is that there's always somebody to take down the license number—they trace the number, find out who owns the automobile, and then you're pestered to death with real estate salesmen trying to interest you in that property or selling you something else. You always prefer starting out in your car but take a taxi for the last part of the trip. Do you understand?"

Mrs. Harlan nodded.

"So," Mason said, "you then remember something you have to telephone about. You get out of your car at a telephone booth. You telephone the Drake Detective Agency. Here's the number. I've written it on one of

my cards. You ask for Paul Drake. You tell him who
you are. Now then, Paul Drake will tell you where to
drive. You drive to this address, stop at the first avail-
able parking space, park your car and get out.

"Within a few minutes a taxicab will come along. Now,
be sure it's a Red Line taxicab. Try not to pay too much
attention to it, and don't be too conspicuous. You settle
back in the car and tell the driver to drive on down
the street, that you want to look at several pieces of
property. Tell your friend that you have suddenly discovered you're short of money but that if she'll pay for
the cab and save the receipt, you'll give her the money
later. Tell her to be sure to save the receipt so that you
can have a proper voucher for your income tax deduc-
tion."

"Mr. Mason, this is all terribly complicated and——"

"Shut up," Mason said. "Listen. We haven't much
time. Do *exactly* as I tell you. Have the cab drive
around several streets while you look at different houses.
When the meter registers a dollar and sixty-five cents,
have him turn around and drive back in the direction
of the place where you have parked your car. Under
no circumstances are you to say anything more than the
bare necessities to the taxi driver. Be sure and get Ruth
to pay off the cab. Encourage her to talk with the cab
driver as much as possible, and when the meter reaches
two dollars and ninety-five cents, apparently come to
the last place you were looking for. Stop the driver
and have Ruth pay off the cab. Tell Ruth to give him
three dollars and a half, and you'll pay her later. Do
you understand all that?"

"I understand it, Mr. Mason. But it seems to me we're
wasting a lot of valuable time, and I don't see why——"

"If you understand what you're to do," Mason interrupted, "you're wasting time talking about it. Just be
sure you understand exactly what you're to do."

She took the card Mason had given her with Paul

Drake's number. "Very well," she said dubiously, "I'll do it and——"

"Now don't misunderstand me," Mason said. "Your life may depend on it. You do *exactly* as I have told you. Follow instructions to the letter. You understand?"

"I understand, but there's no need to do that with Ruth. I can tell her exactly what I'm trying to do, and——"

"Don't do it," Mason warned. "Do exactly as I've told you. You *may* be able to get a lucky break—and you may not."

6

■

MASON UNLOCKED THE EXIT DOOR OF HIS PRIVATE OFFICE.

Della Street looked up from the evening newspaper. "How goes it?" she asked.

"We've got work to do, Della. Thanks for the note."

"Chief, did you notice her shoes and stockings?"

"I didn't see any difference, Della. They looked just the same to me."

"Well, they aren't the same. The other shoes, the ones she wore this morning, were open-toed and had a small design in red leather at the instep. The shoes she had on this afternoon were solid white sport shoes, with no design in color and no open toes."

"What about the stockings?" Mason asked.

"Well, Chief, this morning when she was in I took particular notice of the way she was dressed—you know how we women are about such matters—and I was impressed by the way she had matched every piece of her outer clothing. Her white shoes with just enough red trim to match the off-white jacket with red trim, the white bag and white pleated skirt. But I especially took note of her stockings. They were a very soft flesh shade, so that they blended in with the white skirt and shoes and yet did not make her legs appear too pale, and they were seamless. That was important with that outfit.

"But this afternoon when she was in, she wore hose that were on the beige side—and they had seams."

"Well, of course, she could have changed them," Mason said.

"When? Didn't she take you up there to the house and then go directly to the beauty shop?"

"I think that was her plan. I didn't cross-examine her to find out if she'd changed her plans."

"Why?"

"Because," Mason said, grinning, "I thought it would be better not to know the answers. Thanks for the tip, Della, but after all, she's our client. We're representing her. We take her story at face value."

"What do we do now?"

"We go down to Paul Drake's office. He's probably got that taxi located by this time, and Mrs. Harlan is going to call his number as soon as she gets a friend of hers located."

"Was her gun in the car?" Della Street asked.

Mason's face was wooden. "Someone had broken into the glove compartment. The gun was missing. Let's go."

Mason held the door open for her, and they walked down the corridor to Paul Drake's office.

The girl at the switchboard looked up, recognized Mason, nodded and pointed to the wooden gate which barred a long passageway, on each side of which were numerous small offices.

Mason worked the hidden catch on the gate, opened it for Della Street, and they walked down to Paul Drake's office.

Drake looked up as they entered, nodded, and then

devoted his attention to earphones which were clamped over his head.

Mason raised his eyebrows in silent interrogation, and Drake threw a switch which put the sound on a loud-speaker.

Mason heard the voice of a taxicab dispatcher droning off directions. "Cab three-twenty-eight to the Brown Derby in Hollywood, a Mr. Culber. . . . Come in, two-fourteen . . . come in, two-fourteen. . . ." A man's gruff voice said, "Cab two-fourteen on a call to eighty-one hundred block on South Figueroa . . ."

Drake switched off the loud-speaker, took one of the headphones from his ear, said, "Hi, Perry. How are you, Della? Just a monitoring chore."

"Keeping track of seven-sixty-one?" Mason asked.

"That's right. I'm on the frequency of the Red Line dispatching office."

Mason said, "Gosh, Paul, I hadn't thought of tuning in on their wave length so as to keep track of their cabs. I thought you'd have to put out operatives. Where did you get that gadget?"

"Oh, we keep them around," Drake said. "Occasionally, it's a good thing to monitor police calls, find out about taxicabs, and so forth. It saves us a lot of leg work, and sometimes the cab companies don't want to give out that information."

"Heard anything from Mrs. Harlan?" Mason asked.

Drake shook his head, then said, "Wait a minute. Here's cab seven-sixty-one now."

Drake made a note on a pad of paper and said, "He's out in Beverly Hills, coming in on Sunset toward Holly-wood, running empty, has completed a call."

Mason said, "Hang it! I wish we'd hear from that Harlan woman, but after all, she had a few things to take care of."

"What's the idea?" Drake asked.

Mason said, "You should know me better than that,

Paul. I just want to keep a taxicab located, that's all."

"Witness?" Drake asked.

Mason grinned, winked at Della Street and said, "Witness."

They waited for an impatient twenty minutes, then the phone rang. Paul Drake answered the phone, said, "Yes . . . oh yes . . . Mrs. Harlan."

Mason reached for the phone. "I'll take it, Paul. Where's cab seven-sixty-one?"

Drake said, "The last reports we had he'd picked up a fare and—wait a minute, here's something coming in now."

"You ready, Mrs. Harlan?" Mason asked on the line.

"All ready."

"You have Ruth Marvel with you?"

"Yes."

"Good girl," Mason said approvingly. "Hold on for a minute."

Drake said, "Cab seven-sixty-one has picked up a fare in Hollywood and is going out to the end of North La Brea. There's a movie actress has a swank place out there, and he has a call to her house."

"This is made to order, Mrs. Harlan," Mason said. "Go out almost to the end of North La Brea, park your car and wait. The Red Line cab will be cruising back toward town, looking for fares. Be sure you get out past the point where Franklin Street runs into La Brea. And be sure you take the Red Line cab going south. I'll wait here until you phone me. Now make it fast. You can just about make connections with the cab. If I don't hear from you in fifteen minutes, I'll assume that you have made connections. If you haven't, call me back in fifteen minutes. Is that clear?"

"That's clear."

"Get going," Mason said.

"I'm going," she said, and he heard the click of the telephone.

Mason dropped into one of Drake's chairs, said, "Why don't you get some decent chairs here, Paul?"

"I can't afford it," Drake told him, grinning.

"I pay you enough so you could have——"

"It isn't that," Drake interrupted. "I can't afford to have my clients relax the way you do. I want to keep them on the edge of the chair. Still want me to monitor seven-sixty-one?"

"Yes," Mason said. "I'd like to see if he makes a pickup coming back from his run."

Mason lit a cigarette, picked up one of the late issues of the *Journal of Criminal Law, Criminology, and Police Science,* and became immersed in the section dealing with criminal law, case notes and comments.

Della Street sat quietly, waiting, knowing that this period of suspense would start Mason pacing the floor unless his mind was kept occupied. She raised her forefinger to her lips in a signal to Paul Drake.

Drake nodded to show that he understood.

The office became silent, Drake holding the earphones, from time to time making notes, Mason completely absorbed in his reading, Della Street occasionally exchanging signals with Drake.

Drake, at length, looked up at Della Street, nodded, held thumb and forefinger together in a circle.

Della Street started to say something, then changed her mind and waited until Mason had finished reading the journal and tossed it to one side.

"Any news, Paul?"

"Cab seven-sixty-one reports that it picked up a fare on North La Brea and is on a trip to look at some property that's for sale in the southwestern part of the city."

Mason grinned at Della Street. "Okay, Della, let's go back to our office and wait this one out. Then I'll buy you dinner."

"How about me?" Drake asked.

"What about you?"

"Dinner?"

"Oh, sure," Mason said. "Good Lord, Paul, I wouldn't want you to sit here and work without dinner."

Drake took off the headphones, clicked the switch, stretched and yawned. "A good steak and French-fried potatoes will go good after all the——"

"It'll be a job getting it sent up," Mason interrupted.

"Now, wait a minute," Drake protested. "You mean I can have dinner but I can't go out?"

"Sure," Mason said. "Get anything you want sent up, but stick around on the end of that telephone for a while. Things are going to happen."

Drake sighed. "I should have known it. I've ruined my stomach earning per diems and eating hamburgers, while you and Della are collecting big fees and reveling in juicy steaks."

"Just one of the inequities of the world," Mason assured him, grinning. "Want me to order a couple of hamburgers for you, Paul? How do you want them— with relish and chopped onion or——?"

"Go to hell," Drake said.

Mason grinned at him, motioned to Della, and they walked out.

"Can you," Della Street asked, "tell me what you're up to?"

Mason shook his head. "Better not. See if you can get Herbert Doxey on the telephone, Della."

Della Street walked rapidly down the corridor, fitted her latchkey to the lock of the door to Mason's private office. They entered and Della Street ran through the telephone directory, jotted down a number.

"Got it?" Mason asked.

"I think so."

Della Street dialed the number, then after a moment said, "Mr. Doxey . . . ? Just a moment. Mr. Mason wants to talk with you."

She nodded, and Mason picked up his own telephone, said, "Mr. Doxey, Perry Mason talking. I would like to know a little more about the holdings of the Sylvan Glade Development Company. Can you tell me just how many acres are in the property, how much of it is level property, how much of it is on the hill, and whether there has been a survey to determine the exact boundary on the north?"

Doxey cleared his throat importantly. "I have all that information in the form of an estimate by contractors as to the cost of leveling and hauling. You see, Mr. Mason, at the time we started it hadn't occurred to us that it would be possible to sell the dirt for the freeway fill. So we had bids as to the estimated amount of yardage and the cost of moving. There was a survey of the northern boundary, but the stakes aren't there any more."

"Where are they?"

"Some of them went down with that slide which followed the rain and some of them caved in when the contractor was taking out dirt on the Claffin property."

"I see," Mason said. "In other words, they deliberately excavated some of our property?"

"Not exactly, but they excavated close enough to it so that there was a cave-in."

Mason said, "I would like to see Mr. Lutts at the earliest possible moment."

"You and about ten other people," Doxey said.

"How's that?" Mason asked.

Doxey laughed. "Your little stock transaction set off a chain reaction. Everybody wants to know how much you paid for that stock, and somehow there seems to be a rumor that my father-in-law is in the market for a lot more stock in the company."

"To take the place of the holdings which he sold me?" Mason asked.

Doxey said, "He doesn't confide in me. I was merely giving you the rumor which has resulted in a whole flock of phone calls. I've been trying to find him myself."

"If he should come in," Mason said, "tell him that I'm looking for him."

"Thank you," Doxey said. "I will. Can you leave a number where he can call you?"

"Have him call me at my office."

"Won't your switchboard be disconnected?"

"No, I'm connecting the main trunk line through to my private office."

"Very well, I'll have him call."

"As soon as he comes in," Mason said.

Doxey said dubiously, "Well, there are quite a few other messages, Mr. Mason. It seems as though everyone wants him to call the minute he comes in. However, I'll see that he gets your message."

"Thank you," Mason said. "Tell him that it's important."

Mason hung up, said to Della Street, "The board is connected so that incoming calls will be received in here, Della?"

She nodded.

After a while, Della Street said, "Chief, are you in the clear, protecting Mrs. Harlan on this thing?"

"I don't know. Of course, I only know what my client told me, and that's a sacred confidence."

"What about the canons of ethics?"

"The first duty of a lawyer is to protect his client. You have to understand the relative values, Della.

"Take, for instance, the case of a doctor speeding to the bedside of a patient who is critically ill. He's probably violating a whole assortment of traffic laws, but the emergency makes it advisable to do so. He has to use his own judgment."

Della Street shook her head. "Every time I argue with you, I get the worst of it. And yet——"

The telephone rang. Della Street picked up the receiver, said, "Perry Mason's office. . . . Yes, he is, Mrs. Harlan. I'll put him on."

She nodded to Mason and he picked up the telephone on his desk, while Della Street continued to listen in on her telephone.

"It's all right, Mr. Mason. I'm back home."

"It's all right to talk?"

"Yes."

"You recognized the cab driver?"

"Yes, of course."

"It's the same one?"

"Yes."

"No question about it?"

"No, none whatever."

"He didn't recognize you?"

"He didn't pay the slightest attention to me, Mr. Mason. I had Ruth flag him down. After we got in the cab I told him where I wanted him to go, but I was seated in such a position that I was directly behind his back. He turned around and saw Ruth, but I don't think he even gave me a good look—and, of course, I was dressed differently."

"You have the taxicab receipt, showing a meter reading of two dollars and ninety-five cents?"

"Yes."

"That's fine," Mason said. "Leave that receipt in your purse."

"And what do I do now?"

"Now, you simply relax and forget everything—provided you've been telling me the truth and you *didn't* pull any triggers."

"I *have* been telling you the truth, Mr. Mason."

"All right, fine. Go ahead and enjoy your fifth wedding anniversary."

"You can't enjoy a wedding anniversary without a husband."

"You expect him home, don't you?"

"I *expect* him home, yes. I'm all jittery. I'm so nervous I don't feel that I can——"

"Do what I told you to do," Mason said. "Forget everything. This is a crucial period as far as your marriage is concerned. You've sacrificed a lot in order to get this opportunity. Now, go ahead and capitalize on it."

"I'll . . . I'll do my best."

"And that," Mason told her, "should be pretty good."

"Make no mistake about it, Mr. Mason, it's going to be damn good," she said and hung up.

7

∎

MASON LOOKED AT HIS WATCH. IT WAS SEVERAL MINUTES since Mrs. Harlan had called. "I thought we'd hear from Doxey before this. He should be getting worried. I'd like to get some action before dark. I hate to do this to you, Della, but you're going to have a late dinner. Get Doxey again, will you please?"

Della nodded, put through the call, and said, "Just a moment, Mr. Doxey. Mr. Mason again."

Mason said, "Hello, Doxey. I'm just leaving the office. Any word from your father-in-law?"

"No," Doxey said. "I'm worried. We dine at seven o'clock every night. It's a schedule that is like clockwork, and Daddy Lutts doesn't let anything interfere with dinner. Once or twice, when he has been in the middle of a big business deal that he couldn't conclude he's telephoned to let us know that he couldn't be here. But tonight we haven't heard a word. He's nearly an hour late, now. We went ahead and had dinner."

"Oh, well, he'll probably show up all right. I'm——"

"But there's something wrong, Mr. Mason. He's been in an automobile accident or something. He would have shown up or telephoned. He's a stickler for dinner. He wants it on the table right on the dot—that's been one of the things that has bothered us in connection with our housekeeping help. He doesn't realize that some of these things can create rather difficult problems."

"Well," Mason said, "it'll probably turn out all right. I wanted to get him to take me out to show me the actual location of that north boundary line on the ground. He promised me he'd co-operate in every way he could. I wanted to get out there before dark."

"Yes, I'm certain he'll help you all he can. He appreciated the fact that you didn't do any haggling and that you were most considerate in your dealings with him."

Mason said, "I'm very much interested in this thing. I'm going to need certain information tonight. Would it be possible for *you* to go out there and show me the location of that line? Even with daylight saving time, we haven't very many minutes of daylight left."

"Well . . . you know where the property is, of course."

"I've been there."

"Well, the line is just to the north of the building. You can see one of the stakes and——"

"I'd like very much to have you show me. It wouldn't take long. I could drive by and pick you up."

"Very well," Doxey said. "It isn't a long drive from here. We could get there in about seven minutes from my house. Do you know where I live?"

"I have the address from the phone book," Mason said.

"Well, that's right. Just drive up and tap on your horn. I'll be right out. My wife is a little worried."

"Try calling the police and the hospitals. If he's been in an accident, there'll be a record of it."

"I've thought of that. I don't like to do it, however, because it will worry my wife when she hears me placing the calls."

"He might be at the office and just not answering the phone."

"No, I've been up to the office. He isn't there."

"Well, don't worry about it," Mason told him. "He'll show up all right. I'll be out in about . . . well, it'll take me about fifteen minutes from here, I guess."

"I'll be looking for you," Doxey said.

Mason hung up the telephone and said to Della Street, "Okay, Della, you'll have to wait, and——"

"I'm going with you. You can't shake me that easily. You'll need me to take notes."

Mason shook his head.

"Yes, Chief, please. You'll need someone to——"

"You know what's going to happen," Mason said.

"I won't give the show away."

"All right," Mason conceded. "Bring along a notebook and some pencils. Sit in the back seat and keep notes on any conversation. Let's go."

They drove out to Doxey's house, which they found without difficulty. It was a large white stucco, red-tile roofed house, a traditional California type of Spanish architecture. There were two palm trees in front of the doorway to the porch, a wide cement walk crossed a velvety, grassy lawn to the sidewalk. Mason tapped the horn button twice, and almost instantly the door opened and Herbert Doxey started out, turned, said something over his shoulder, closed the door and came running down the walk.

"Heard from Lutts?" Mason asked.

"Not a word. We're really becoming quite apprehensive about him."

Mason introduced Doxey to Della Street.

"Don't you want to ride up in front?" Doxey asked. "I'd just as soon——"

"No, she's fine," Mason said. "I'd like to talk with you. Sit up here and tell me something about the affairs of the company."

"I'm afraid there's not very much I can tell you, Mr.

Mason," Doxey said, getting into the front seat. "I think you're fully conversant with the plans of the company, that is, the plans the company did have before this afternoon's meeting."

"And now what's happened?" Mason asked.

"Well," Doxey said, laughing, "there's been a sharp division of opinion. You'll appreciate my position. As an officer of the company I want ot give you all the information you want, but I have to remain neutral."

"I understand," Mason told him, "and I appreciate your courtesy. You mentioned a divided opinion. Just how is the opinion divided?"

"Well, Mr. Mason, a peculiar situation has developed. I . . . I don't feel that I can tell you any more until I talk with Daddy Lutts."

"What's the book value of the stock?" Mason asked.

"I— Well, there again it's a matter of opinion."

"What's the book value per share with reference to the money the company has invested?"

"Oh, that's quite low, Mr. Mason. Undoubtedly, *very, very* much below the market price. You see, the company made a rather speculative buy, and circumstances have developed that have made the original value important only from a bookkeeping standpoint."

"I see," Mason said dryly, then asked, "any recent transfers of stock?"

"Well, I— Your transfer was recent."

"Been any since then?" Mason asked.

Doxey hesitated.

"After all," Mason told him, "there's no use being mysterious with me. I'm a stockholder in the company. I'm entitled to information."

"Some sales were made late this afternoon," Doxey said noncommittally.

"Who sold?"

"Some of the others on the board of directors."

"Who bought?"

"I . . . I . . . know certain things in confidence, Mr. Mason. I——"

"You'll learn them officially as soon as the shares are surrendered for transfer?"

"Yes, I suppose so."

"Have they been surrendered for transfer?"

"To what shares are you referring, Mr. Mason?"

Mason said, "I'm referring to any shares that were sold this afternoon. Now don't get so damned technical; if you're going to get along with me, don't start by trying to hold out information."

"There are others to get along with," Doxey said. "I'm in the position of being between two fires."

"Where's the other fire?"

"I think you can figure that out, Mr. Mason."

"All right," Mason said, "let's get down to brass tacks. How many transfers of stock have you entered this afternoon, *after* the transfer of my shares this morning?"

"One," Doxey said.

"Who to?"

"Daddy Lutts bought some shares."

"Who sold?"

"Regerson B. Neffs."

How many shares of stock?"

"The certificates that I entered for transfer on the books of the corporation amounted to three thousand shares of stock."

"What did Lutts pay for them?" Mason asked.

"The consideration didn't show on the transfers. It was a private matter."

"Neffs is sort of a stuffed shirt, isn't he?" Mason asked.

"I'm sorry," Doxey said, laughing, "but the corporation doesn't pay me to discuss members of the board with the stockholders."

Mason glanced sidelong at Doxey. They were silent for a while; then Doxey shifted his position and said,

"I've got a sunburned back. You could do me a very great personal favor, Mr. Mason."

"How?"

"By telling me what you paid for Daddy Lutts' stock."

"Why?"

"I might do a little speculating."

"And you might get your fingers burnt."

"I'll take a chance on that. I know that Daddy Lutts is . . . well, he's . . . uh——"

"Exactly," Mason said. "He's greedy. He's decided that something has happened to make the stock worth a lot more money than the directors think it's worth. He's out buying more stock. Tha's why he forgot all about dinner tonight."

Doxey said irritably, "Well, at least he could have rung up Georgiana."

"Georgiana is your wife?"

"That's right. Daddy Lutts' daughter. His name is George. He wanted a son, but when it turned out to be a daughter, they called her Georgiana. That was as close as they could come."

"I see," Mason said.

"You still haven't answered my question," Doxey told him.

"I'll put it this way," Mason said. "I paid too damn much for the stock."

"Yes," Doxey said sarcastically, "I have a picture of the great Perry Mason going around buying things at too high a price."

"We might make a trade," Mason suggested.

"In what way?"

"You may have some information that I want."

"What?"

"Does Lutts know who my client is?"

Doxey glanced at Mason, hesitated, then said, "I think he does."

"Do you know?"

"No."

"How did Lutts find out?"

"I couldn't tell you that. He might have traced the check that your client gave you. He has a bank teller who's under obligations to him. That's all I know. Now, it's your turn."

Mason said, "I paid thirty-two thousand seven hundred and fifty dollars for Lutts' two thousand shares of stock."

Doxey regarded Mason as one might look at an individual who had just started to put on water wings to jump from the upper deck of the *Queen Mary* in the middle of the Atlantic. "You paid *what?*" he asked.

"You heard me."

"Good heavens, Mr. Mason! That— Why . . . why if you'd only let me know, I could have bought all the stock you wanted at eight dollars a share. There have been some sales at seven."

"That's the point," Mason said. "I told you I paid too much money for it."

"Why?"

"Now that," Mason said, "is something that I can't discuss. You can, of course, draw your own conclusions."

"You mean that you wanted . . . you wanted Daddy Lutts out of the corporation?"

"He bought right back in again, didn't he?" Mason asked.

"Yes, of course. But during the period when he wasn't a stockholder he had to resign from the board of directors because he wasn't properly qualified. Look here, Mr. Mason, you're playing some sort of a deep game, with the control of this corporation at stake."

Mason grinned, turned the car into the bumpy, ancient road which led up to the property of the Sylvan Glade Development Company. He made the sharp turn at the foot of the hill. The car crawled up the hill, and then, as they reached the top, Doxey exclaimed excitedly, "Good heavens, Mr. Mason! That's Daddy Lutts' car. He's up here himself."

"That's fine," Mason said. "I want to see him."

"I simply can't imagine why he didn't come home," Doxey said. "But it's a relief to me to know that he's all right. I suppose it's some new business angle he's working on. He's sure a sharpshooter."

There was envy and a certain sharp-edged jealousy in Doxey's voice.

Mason parked the car. He and Doxey got out.

"You may as well wait here, Della," Mason said casually.

"We'll be right back, Miss Street," Doxey said reassuringly.

"Can we get into the place?" Mason asked.

"We can if Daddy Lutts is in there. The door is kept locked, but he has the key."

Doxey tried the door. "It's unlocked," he said. "Come on in."

"What a dirty place," Mason announced.

"The people who moved out knew it was going to be torn down," Doxey explained. "They just pulled out and left all of this junk behind them."

"Better call to Lutts," Mason said, "and get him to come down."

"He might not like that. There's a certain protocol in connection with being a son-in-law," Doxey said, grinning. "I'll go up and see what he's doing."

"It's fairly dark in here," Mason said. "Even with daylight saving time, it's rather late. Be careful."

"I can see all right," Doxey said, and groped his way up the stairs. Suddenly he stopped partway up the second flight.

"What's the trouble?" Mason asked.

"Come . . . come up here," Doxey said in a harsh, rasping voice.

"What's the trouble?"

"Come up here."

Mason climbed the stairs. Doxey was bending over Lutts' body.

"Good heavens!" Mason said. "He's lying there head down . . . what is it? A heart attack? How long do you suppose he's been there?"

Doxey struck a match, shielded his eyes from the flame, said, "Look at that blood—it's come from that hole in his chest."

"Try his pulse," Mason said.

Doxey bent down, then after a moment said, "I think he's dead. His body's begun to cool off. It feels sort of . . . well, you know—dead."

Mason said, "All right. We'll notify the police."

"Shouldn't we move him and get him around . . . so his head isn't——"

"Don't touch the body," Mason warned. "Get the police."

"Oh, good Lord," Doxey said. "This is one hell of a mess. What am I going to do? How am I going to tell Georgiana? We can take his car. You drive yours and I'll drive his and——"

"You leave everything *exactly* as it is," Mason said. "Don't touch a single thing. I'll stay here and see that nothing happens, and you take my car, go down the hill and call the police."

"I'll stay, and you can go——"

"Not me," Mason said. "The police don't like it when I report that I've discovered a corpse."

"Well, you were along on this one," Doxey said. "I want you to remember——"

"Oh, sure," Mason told him. "I'm going to be right with you in the thing, but you were the one to discover it, and you'll be the one to report it."

"You want to wait here?"

"I'll wait right here. You explain to Miss Street that there's been an accident."

"She could sit in his car and——"

Mason shook his head. "The police wouldn't like that. They'll want to go over his car, trying to find fingerprints. Go call the police. I'll wait."

"All right," Doxey said. "What department do I call?"

"Just tell whoever answers that you want to report a homicide," Mason said, "and tell them you're in a hurry. They'll put you through."

"All right," Doxey said. "I'll . . . do you think I'd better tell Georgiana?"

"I wouldn't quite yet," Mason told him.

Doxey ran back down the stairs. A few moments later Mason heard the car start, then take off down the hill. Mason walked back to stand in the doorway.

It was nearly ten minutes before Doxey returned, and Mason could hear the sound of the siren as a police car followed him. The lawyer walked out away from the doorway.

Doxey parked Mason's car off to one side. The police car ground to a stop. One of the radio officers came bustling up to Mason. "Hello, Mr. Mason. How are you mixed up in this thing?"

"I'm not," Mason said. "I was just standing guard until you arrived."

"That isn't what I meant."

"Well," Mason told him, "that's what I meant."

The officer looked at Mason sharply, then took a flashlight and entered the house. The other officer stood by the door, watching the place.

"It's a job for homicide, all right," the first officer called from the interior of the house.

Mason heard the officer in the car making contact on the two-way radiophone.

"You might tell me what you know about it," the first officer said to Mason, emerging from the building.

"Ask him," Mason said, jerking his thumb toward Doxey. "He's related to the man. He found the body."

"I didn't touch anything," Doxey said. "I wanted to straighten him up, but Mr. Mason said to leave him alone."

"That's right."

"How is he related to you?"

"My father-in-law."

"How old?"

"Around fifty-four or -five."

"Where was he living?"

"With us."

"How did you know he was up here?"

"I didn't. I came up here on another matter and then saw his car."

The officers continued to question Doxey about various matters until a car from Homicide Squad came laboring up the hill.

"Well, well, well, well," Sergeant Holcomb said, "look who we've got here! Look who's discovered another body!"

"Not me," Mason said.

"How'd you happen to come up here?"

"Looking over property."

"And this was all a big surprise to you," Sergeant Holcomb said.

"That's right."

Holcomb said, "You should have some kind of a rubber stamp or pocket recorder so you could play this same record over and over. It would save wear and tear on your vocal cords."

Mason said, "You'd better get in there and look around, and you'd better talk with that man over there. He's the one who discovered the body."

"Yeah, I know," Sergeant Holcomb said sneeringly. "You arranged this one a little different."

Mason walked over, climbed into his car and sat down.

"Want any notes?" Della Street asked.

"No, not yet. Did Doxey call his wife?"

"No. He called the police. They told him to wait right there at the phone booth and they'd have a radio car there within five minutes."

"Good work," Mason said.

Sergeant Holcomb and two detectives from Homicide

Squad entered the place, leaving one of the radio officers on guard.

After a while, Holcomb came out, talked briefly with the officers, and then came over to Mason.

"What did you find?" Mason asked.

"How did you happen to come up here, Mason?"

"I'm representing a client."

"Who?"

Mason shrugged his shoulders.

"We'll find out."

"Go ahead. That's your duty and privilege. It's my duty to protect my client."

"What did you come up here *for?*"

"Specifically," Mason said, "I came up to look at the boundaries of this property. Does that satisfy you?"

Sergeant Holcomb regarded him for a moment, said, "No," and abruptly turned away.

Mason nodded to Doxey. "Let's go, Doxey," he said. "They've got everything they need from us."

"I'm not so sure," Sergeant Holcomb said, turning around.

"Well, I am," Mason told him. "There aren't any other questions you want to ask, are there?"

"They may turn up later on."

"Then get in touch with me later on," Mason said. "You coming Doxey?"

Doxey glanced apprehensively at the officers, said, "Yes . . . I guess so," and got in Mason's car.

"I'll take you home," Mason said, easing the car into motion, "and you can break the news to your wife personally. That'll be better than trying to do it over the phone."

Doxey nodded, presently blew his nose, surreptitiously wiped the corners of his eyes. "I'd be a damned liar if I told you there weren't times when Daddy Lutts was hard to get along with, but I was very fond of him and— The poor guy."

"It wasn't suicide?" Mason asked.

"Heavens, no. At least, I don't think so. He was in good spirits until after you bought his stock, and then he . . . and then he thought of a way of getting stock to take the place of the stock he had sold you, and still have some gravy, and that made him feel even better."

"After he got to thinking it over," Mason said, "he may have thought it would have been better if he'd left the situation the way it was."

"Not Daddy Lutts. He worries about something of that sort. He just couldn't understand why you wanted stock in the company, and the more he thought of it, the more worried he became. He's a gambler at heart. A situation like this was made to order for him. When I say he was worried, I don't mean it the way you'd be inclined to take it. I mean that he was afraid there was something going on beneath the surface that he couldn't get a line on—you know what I mean—that he couldn't . . . well, if there were any gravy trains going by, he wanted to get aboard."

"Nothing in his accounts," Mason said. "He wouldn't be short of money or anything?"

"Anything but! Why, the guy's worth a million. He played the cards close to his chest, but he had lots of chips."

"Well," Mason told him, "I extend my sympathies. You'll have to break it rather gently to your wife. Was she fond of him?"

"In their respective ways, they were *very* fond of each other. But they were . . . well, they were a lot alike. Their temperaments would clash, but they loved their little squabbles. She's going to be terribly broken up."

"Does she have any stock in this company?" Mason asked.

"No. Daddy Lutts told her she'd have plenty when he died, but while he was alive he was going to hang on to every cent. That's the way he was—always joking, telling her about the too indulgent and credulous parents who gave it all away and then were thrown out. It's hard to explain. When I tell it, it doesn't sound like a joke, but Daddy Lutts and Georgiana always used to kid about it. It was the way they joked back and forth. She'll miss him terribly."

"Well, it's a horrible jolt," Mason said.

Again Doxey blew his nose, then turned his head, ostensibly interested in the scenery.

Mason paused at the first service station where there was a telephone. "I'll only be a minute," he told Doxey. He called Paul Drake's office. "Paul, do you still have contacts with the newspaper reporters who cover police headquarters?"

"Sure," Drake said. "Why?"

"Because," Mason told him, "a man by the name of George C. Lutts was murdered in a deserted house in an outlying real estate development project late this afternoon. I want all of the dope just as fast as it comes into police headquarters. I particularly want to know whether they have recovered the murder weapon, where the man was standing when he was shot, how long he lived after being shot, the direction from which the shot was fired, and whether police feel there was a woman involved in the case."

"Anything else?" Drake asked sarcastically.

"Certainly," Mason said. "I want *everything* else— fast."

"Okay," Drake said. "Here's something else for you, Perry."

"Hurry up, Paul. I'm in a rush."

Drake said, "Mrs. Harlan phoned . . . said she wanted me to give you a message. Said to tell you that everything was working out fine, that the third corner of the triangle already had her husband on the defensive, that Roxy and Mrs. Harlan's husband had been to see Roxy's lawyer and that her husband had finally awakened to the fact that it was their fifth wedding anniversary. She said that I was to tell you, quote, 'He is behaving in a most satisfactory manner and exactly as anticipated.' "

"Well," Mason said, grinning, *that's* something."

"I take it it makes sense to you," Drake said.

"It makes sense to me. How long will it take you to get some of the dope on this Lutts murder case, Paul?"

"About the time Homicide Squad gets back and makes a report. The newspaper boys will pick up everything they're releasing to the public."

"You had dinner?" Mason asked.

"Oh, sure," Drake said sarcastically. "I had two sandwiches and coffee, and now I have just had my dessert of four tablets of bicarbonate of soda. I'm right back in my stride."

"That's fine," Mason told him. "You stay there and get the dope. Della and I are going out to dinner. Mrs. Harlan didn't leave any more messages for me, did she?"

"Yes," Drake said. "She said that she didn't want to be disturbed any more this evening, that she would appreciate anything you cold do along those lines."

"Yes, I take it she would," Mason said dryly. "Okay, Paul, see what you can find out. We'll call you later."

Mason hung up, returned to his car. "Sorry to keep you waiting, Doxey."

"It's okay. I'm dreading going home, breaking the news."

"Would it help any if I went in with you?" Della Street asked. "Or I could phone and tell her that you were on your way in and that you had some disturbing news—sort of break it to her gently."

"No, thanks. I appreciate your offer, but I'll have to face the situation, and I think the best way is to tell her all at once, not beat around the bush."

"You're the doctor," Mason told him. "But Miss Street wants you to know that anything we can do, we'll be glad to do."

"Thanks. This is one thing I'm going to have to face alone."

8

■

PERRY MASON, FRESH AND DEBONAIR, LATCHKEYED THE
door of his private office.

Della Street, who had been opening mail, looked up
at him with a smile.

"How's everything coming, Della?" Mason asked.

"So-so. Drake says he has a more complete report on
what happened than he was able to give us when we
phoned last night."

"That's fine," Mason said. "Give him a ring and tell
him to come in. What's in the mail?"

"The usual assortment of trouble. Letters from mothers,
telling you of their sons who have been convicted on
perjured evidence. A letter from Cleve Rector, stating that
he would like to discuss a business matter with you at
your earliest possible opportunity. A letter from Ezekiel
Elkins, stating that he would like an appointment regarding a matter in which you have a mutual interest.
An attorney named Arthur Nebitt Hagan has telephoned
twice; he says that he is representing Roxy Claffin and
that because of statements which you made to the board
of directors of the Sylvan Glade Development Company,
she finds herself suffering a pecuniary loss, that your
statement misinterpreted the law and misstated the facts.
It seems Mrs. Claffin wants you held strictly accountable,
but that Attorney Hagan is counseling moderation and
is suggesting that she hold off any action until after it
has become fully apparent that, as her representative, he
can't work out any amicable basis of approach."

"How interesting," Mason said.

"He wanted you to call him as soon as you came in."

"Get Paul Drake," Mason said. "Tell him to come in."

Mason busied himself reading the mail while Della Street phoned Paul Drake.

"No word from Mrs. Harlan?" Mason asked.

"Not yet."

"Paul Drake coming down?"

"He said he'd be in right away. He—here he is now."

Drake's code knock sounded on the door of the office, and Della Street opened it.

"How are you feeling this morning, Paul?" Mason asked.

"Terrible," Drake said, "I had acid indigestion all night."

"Comes from taking too much soda," Mason told him. "You destroy the alkaline balance in your system."

"I know," Drake said, "but taking too much soda comes from eating too many soggy hamburgers, and eating too many soggy hamburgers comes from working for a lawyer who wants everything fast. Actually, the way things developed, I could have gone out last night, had a nice dinner and then come back about eleven o'clock and got all of the information you needed."

"I know," Mason said, "but then we would have missed Mrs. Harlan's message about her fifth wedding anniversary."

"Yes, wasn't it wonderful. How are you connected with this Lutts' murder, Perry?"

"*I'm* not connected with it. Lutts was on the board of directors of a corporation in which I have invested a fairly large amount of money. I'm afraid his death may upset the balance of power."

"Then," Drake said, "why worry about the circumstances of his death? All you needed was a physician's certificate that he was dead. I could have told you that within a few minutes after you telephoned. He was dead as an iced mackerel."

"Anything else, Paul?"

"It seems the police found you at the scene of the murder."

"Yes. It was most unfortunate. I went out to inspect the property, and the corpse of Mr. Lutts made it impossible for me to carry out my inspection. The police were rather narrow-minded about the entire procedure."

"They're inclined to be that way," Drake said. "Then you know all about the place where the body was found?"

"That's right. An old three-story building which has been abandoned for some little time. This company Lutts was with was making a real estate development out of it. Lutts evidently went out there to look it over just before I arrived, and somebody shot him."

"That's right. With a thirty-eight revolver, right in the chest from a distance of about eighteen or twenty inches."

"In the chest?"

"Yes. Severed the aorta or something. Death was almost instantaneous."

"He was facing the person who shot him?"

"That's right."

"About eighteen inches away?"

Drake nodded. "Eighteen or twenty."

"They got that from a powder pattern, I presume," Mason said.

"That's right. They processed the vest and shirt at the police laboratory. The chemical pattern reaction of powder stains shows about eighteen inches—assuming that the weapon used was an ordinary thirty-eight caliber revolver with a standard barrel."

"When?" Mason asked.

"Probably around four-thirty yesterday afternoon."

"How do they fix the time?"

"They know that he didn't go to lunch until after a directors' meeting. They know just what he ate and exactly when. The post-mortem shows the condition of food in the stomach. Also, there's a question of body temperature. Police feel that they can fix the time of death within not more than a thirty-minute period. In other words, that the maximum period of variation will be fifteen minutes either way."

"I take it they haven't found the gun?"

"Not yet. They do have one clue."

"What?"

"When they broadcast the news of the murder—now this is confidential, Perry; it hasn't been released to the public yet——"

"Yes, yes, go on, never mind that."

"Well, a taxi driver came forward, a fellow by the name of Jerome C. Keddie. He's a Red Line cab driver. The cab number is seven-sixty-one."

"All right," Mason said, "go ahead. What are you looking at me like that for, Paul?"

Drake said, "I was just wondering why you had me locate cab number seven-sixty-one yesterday evening."

"Go on," Mason said, his face expressionless. "Tell me what Keddie told the cops."

"He said that he had picked up a very mysterious passenger, a young, attractive woman, dressed almost entirely in white, that is, a white skirt, white shoes and a sort of cream-colored jacket with red trim. He picked her up just a short distance from where the body was found. He was returning empty from the country club. There was something about his fare that impressed him. He noticed her particularly."

"What did he say impressed him?"

"He thought she'd been through some very harassing experience. He knew she'd been running. She seemed very upset. Her face was pale underneath her make-up. He thought that perhaps she had been out with a man who had tried to assault her and that she'd either been forced to get out and walk, or had hit him over the head in self-defense or something. He tried to sound her out in conversation, but couldn't get her to open up at all. He took her to the Union Station. He felt certain that she intended to catch another cab at the station and go to some other destination. She didn't have any baggage. She said her husband was going to meet her at the train. The cabbie said he thought she was lying.

"Keddie admitted he'd been listening to the radio broadcasts and that he'd read the morning newspaper, wondering if he wouldn't find something had happened out on that road—either that there'd been a hit-and-run accident or that some crime had been committed."

"He can identify this woman?" Mason asked.

"He can identify her," Drake said.

"That's nice," Mason observed quietly.

"So," Drake said, "I wonder where that leaves me, Perry."

"Why should it leave you anywhere?"

"I was scouting this cab for you."

"You don't need to tell the police that."

"Well, it depends on why I was doing it."

"You don't know why you were doing it."

"I suppose," Drake said, "you wanted to put one of your client's friends in this cab who could sort of pump the guy and see what happened. That bothers me a lot. But suppose it should turn out that this person he picked up was your client. That might leave us both in a predicament."

"Why?"

"Tampering with the evidence."

"Tampering with what evidence?"

"With the testimony of a witness."

"How?"

"Well, trying to influence him."

"Influence him to do what?"

"I don't know what was said by the people who were in that taxicab."

"Then," Mason said, "there's no need for you to worry. What else do you know?"

"Isn't that enough?"

"Not if there's anything else."

"Well, of course, the police felt that Keddie had the right idea. They're covering taxi drivers who were at the Union Station, seeing if they can find a taxi driver who remembers picking up a fare dressed as this woman was dressed."

"I see," Mason said.

"You're awfully damned noncommittal about this thing," Drake blurted out.

"Who did you want me to commit?" Mason asked. "Myself?"

"Well," Drake told him, "I thought you should know that——"

The telephone rang. Drake said, "That may be for me, Perry. I left word that if anything important came up in this case, they were to call me here."

Della Street picked up the telephone and nodded, said, "It's for you, Paul."

Drake picked up the receiver, said, "Yes, this is Paul. . . . Give me that again, will you."

Drake said, "Okay, I'll pass the word on to Mason. Nothing else, is there? . . . Okay. Thanks."

"Okay," Drake said wearily to Mason. "Here we go again."

"Where?" Mason asked.

"On one of those wild run-arounds of yours. The police have found the murder weapon."

"Where?"

"Someone had thrown it down on the bank to the north of the house."

"How nice," Mason said. "What did they find out from the weapon?"

"They found that it was a Smith and Wesson thirty-eight caliber revolver, with a five-inch barrel, that it had been fired three times, that the number on the gun had not been tampered with, that, tracing the number, the police found the sale had been made to Enright A. Harlan of 609 Lamison Avenue.

"At about the same time, the police got a lead from a taxi driver who had picked up a fare at the Union Station whose description matched the girl's they were looking for. This cabbie remembered that he had gone to someplace on Lamison Avenue, but he couldn't remember the exact number. It was someplace between Fifth and Ninth.

"So police got the taxi driver to see if he could locate the house, and it was 609 Lamison Avenue. Police went in and invited Mr. and Mrs. Enright A. Harlan to headquarters for a little chat with the district attorney. They're there now."

"Well," Mason said, "that's going to make an interesting case."

"You make such masterpieces of understatement," Paul Drake groaned. "That's going to make an exciting case, and if they should find out what you did with that taxi driver——"

"What did I do with him?" Mason asked.

"You did—Hell, I don't know *what* you did with him. Probably, you've arranged to confuse the issues in some way. You've——"

The telephone rang again. Della Street picked it up and again nodded. "For you once more, Paul."

Drake picked up the telephone, said, "Okay, shoot. This is Paul. . . . Who is it, Jim? . . . Oh, I see. They are? . . . Well, let me have it."

Drake was silent for almost a minute, then he said thoughtfully, "Well, I guess that's all there is to it, Jim. Just keep me posted. Thanks for letting me know."

Drake hung up the telephone and said, "Well, you were being so damned smart, Perry, you should have advised your client to use a little more care."

"In what way?" Mason asked.

"Police opened her purse and found the receipt issued by the taxi driver for the run down to the Union Station. The amount was two dollars and ninety-five cents, which is exactly the way the cab driver remem-

DELUXE LENGTH

KENT

WITH
THE FAMOUS MICRONITE FILTER

King Size
or Deluxe 100's.

Micronite filter.
Mild, smooth taste.
America's quality cigarette.
Kent.

Kings: 16 mg. "tar," 1.0 mg. nicotine; 100's: 19 mg. "tar," 1.2 mg. nicotine;
Menthol: 18 mg. "tar," 1.3 mg. nicotine; av. per cigarette, FTC Report Sept. '73.

Try the crisp, clean taste of Kent Menthol.

The only Menthol with the famous Micronite filter.

Warning: The Surgeon General Has Determined That Cigarette Smoking Is Dangerous to Your Health

bers it because he remembers she gave him three and a half, which left him a fifty-five-cent tip. The number of the taxi cab, number seven-sixty-one, is on that receipt. It seems to me, you might at least have had foresight enough to have your client drop that receipt in a waste-paper receptacle someplace. Now, we're hooked."

"Who's hooked?"

"You and I."

"You haven't anything to do with it."

"I wish I didn't—you had me locating that cab."

"Now look here," Mason said. "You do a lot of work for me, Paul. The things that you do for me are confidential."

"What if the police ask me? I can't lie to them."

Mason said, "Paul, your stomach is bothering you. You're living on greasy hamburgers and half-fried onions. You're eating entirely too much fried food. You're eating at irregular hours. You need a good rest—start taking it."

Drake looked at him in surprise.

"I have a job in La Jolla that I want you to work on," Mason told him.

"What is it?"

"I'll phone you details after you get down there."

"I'm to leave now?"

"Immediately," Mason said. "Get a nice unit in a motel, enjoy the ocean breezes and relax."

"I think I'm going to like this," Drake said.

"I knew you would," Mason told him. "Who's going to handle your office while you're gone?"

"Harry Blanton. I'll have to go to the bank to get some money."

"Give Paul some money out of the safe, Della," Mason said.

She nodded.

"So," Mason said, looking at his watch, "there's nothing holding you back, Paul."

9

■

Perry Mason sat in the visitors' room, while on the other side of the table and separated from him by a mesh screen, Sybil Harlan smiled happily.

"Well," Mason said, "you don't look like a girl who's in trouble."

"I'm not. I'm happy as a lark."

Mason said, "You're going to be charged with murder in about fifteen minutes, as soon as the district attorney can get the papers filed."

"Then what?"

"Then," Mason said, "you will be arraigned and a date set for a preliminary hearing."

"What happens at the preliminary hearing?"

"Actually, it's a hearing before the magistrate to determine if there is probable cause for believing you guilty. If the magistrate finds that a crime has been committed and there is probable cause to believe you committed the crime, he will hold you over for the Superior Court. Then the district attorney will file an *information,* and after that you'll be tried before a jury."

"Well?" she asked.

"Everything depends on that taxi driver. That's going to be the district attorney's case."

"You mean at the preliminary?"

"Yes."

"Can you upset that?"

"If you can keep your mouth shut, I think I can."

"I've kept it shut. That's why I'm here. The district

attorney told me that if I'd explain just what I was doing out there on the road, just where I had been, and how I happened to take the taxicab, he wouldn't file any charges against me. Otherwise, he'd have to proceed."

"What did you do?"

"I smiled sweetly at him and told him that I didn't think my lawyer would want me to answer any questions unless he was here."

"Now that you've phoned for me, won't your husband suspect that you were the one who had me buy the stock?"

"No. I think I did it very cleverly, Mr. Mason. He started talking about what you did at that directors' meeting, and I told him that if I ever got in trouble I'd most certainly ask for you.

"So when the police came, I told them I didn't like their attitude and I'd have to see a lawyer before I so much as gave them the time of day. That was when Enny said, 'Get Perry Mason, honey.' And so I told him I was going to. It was his own suggestion."

"What about your fifth wedding anniversary?"

Her eyes became dreamy. "I have him back, Mr. Mason."

"Want to tell me about it?"

She nodded. "It happened exactly the way I had hoped it would happen," she said. "Roxy had been leading Enny on with all of those languishing sighs and sidelong glances. But the minute it began to look as if Enny had got her into a business deal which might terminate in a lawsuit, that woman's real character came to the front.

"She dragged Enny off to her lawyer, her lawyer made the mistake of trying to browbeat Enny, telling Enny that he would be responsible because his client had acted on Enny's advice, and Roxy sat there and nodded her head, with all of her selfish, scheming disposition showing in her eyes, and Enny got so disgusted he felt he never wanted to see her again as long as he lives."

"So then what happened?"

"So then he came home to me, wanting to confess his infidelities and be forgiven."

"And what happened?"

"I never gave him the chance to confess," she said. "I told you that a woman should never forgive a man for his infidelities. It puts them both in an embarrassing position. She should simply be ignorant of them. I told him that, of course, I knew in making business deals with women like Roxy, he had to use a little sales appeal. I said I expected that, and then I smiled and asked him if he remembered the first time he had met me, and all of a sudden, I was the body beautiful and Roxy Claffin was just a legal headache."

"And how did you explain about me?"

"I didn't have to explain. He told me all about you and about what you had done at the directors' meeting, and I just lay in his arms and stroked his hair and smoothed his forehead and let him tell me his troubles. And he told me that Roxy's lawyer had said that you were the most diabolically ingenious attorney of the whole California Bar; so I said, 'Well, that's fine. If I ever get in trouble, I'll call on Perry Mason.' And he said, 'You'll never get in trouble, but if you do, he's the man you want.'

"So then, when the officers came out and started asking him questions about the gun and interrogating me and . . . and when they found that receipt from the taxicab in my purse—Mr. Mason, do you think it was wise having me leave that receipt in my purse? Shouldn't I have destroyed it and——"

Mason said, "No, no, that's just the way I want it. Tell me, what about the gun?"

"Well, it's one of Enny's guns, all right."

Mason said, "Is that the gun you had in your glove compartment?"

"Apparently."

"Did you take it from Enny's collection?"

"He gave it to me."

"How did it get up there at the scene of the crime?"

"There's only one way—someone broke into my glove compartment and stole it."

"When?"

"It could only have been after—afterwards. I can tell you one thing, Mr. Mason—*that* gun never killed George Lutts."

"Ballistic experts say it did."

"Then the ballistic experts are lying."

"How do you know it didn't kill Lutts?"

"I . . . I'm *sure* it didn't. Mr. Mason, you can pin your whole defense on cross-examining those ballistic experts. They just can't make that theory stand up. That's *not* the fatal gun."

"They can identify bullets and guns with scientific accuracy," Mason warned.

"I don't care what they can do. They're bluffing, trying to get us to make some admission. I'll absolutely guarantee that's not the fatal gun, Mr. Mason."

"All right," Mason told her. "Here's the hard part. Look me right in the eyes."

"I'm looking."

"Did your husband kill George Lutts?"

"Good heavens, no!"

"How do you know he didn't?"

"Why, he wouldn't do a thing like that and . . . and then, besides, at the time Lutts and I were up at that old house Enny and Roxy were just getting ready to leave for an appointment with Roxy's lawyer."

"Are you sure?"

"Of course. Enny told me all about it. They had an appointment with Arthur Hagan. He'd been in court all day, but he said he'd see them after five o'clock.

"I saw Enny drive up while I was up there on the

hill. That is, I guess it was Enny. It was his car. He wanted to take Roxy with him to see the lawyer."

"You didn't see him drive away?"

"No."

"Did you see Roxy?"

"Yes. She was running around down there, and Enny honked the horn a couple of times to hurry her up. He hates to be kept waiting."

"But you saw both of them down there."

"Yes. That is, I saw Roxy and I saw Enny's car with someone in it. I presume it was Enny."

"You're certain of Roxy?"

"Oh yes, there's no mistaking that little minx. I wonder how she's feeling, now that she realizes she made a play for Enny and lost him."

"She may be feeling pretty good," Mason said significantly. "She knows that you're being questioned about the murder of George C. Lutts, and it just *may* occur to her to think of something that would enable her to help the prosecution with its case. That would put you out of the way for a nice long time and leave your husband where she could get her claws into him again."

"She'll never get her claws into *him* again," she said. "Enny isn't entirely a fool, and I guess her true character came to the surface when she got Enny into the lawyer's office."

"When did that happen?"

"Sometime around five o'clock, I think."

Mason said, "The point I've been trying to make is that despite the fact it was your husband's gun that was used in the murder, the police seem to be leaving *him* pretty much alone."

"That's because he has such an ironclad alibi. They've checked it. He was in his own office until shortly after four; then he dashed out to get Roxy and went to see her lawyer. They were with him until six-thirty. Apparently, Mr. Mason, you threw a double-barreled scare into everyone. That legal point you thought up must have been a dilly. I understand that Roxy's lawyer is pretty much worried. And, of course, that made Roxy get in a panic—she may be liberal with her affections, but that's the extent of her generosity. She's tight as wallpaper with her dollars."

"All right," Mason said. "What did you tell the officers?"

"Not one thing."

"Nothing?"

"Nothing."

"Not even on preliminary questions?"

"No. I told them I left the beauty parlor, because I knew they'd find out about my going there. In fact, I'd told my maid to tell anyone who called that that's where I was. But aside from that I told them nothing. I said I'd been attending to some very private business and I didn't care to make any comment."

Mason said, "Do you mean you didn't even tell them——"

"Mr. Mason, I told them nothing!"

"Good girl," Mason told her. "Don't tell them anything until we know where we stand—but it isn't going to be pleasant."

She smiled. "I can take it. I can take anything now."

"All right," Mason told her. "Keep a stiff upper lip and I'll do everything I can."

The lawyer signaled to the matron that the interview was over, watched Sybil Harlan being led away, then went to a telephone and called Harry Blanton at Paul Drake's office.

"I want to know where certain people were at exactly four-thirty on the afternoon of the third. Can do?"

"Sure. It'll cost you money, but I can get the information if it's at all possible. Of course, sometimes you have to take a guy's unsupported word for where he was."

"In that case, I want to know that he has no one to support his word," Mason said.

Blanton said, "Okay. Give me the names, Mr. Mason. We'll do our best."

Mason took a list from his pocket. "Herbert Doxey, Lutts's son-in-law; Roxy Claffin; Enright Harlan; Ezekiel Elkins, a director of the Sylvan Glade Development Company; Regerson B. Neffs, also a director; Cleve Rector, another director."

"Okay. Anybody else, Mr. Mason?"

"That'll do for now. Get busy on them," Mason said. "However, there's one more thing. The murder gun had been fired three times. One of the bullets entered Lutts' chest. Try to find out where the gun was fired when the other two shells were discharged."

"Now, that may be where we fall down," Blanton said. "We have contacts, but the answer to that question is probably bothering the police right now."

"Well, do the best you can," Mason said and hung up.

10

■

HAMILTON BURGER, THE MASSIVE DISTRICT ATTORNEY OF the county, arose as Judge Hoyt called, "Case of the People of the State of California versus Sybil Harlan."

"Your Honor," Burger said, "this is a preliminary hearing. The object of a preliminary hearing is to determine whether a crime has been committed, and if so, whether there is probable cause to believe the defendant guilty of that crime.

"In ordinary cases, preliminary hearings proceed in an orderly manner to a speedy conclusion. But in cases where Mr. Perry Mason is the attorney on the other side, we seem destined to have legal pyrotechnics, spectacular cross-examinations, dramatic assertions, and a whole series of procedures which, in the opinion of the prosecutor's office, have absolutely no place in a preliminary hearing. I have, therefore, decided that I will conduct this preliminary hearing in person for the purpose of eliminating all of these extraneous dramatics."

Judge Hoyt glanced sternly at Perry Mason. "The Court has no desire to deprive the defendant of any of her rights. But the Court does recognize the fact that in some instances preliminary hearings have been skillfully and very adroitly manipulated so that they have been taken far beyond the scope which the Court feels the framers of the law had in mind. Do you wish to make any statement, Mr. Mason?"

"None whatever," Mason said, his face a mask of cherubic innocence. "I take it the Court is not insinuating that counsel for the defense is to be deprived of the right of cross-examination."

"Certainly not," Judge Hoyt snapped. "But the cross-examination will be conducted decorously and within the strict technical limits of the law."

"Thank you, Your Honor," Mason said, as though the judge had conferred a great favor upon him.

"Proceed," Judge Hoyt snapped at the district attorney, obviously irritated at Mason's attitude, yet unable to find anything which would furnish a ground for rebuke.

"I will call Dr. Jules Oberon," Hamilton Burger said.

Dr. Oberon took the stand and qualified himself as a physician, surgeon, a deputy coroner, and an expert in the field of pathology. He stated that he had performed the autopsy on the body of George C. Lutts.

"What did you find as the cause of death?"

"A thirty-eight caliber revolver bullet, which had penetrated the chest and partially severed the left common carotid artery."

"That was the cause of death?"

"Yes, sir."

"Where was the bullet?"

"I found it in the body when I performed the autopsy."

Dr. Oberon took a small phial from his pocket, said, "This is a sealed phial. I, personally, placed the bullet in it along with a slip of paper containing my signature, and then sealed the glass stopper in place. I removed the bullet only to let the ballistic expert examine it, then replaced it and resealed it."

"Did the victim die instantly?"

"I think he may possibly have staggered a few steps."

"Assuming, Doctor, that the body was found lying head downward on the stairs, would you state that from the nature of this wound, the victim could have started for the stairs before death overtook him?"

"Yes, he could have taken a few steps to the head of the stairs and then fallen down the stairs."

"What was the course of the bullet?"

"Upward. The man was facing his murderer and the assailant must have been holding the gun at about the level of his hip."

"Do you have an opinion as to the time of death?"

"Yes, sir. Mr. Lutts died between four-twenty and four-forty."

"How do you determine the time of death?"

"By temperature of the body and by the state of the food in the stomach."

"Do you know, of your own knowledge, when the food was ingested?"

"Only by hearsay."

"Then I won't ask you about that now," Burger said. "You may cross-examine."

Judge Hoyt said, "Now, Mr. Mason, I wish to give the defendant every possible right, but I would like to caution you at this time that the Court will brook no extraneous questions. Cross-examination must be confined to the questions asked on direct examination."

"No questions," Mason said.

Judge Hoyt frowned.

"Call Herbert Doxey," Hamilton Burger said.

Doxey came forward, took the witness stand, testified to his relationship to George Lutts, to the fact that he had seen the decedent on the day of the murder, that his last contact with the decedent had been when they left the office of the corporation and had driven to a restaurant, where the decedent had eaten a bowl of vegetable soup, a hamburger with onions, a cup of coffee and a piece of pumpkin pie.

"What time was that?"

"That was at three-twenty."

"And then what happened?"

"Mr. Lutts said he had some business to attend to, and I went home."

"You're certain as to the time?"

"Yes, sir."

"What makes you certain?"

"I noticed the time."

"Where?"

"In the restaurant."

"In what way?"

"I looked at my wrist watch and compared the time with an electric clock on the wall."

"Was your wrist watch accurate?"

"Within one minute, yes."

"What was the time?"

"Three-eighteen, and the waitress was just bringing our orders."

"Sometime after that you went with Mr. Perry Mason to the house where a certain real estate development is taking place, a house shown on the map I now hand you?"

"I did, yes, sir."

"And what did you find?"

"I found Mr. Lutts's automobile parked in front of the place."

"And what did you do?"

"I tried the door of the house."

"Was it locked or unlocked?"

"It was unlocked."

"And what did you do then?"

"I walked up the first flight of stairs; then I crossed the landing and had started up the second flight of stairs when I saw the body of Mr. Lutts lying there."

"How was the body lying?"

"On the stairs."

"In what position?"

"Partially on his back, partially on the right side, the head was downward as though he had——"

"Never mind your conclusions. Just give us the facts."

"Yes, sir."

"Was the body that of George C. Lutts, your father-in-law?"

"Yes, sir, it was."

"Did you subsequently see that body at the autopsy room in the coroner's office?"

"Yes, sir."

"And it was the same body?"

"Yes, sir."

"That of George C. Lutts?"

"Yes, sir."

"What time was it when you made the discovery of the body?"

"About eight-fifteen, daylight saving time. I don't know the exact time."

"You may inquire," Burger said to Mason.

"No questions," Mason said.

Judge Hoyt looked thoughtfully at Perry Mason.

"I desire to recall Dr. Oberon for one question," Hamilton Burger said.

"Return to the stand, Dr. Oberon," the judge directed.

Dr. Oberon resumed his position on the witness stand.

"You have heard the testimony of Mr. Doxey as to the time at which a meal was ingested?"

"Yes, sir."

"Assuming that the meal such as he described was ingested at 3:30 P.M., how long was it after the ingestion of that meal before the decedent met his death?"

"I would say from fifty minutes to an hour and ten minutes."

"You feel that you can place the time within twenty minutes?"

"I do, yes, sir."

"You may cross-examine," Hamilton Burger said.

"No questions."

"I'll call Sidney Dayton to the stand," Burger said. Sidney Dayton, a police expert, took the stand, qualified himself as an expert, and turned to Hamilton Burger.

"Can you," Hamilton Burger asked, "tell by any scientific means the distance at which a gun was held when a shot was fired into the body of a man?"

"Yes."

"How?"

"By powder tattooing on the skin or by the dispersion of powder particles in the clothing."

"Will you please explain what you mean by the latter."

"When a shell is fired, there are certain particles of powder which are consumed entirely, and so turned into a gas. There are other particles which are not entirely consumed. These particles are spewed from the muzzle of the weapon. They naturally follow a pattern of expansion. By determining the number of particles and the pattern of their expansion or dispersion, it is possible to tell the distance at which the weapon was held from the body."

"Can you describe, generally, the method by which that is done? I just want to have it very generally."

"The clothing containing the powder chemicals is placed on an ordinary ironing board. A sheet of a special type of photographic paper is placed under the clothing. A blotter containing a chemical is placed over the clothing where it is thought the powder particles are deposited. A hot iron is placed upon that moistened blotter. The iron vaporizes chemicals in the blotter, which in turn cause a chemical reaction with the powder particles, which in turn cause a series of dots on the photographic paper, representing a dispersion of the powder particles."

"Did you make such a test on the clothing of George C. Lutts?"

"I did."

"Did you reach any conclusion as to the distance at which the weapon was held?"

"I did."

"What concludion did you reach?"

"I feel that the person who discharged the bullet into the body of George Lutts was standing at eighteen to twenty inches from the victim at the time the bullet was fired."

"Did you examine the hands of the decedent to see if there were any powder stains on them?"

"I did, yes, sir."

"Did you find any?"

"No, sir."

"If the decedent had been grabbing for the gun, if he had been putting up his hands in front of the gun trying to ward off the bullet, you'd have found powder stains."

"Very definitely. When I say that the weapon was about eighteen to twenty inches from the decedent, I mean the distance from the muzzle of the weapon to the *chest* of the decedent was not more than that."

"At that distance he could then have reached for the gun?"

"He could have, if the bullet hadn't reached him first, which, in this case, it evidently did."

"You may cross-examine," Hamilton Burger said.

"No questions," Mason announced tersely.

Judge Hoyt started to say something, then changed his mind.

"Call Alexander Redfield," Hamilton Burger said.

Alexander Redfield glanced at Perry Mason with a half-smile. He had been cross-examined by Mason many times and knew only too well the skillful manner in which Mason could confuse an uncertain witness or one who was misrepresenting the facts. His manner showed that he intended to be very, very cautious in giving his testimony.

He qualified himself as an expert on ballistics, stated that he had been called to the scene of the crime after the body had been removed.

"At what time?" Hamilton Burger asked.

"It was the next morning."

"What time the next morning?"

"After daylight."

"What was your purpose in going out there?"

"To try and find the murder weapon."

"Did you search the premises?"

"No, I understand the premises had been searched by police the night before. I confined myself to searching the grounds."

"And did you find a weapon?"

"I did."

"How soon after arriving?"

"Within five minutes."

"Wasn't that rather fortuitous?"

"I knew by experience about how far it would be possible to fling an ordinary weapon of ordinary weight under those circumstances, so I went out to the place where I thought such a weapon might have landed. Sure enough, I found a track in the moist soil, indicating that something had struck, bounced, then slid under some loose, moist soil. I probed in this soil and found the revolver."

"What sort of a revolver?"

"A Smith and Wesson revolver with a five-inch barrel, thirty-eight caliber, number S910684."

"What did you do with that gun?"

"I took it to my laboratory, I tested it for fingerprints, and found none. I examined the cartridges that were in it."

"How many cartridges were in it?"

"Six. There were three loaded cartridges and three empty cartridge cases in the cylinder."

"What did you find about the empty cartridge cases?"

"Two of them were Peters, thirty-eight specials. One of them was a U.M.C."

"Did you weigh the bullets that were in the undischarged cartridges in the weapon?"

"I did."

"What did you find?"

"I found that they were Peters cartridges containing lead bullets of one hundred and fifty-eight grains each."

"Now, did you check the fatal bullet to determine the weapon from which it had been fired?"

"I did."

"In what way?"

"My first test was to measure the lands and grooves and get the pitch in order to determine the type of weapon from which it had been fired."

"Did you make such determination?"

"Yes."

"What was it?"

"The bullet had been fired from a Smith and Wesson thirty-eight caliber revolver."

"Did you subsequently make tests to determine whether or not the fatal bullet had been fired from the revolver which you had found in the place that you described?"

"Yes, sir."

"What did those tests disclose?"

"That the fatal bullet had been fired from that revolver."

"Do you have that revolver with you?"

"I do."

Hamilton Burger said, "I move that the fatal bullet now be introduced in evidence as People's Exhibit C and that the revolver be introduced as People's Exhibit D."

"Any objection from the defense?"

"No, Your Honor," Mason said.

"And what about the shells that you found in the chamber of the gun?"

"I photographed those cartridges in place, so that the position of the cartridges could be determined. I made scratches upon the cartridges, numbering them one, two, three, four, five and six, and I made scratches upon the cylinder of the gun so that the position in which the respective cartridges had been found could be determined."

"You have those photographs?"

"I do."

"What do they show?"

"They show the cylinder of the gun. The cartridge chamber marked six is the one that was at the top of the cylinder, that is, the one that contained the U.M.C. cartridge. That would have been the last cartridge fired."

"And what did you do with the shells themselves?"

"I have placed those in receptacles, each one of them numbered according to the places in the cylinder from which they were removed."

"I ask that all of those and the photographs may be received in evidence as appropriate exhibit numbers," Hamilton Burger said.

"No objection," Mason said.

"That's all," Burger said.

"No cross-examination," Mason said.

Judge Hoyt cleared his throat. "Mr. Mason."

"Yes, Your Honor."

"The Court is not unfamiliar with the fact that sometimes attorneys try to take advantage of the Court."

"Yes, Your Honor."

"I am not accusing you of doing that."

"Thank you, Your Honor."

"I am aware, however, that a desperate and resourceful attorney might seek to refrain from cross-examining witnesses and then raise the claim that the attorney had been intimidated by the remarks of the prosecutor and the remarks of the Court. I therefore charge you, Mr. Mason, that not only is the Court not trying to restrain you from any *proper* cross-examination of witnesses, but I believe it is your duty as the attorney representing the defendant to cross-examine witnesses who are called against her."

"Yes, Your Honor."

"Now then, in view of that statement do you wish to recall any of these witnesses for cross-examination?"

"No, Your Honor."

Judge Hoyt said, "Let the record show that the Court has again given the defense an opportunity to cross-examine witnesses and that the attorney for the defense refuses to make such cross-examination."

"So stipulated," Mason said cheerfully.

Hamilton Burger glowered at him.

"Harold Ogelsby take the stand," Hamilton Burger said.

Ogelsby came forward, was sworn, identified himself as being a police detective.

"Did you have occasion to interrogate the defendant on the morning of the fourth of this month?"

"I did, yes, sir."

"That was the day after the body of George C. Lutts had been discovered?"

"Yes, sir."

"Did you ask her to make any statements?"

"I advised her of her rights. I told her that if she made any statements, they might be used against her. I told her that if she could make any explanation as to why she had been out in the vicinity at the time, that is, any explanation which would be reasonably satisfying, we would release her."

"And did she make any statement?"

"No."

"Just a minute," Judge Hoyt said. "Do you wish to object to that, Mr. Mason?"

"No, Your Honor."

"Well, the Court interposes an objection for you," Judge Hoyt said. "There is no obligation on the part of a defendant to make a statement. I note that this is not a case where the defendant has specifically been accused of crime and fails to deny it. This is a case where the defendant was called on to make a statement, and she remained silent. The Court will strike the answer from the record. The Court will object to it on behalf of the defendant."

"Very well, Your Honor," Hamilton Burger said. "The point was merely preliminary."

"Then get to the point you're trying to make," Judge Hoyt snapped, his nerves badly frayed.

"Yes, Your Honor." Hamilton Burger was smiling now, suave and triumphant, all but ready to close his case, visualizing newspaper comments that, while Perry Mason had on occasion transformed the court of a committing magistrate into a three-ring circus, his pyrotechnics had signally failed to materialize when Hamilton Burger himself had taken over all phases of a preliminary hearing.

"Now then," Hamilton Burger said, "did you have occasion to search the purse of the defendant?"

"I asked her if she would let me look in it."

"Did she raise any objection?"

"No."

"Did you look in it?"

"Yes."

"Now, I am not going to ask you about all of the things that you found, many of which may be irrelevant, but I am going to ask you if in that purse you found a piece of paper?"

"I did."

"And what was the nature of that paper?"

"It was a receipt from the Red Line Cab Company, receipt for cab seven-sixty-one, trip nine-eight-four, in an amount of two dollars and ninety-five cents."

"You say that was cab seven-sixty-one?"

"Yes, sir."

"You have that receipt here?"

"I do."

"You found it in the defendant's purse?"

"Yes."

"I ask that it be introduced in evidence," Hamilton Burger said, "and if the Court please, I will connect it up."

"No objection," Mason said cheerfully. "Stipulate that it may be received in evidence."

"Cross-examine," Hamilton Burger said.

"No questions," Mason said.

Judge Hoyt again started to say something, then checked himself.

"Call Jerome C. Keddie to the stand," Hamilton Burger said.

Jerome Keddie came forward, was sworn, gave his name, address and occupation as that of a taxi driver for the Red Line Cab Company.

"On the third of this month, were you operating a taxicab for the Red Line Cab Company?"

"I was."

"What was the number of that cab?"

"Number seven-sixty-one."

"Where were you operating that cab at about four-forty-five on the afternoon of the day?"

"I had deposited a fare at the country club at just about four-thirty. I was running back empty toward the city."

"Did you follow a course which would take you near the point shown on this map, People's Exhibit A?"

"I did, yes, sir."

"What, if anything, happened as you approached the intersection of this roadway?"

"Well, when I came to the intersection I saw a very good-looking woman, dressed in a white skirt and white shoes and a sort of sport jacket with red trim, hurrying out of this road that——"

"Just a moment. Indicating on this map by the words 'this road,' what do you mean?"

The witness walked over to the map and indicated the road.

"Let the record show that the witness is indicating the road, in fact, the only road, leading from the property where the body was discovered to the main highway," Hamilton Burger said. "Now then, just resume your position on the stand, Mr. Keddie, and tell me what happened."

"This woman seemed very agitated and upset, very nervous. She flagged me down, and, of course, I was anxious to get a fare, so I pulled the car to a stop—I'd slowed down as soon as I saw her. I thought maybe she'd be looking for a cab. Well, she sure was. She was sure nervous and upset. She couldn't tell me at first the way she wanted to go. She told me just to drive on toward town. I could see she was thinking.

"Well, then she told me that she wanted to go to the Union Station. Well, I knew that was a blind because——"

"That will do," Judge Hoyt snapped. "If it is incumbent upon the Court to protect the rights of the defendant, the Court will endeavor to do so. The witness will give none of his conclusions. Simply state the facts."

"Yes," Hamilton Burger said virtuously, "just state the facts."

"Well," Keddie said, "she told me she wanted to go to the Union Station, and I took her there."

"Did you have any other conversation?"

"I asked her if she might be in trouble of some sort or other, if there was anything I could do to help."

"What did she say?"

"She said she was all right."

"Did you notice her particularly?"

"I sure did."

"Who was that woman?"

"The defendant."

"Point to her, please."

The witness pointed to Sybil Harlan.

"Let the record show the witness is pointing directly at the defendant, Sybil Harlan," Hamilton Burger said.

"So stipulated," Mason said affably.

Judge Hoyt frowned at him.

"Then what did you do?" Burger asked.

"Well, I took her to the Union Station and drove away."

"How much was the fare, do you remember?"

"I remember exactly. The fare was two dollars and ninety-five cents. She gave me three dollars and a half, which made a fifty-five cent tip."

"Did you watch to see where she went?"

"She walked into the station, then turned toward the cab stand out at the back. I knew she was going to——"

"Never mind your conclusions," Judge Hoyt said. "The Court doesn't want to have to warn you again, Mr. Keddie."

"Yes, sir."

"Call me 'Your Honor.'"

"Yes, Your Honor."

"Go ahead," Hamilton Burger said.

"Well, that was all."

"Now, just a moment," Hamilton Burger said. "Your taxicab, in common with all Red Line Cabs, is equipped with a taximeter which starts in operation when you pull your flag down, is that right?"

"Yes, sir."

"And that meter is coupled with the speedometer and a clockwork mechanism so the amount of the fare is registered?"

"Yes, sir."

"And when you manipulate the flag at the termination of the trip, that causes the amount to be rung up on the meter in the nature of a register and a slip of paper comes out which you give to the customer?"

"Yes, sir. Most of them don't take it, but the paper's there."

"And did that happen in this case, when you terminated the trip at the Union Station?"

"Yes, sir."

"And what did the defendant do, if anything?"

"She took the paper and put it in her purse."

"Now then," Hamilton Burger said, "I'm going to show you this piece of paper and ask you if you know what it is."

"Yes, sir."

"What is it?"

"It's the receipt from my cab which I gave the defendant in this case."

"When?"

"There at the Union Station."

"At what time?"

"Oh, I reckon it was just a minute or two after five when we got there."

"And what does that paper show?"

"It shows that this was trip nine-eighty-four, that it was my cab, number seven-sixty-one, that the amount of the meter was two dollars and ninety-five cents."

"That's all," Hamilton Burger said.

The witness got up and started to leave the stand. "Just a moment," Mason said. "With the indulgence of the Court, I have a few questions to ask on cross-examination."

Judge Hoyt, who had been somewhat apprehensive, settled back with an expression of relief on his face.

"You recognize this slip?" Mason asked.

"Yes."

"And you recognize the defendant?"

"Yes, sir."

"You first saw the defendant that afternoon at the point you indicated on the map?"

"Yes, sir."

"So far as you know, had you ever seen her before?"

"I never saw her before in all my life, as far as I know."

"When did you see her next?" Mason asked, quite casually.

"When I was asked to pick her out of a lineup down at police headquarters."

"When was that?"

"Sometime on the morning of the fourth, about ten or eleven o'clock."

"Did you pick her out?"

"I certainly did."

"You hadn't seen her from the time you deposited her at the Union Station until you saw her again in that lineup?"

"That's right."

"Isn't there a chance you're mistaken?"

"None whatever."

"Isn't there a chance that some other time on the third you may have had this young woman in your cab and that you have confused her identity in your own mind?"

"None whatever."

"You feel certain that you would have noticed this defendant if you had seen her again prior to the time you picked her out of the lineup?"

"You mean after I saw her out there when she got in the cab that afternoon?"

"Yes."

"Sure, I'd have known her. I knew her the next morning when I picked her out of the lineup, didn't I?"

"Now then," Mason said, "you keep some sort of a record of your own, do you not, in regard to your trips?"

"That's right. I make a note of all the trips I make."

"And you telephone in to cab headquarters, announc-

ing when you're making a trip. In other words, you telephoned in when you started out to the country club?"

"That's right."

"And when you started back, you reported that you
were coming back empty?"

"Yes, sir."

"And then when you picked up a passenger, did you
report that fact?"

"That's right, and I marked the Union Station down
on my trip sheet."

"That's right. You marked on your trip sheet the fact
that you were going to the Union Station."

"That's right."

"Do you have that sheet with you?"

"I do, yes, sir."

"Let me look at it, please."

"Objected to as incompetent, irrelevant, immaterial, not
proper cross-examination and not the best evidence,"
Hamilton Burger said. "That sheet is not part of the of-
ficial records of the company, that sheet was never
shown to the defendant. It is only the personal record
of the witness. It has no proper bearing, nor were any
questions asked about it on direct examination."

"Overruled," Judge Hoyt said.

Hamilton Burger smiled triumphantly. Now he had
the record in such shape that the impartiality of the
Court could not be questioned. Not only had Perry Mason not been curtailed in his cross-examination, but the
Court had overruled the district attorney's objection to
one of Perry Mason's questions.

"May I see the sheet, please?"

The witness took a folded sheet of paper from his
pocket, handed it to Perry Mason, and said, "I keep
this in connection with my own books. I check in with
the trips at the taxicab company about once a week in
order to make sure we've got them straight."

"I see," Mason said. "What time do you go to work?"

"Well, it varies, depending which shift I'm on."

"On the third of this month what time did you go to work?"

"I went to work at four o'clock in the afternoon and got off at midnight."

"So you'd picked up your cab around four o'clock?"

"Around there—actually, about ten minutes before four."

"The trip to the country club was then your first trip of the afternoon?"

"No, that was the second trip. I'd picked up a man who wanted to go to the Jonathan Club. That was the first trip. Then I picked up this fare for the country club. That was a good trip."

"How long did it take you to get out there?"

"Right around twenty minutes."

"So then you had started that trip around four-ten in the afternoon?"

"I guess so, right around there."

"And you had picked up your cab at what time?"

"Well, my partner who ran the cab before I did was a little early getting in, about ten minutes early—we like to have them right in on time, but of course you can't help it sometimes when you're out on a call. You have to learn to take things like that; if they're not over ten or fifteen minutes late, nobody ever says anything. But we try to be on time or perhaps a little early. Of course, each driver wants to get as much use out of the cab as he can. I have to have it back in the lot there at twelve o'clock midnight. I want to get as much out of the bus as I can in the line of trips and tips, but I also want to give the next driver a break. If a man is over fifteen minutes late or if he makes a habit of being late, why then, you sometimes make trouble, but this time the man before me came in a little early."

"So you started out a little before four. You had one fare, which took you to the Jonathan Club. Then where did you go?"

"Well, then I went down and got in line at the Biltmore

Hotel. At that hour of the afternoon you can pick up a fare there without waiting very long. I waited there for about . . . oh, I don't know . . . I guess for four or five minutes and then soon as I got in position the doorman gave me this fare with the big bag of golf clubs. I knew that was going to be a good trip as soon as I saw the golf clubs."

"So," Mason said, "the trip which you made with the woman that you think is the defendant would then have been the third trip of the day."

"That's right."

"Now then," Mason said, "I notice that when you took over this cab your sheet shows that you took it on at trip number nine-sixty-nine."

"Well, that's right if that's what it shows."

"And what would that mean?"

"That would mean that the man who'd checked out before me had had up to and including trip nine-sixty-eight. My first trip would be nine-sixty-nine."

"That would mean the trip to the Jonathan Club."

"That's right."

"Then your trip to the country club would have been trip nine-seventy."

"That's right."

"And your trip with the defendant would have been nine-seventy-one."

"I guess so. You've got the sheet. I haven't."

"Well, look at it, please," Mason said, walking over to the witness and showing him the sheet.

"Okay, I'm looking at it."

"And that was correct? That was trip nine-seventy-one?"

"That's correct. Trip nine-seventy-one she is."

Mason said, "How does it happen, then, that this receipt you have identified as being the receipt you gave the defendant at the Union Station shows that it is for trip nine-eighty-four?"

"What?"

"Just a moment, just a moment," Hamilton Burger shouted. "Just a moment. Let's get this straight. Before the witness answers that question, I want to inspect the paper. I object to this method of interrogation. I object to the question as assuming facts not in evidence. I object to it as not being proper cross examination."

"It's proper cross-examination," Judge Hoyt said, "but the witness will refrain from answering until the Court and counsel have had an opportunity to examine those papers."

Hamilton Burger strode angrily up to stand beside Perry Mason, his thick, powerful fingers all but snatched the paper from the hand of the witness, and he said to the clerk, "Where's that taxi receipt? Let me take a look at that."

"Just a moment," the judge said, "the Court wants to look at those papers, too, Mr. Prosecutor."

"Yes, Your Honor, of course, certainly."

"Pass them up here, please."

Hamilton Burger passed up the trip sheet and the taxicab receipt.

He said, "I submit, if the Court please, that there's some technical error, something that can be explained. Perhaps it's a misprint. I object to counsel asking questions about this trip sheet of this witness on the ground that they are argumentative. The facts speak for themselves. We'll try to get this situation unscrambeld later, without having the witness become hopelessly confused trying to explain some typographical error."

Judge Hoyt said, "The objection to the question will be . . . well, just a moment. The Court will reserve ruling. The Court will ask the witness some questions, and the counsel for each side will refrain from interrupting.

"Mr. Keddie, do you understand this?" Judge Hoyt asked the witness.

"Well, I don't understand how that number got on the receipt."

"You understand your trip sheet?"

"Yes."

"And is there a chance that your trip numbers on the trip sheet could have been in error?"

"Well, now let's see. If I had made a mistake in copying down the trip number from the record on the meter, the real trip number that I should have copied would have been . . . let's see . . . nine-eighty-one, and that would have been my first trip to the Jonathan Club. Then nine-eighty-two . . . now, now wait a minute, it would have been nine-eighty-two, my trip to the Jonathan Club. Nine-eighty-three would have been my trip out to the country club, and nine-eighty-four would have been my trip with this woman here. Now, it doesn't seem I could have made a mistake and copied down nine-eighty-two—I mean, it doesn't seem as though I could have copied nine-sixty-nine when I was trying to write nine-eighty-two."

"Do you sometimes make mistakes?" Judge Hoyt asked.

"Well, I suppose I do. I've made mistakes. Sometimes I get a number wrong and sometimes I'll plumb forget to put down a trip, but that doesn't happen very often. The records are all checked over by the main office about once a week. We get in and check these things over. They keep track of where we are . . . well, you know how it is, there's always a temptation for a cabbie to knock down if he can do it, and they try to keep their records so they show what the cabs are doing and what the drivers are doing and . . . well, so nobody can knock down on 'em."

"Now let me see," Judge Hoyt said. "If you had taken over at nine-sixty-nine, then you would have gone to the Jonathan Club on trip nine-seventy?"

"That's right."

"And this trip that you say you made with the defendant would then have been trip nine-seventy-one?"

"Well, that's the way it should be, but that receipt sure shows nine-eighty-four."

Hamilton Burger said, "Now just a minute, just a minute."

The judge said, "Don't interrupt me. I'm trying to check these things. Let's see, I'm going to count these trips on your trip sheet. This would have been trip nine-seventy-one . . . seventy-two . . . seventy-three . . . seventy-four . . . seventy-five. . . ."

Judge Hoyt counted down the trips, turned the page, adjusted his glasses, frowned at the sheet, looked over at Hamilton Burger, and said to the witness, "Well, Mr. Keddie, I notice that what would have been trip number nine-eighty-four on your sheet if you had started out at trip number nine-sixty-nine, as you said you did, would have been a trip which you have marked 'Looking at property.' "

"Let me see," Keddie said.

He took the sheet of paper and frowned over it. "Well, now, just a minute," he said. "Wait a minute. I can remember that trip. A couple of dames I picked up on North La Brea somewhere. They wanted to go look at some property. They told me to drive out and look at some property, and then they told me to drive down some street and all of a sudden one of 'em said, 'Here it is. Stop right here.' She started all at once yelling at me to stop. I stopped and they got out and paid off."

"Was one of those women this defendant?" Judge Hoyt asked.

"Nope. I didn't see her from the time I picked her up out there until I saw her in the lineup the next morning."

"Are you sure?" the judge asked. "Do you remember? You say there were two women?"

"Well, now let's see," Keddie said. "One of those women was a little chunky and the other one . . . I can't remember her very well, Judge. You pick up lots of people and———"

"The point is, can you swear that she wasn't the defendant?"

"Well, I can't remember her so clearly, but I never saw this defendant until the lineup the next morning . . . I mean, after that trip when I picked her up out there at that intersection."

"Are you positive you never saw the defendant from the time you picked her up out there at the point indicated on this map until you saw her in the lineup the next morning?"

"Oh, if the Court please," said Hamilton Burger, "I think now we are beginning to see the pattern of this———"

"Just a minute," Judge Hoyt said. "Just a minute. I don't want counsel for either side to interrupt me. I want to finish this line of questioning in my own way."

"Yes, Your Honor," Hamilton Burger said.

"I, too, would like to ask a question," Mason told the Court.

"You may ask it when I finish," Judge Hoyt snapped.

"I submit," Mason said, "that in a matter of this sort, counsel should not be precluded from cross-examining the witness. My rights have been somewhat curtailed, and I———"

"The Court will do the questioning at this point," Judge Hoyt said. "Counsel will be quiet.

"Now, I want to have this definitely understood," Judge Hoyt continued, turning to the witness. "Is there any reasonable chance that this receipt, which was apparently taken from the defendant's purse, is the receipt for a trip made later in the evening, the trip that you have referred to as the pickup of two women at North La Brea?"

The witness fidgeted a bit on the witness stand.

"Yes or no?" Hoyt asked.

"Yes, there *is* a chance," the witness admitted.

"How much of a chance?"

"Well, if you're going to put it that way, Judge, Your Honor, I suppose there's a pretty good chance."

"That's what I wanted to know," Judge Hoyt snapped.

"I want to ask a question," Hamilton Burger said.

"I beg your pardon," Mason told him. "I think I was cross-examining the witness. I haven't finished with my cross-examination."

"Well, I think I'm entitled to ask a question at this time, anyway, in order to get this thing straightened out for the Court," Hamilton Burger said.

"The Court is quite able to straighten things out for itself, if they can be straightened," Judge Hoyt said. "The Court doesn't need a guardian or an interpreter."

"Your Honor, I think the answer is obvious," Hamilton Burger said. "This defendant undoubtedly knows one of the women who made that trip out from North La Brea and got this receipt from that woman. It's very easy to see the way the thing was manipulated. The women cruised around without giving this taxi driver any definite directions. As soon as the meter had reached the amount of two dollars and ninty-five cents, these women got out, took the receipt and, undoubtedly, following the instructions of adroit counsel, delivered the receipt to the defendant so that it would be found in her purse, thereby laying a trap for the witness.

"That, Your Honor, not only constitutes unprofessional conduct, but it's the strongest declaration of guilt we could possibly have because it shows that even at that time, the defendant knew she was going to be questioned about this trip and participated in arrangements to trap the law enforcement officers."

"Do you have anything to say on that point, Mr. Mason?" Judge Hoyt asked.

"Why should I?" Mason asked. "That's the district attorney's theory. He isn't under oath. He doesn't know what happened. In the due course of time, at the proper time and place, I will show what happened. I will prove that this man has testified to certain things which simply

aren't so. He is the victim of his own mistaken recollection."

Judge Hoyt stroked the angle of his chin. "Well," he
said, "you go ahead, Mr. Mason, and continue with
your cross-examination. The Court will state, however,
that this is a most unusual situation and one which the
Court feels should be investigated."

"I'll say so," Hamilton Burger muttered disgustedly.

Mason turned to the witness. "When you say that
you picked up the defendant out there at the point you
indicated on the map, around a quarter to five in the
afternoon, did you pay particular attention to her
clothes?"

"I did."

"Did you pay particular attention to her face?"

"I noticed it was pale."

"Did she have a hat, or was she bareheaded?"

"She . . . well, now, wait a minute . . . I——"

"Don't say unless you're sure," Mason said.

"To tell you the truth, I'm not sure."

"Was she wearing earrings?"

"I don't know."

"Did she carry a handbag?"

"Yes, she carried a handbag, I know, because she
took the money out of it."

"Now, you noticed her face particularly?"

"I noticed it was pale."

"And you say positively that it was this defendant?"

"Well . . . I *thought* it was this defendant."

"But now that you think things over, there is a possibility that you have confused the face of that woman
with the face of a woman who was in your cab later
on in the evening, and when you saw the defendant in
the lineup, you simply knew that her face was familiar
and therefore picked her out."

The cab driver again shifted his position.

"I don't think that's a fair question," Hamilton Burger
said.

"What's unfair about it?" Judge Hoyt asked.

"He's trying to trap the witness," Burger said.

"He has a right to," Judge Hoyt snapped. "Objection overruled. The witness will answer the question.

The embarrassed taxi driver said, "Well, to tell you the truth, now you've got me confused and I don't know just what *did* happen."

"You now think there is a possibility that your memory played a trick on you?" Mason asked.

"It's a possibility all right."

"And that the time that you saw this defendant was later on in the evening, and the person you picked up there at approximately quarter to five might have been someone other than the defendant?"

"To tell you the truth, I don't know what happened," the cab driver said. "I thought I did, but now I don't."

"That's all," Mason said.

Hamilton Burger pounced on the witness. "Now don't let some smart lawyer mix you all up," he said. "You know what you saw and what you didn't see. Now, you saw the defendant on the third of this month."

The witness hesitated.

"I saw her sometime on the third, all right, because I knew her on the fourth when I saw her in the lineup."

Hamilton Burger said, "From the time you first saw her on the third, did you ever see her again until you saw her in the lineup on the fourth?"

"No," the witness said. "I'm positive of that. I saw her once before I saw her in the lineup, but I never saw her twice."

"Only once," Hamilton Burger said.

"That's right."

"And to the best of your recollection, the time you first saw her was out there at the point that you have indicated on the map at around four-forty-five in the evening."

"Well, that's the way I did feel about it, but I'm kind of mixed up now. I'm sort of going around in circles. To tell you the truth, I don't know *when* I saw her."

"All right," Hamilton Burger said disgustedly, "if that's the way you want it."

The district attorney walked back and dropped himself into his chair at the counsel table.

"In other words," Mason said suavely, his voice friendly and informal, "when you say you don't know just when you saw her, you mean you don't know what time on the third you saw her."

"That's right, yes."

"You just know that you saw her some time on the third, and therefore when you saw her face in the lineup on the fourth, it was familiar to you and so you picked her out."

"I guess that's what must have happened."

"That's your best recollection at the present time?" Mason asked.

"Now just a moment," Hamilton Burger said. "That question is argumentative. A very apparent flimflam has been worked on this witness to get him confused and——"

"Are you making an objection to the Court?" Mason asked, his voice cracking like a whiplash.

"I am."

"Make it to the Court then," Mason said.

"I object, Your Honor. This is not proper cross-examination. It's incompetent, irrelevant and immaterial."

"Overruled," Judge Hoyt snapped.

"To tell you the truth, Judge," the witness said, "the more I get to thinking of it, the more I feel that maybe she *was* one of those two women I picked up out there on La Brea. I've been sitting here watching her, the way she holds her head and . . . well, it could have been."

"But," Mason said, "You *are* positive that you only saw her *once* on the third?"

"Well, yes."

"But you *think* the time you saw her was on the third

trip you made after starting out, don't you?" Hamilton Burger said.

"Objected to as leading and suggestive," Mason said.

"Oh, Your Honor, this is on redirect examination," Hamilton Burger protested.

"That doesn't give you the right to put words into the mouth of your own witness. I don't care what stage of the examination it is.

"Nevertheless," Judge Hoyt said, "this is a peculiar situation. I'm going to overrule the objection. I want the witness to answer, and I think he's entitled to answer."

"Well," Keddie said, "to tell you the truth, I *thought* that she was this woman I picked up then. Now, I'm just not sure, and that's all there is to it, but I do know that if she is the same woman I picked up out there by the country club, I'd have known her if I saw her a second time."

"Then she *couldn't* have been one of the women you picked up on North La Brea?"

"Not if she was the one I picked up by the country club."

"That's all," Hamilton Burger said.

Mason, smiling affably, said, "Then as I understand it, if it turns out she *was* one of the women you picked up on La Brea, she couldn't have been the woman you picked up out near the country club?"

"That's right. If I ever saw *that* woman again, I'd have known her . . . like I did when I saw her in that line-up . . . only maybe the time I saw her on La Brea—Now wait a minute. I just don't know."

"You do know you saw this woman on the afternoon or evening of June third?" Mason asked.

"Yes."

"And you only saw her once on that day?"

"That woman I picked up by the country club I only saw once on that day, that's for sure."

"That's all," Mason said.

"No questions," Hamilton Burger said disgustedly.

"Is there any more evidence, Mr. Burger?" Judge Hoyt asked.

Hamilton Burger said, "Well, Your Honor, I feel absolutely positive that the gun which has been introduced in evidence was purchased by the husband of this defendant, Mr. Enright A. Harlan. But, at the moment, I am not in a position to prove it."

"May I ask why?" Judge Hoyt asked.

"Well, somebody signed the name Enright A. Harlan to the purchase slip and the firearms register, but apparently that is not the handwriting of Mr. Harlan. It would seem to be the handwriting of a woman."

"The defendant?" Judge Hoyt asked.

"No, Your Honor, I am sorry to say that it is not the handwriting of the defendant. Apparently, some other woman signed the name of Enright A. Harlan. The dealer, at the present time, has no independent recollection of the circumstances surrounding the purchase."

"Can you show possession of the gun?"

"The only way I could show possession of the gun is by the testimony of the husband, and, of course, I would be met with the prompt objection that in an action of this sort a husband can't testify against his wife without the wife's consent."

"I see," Judge Hoyt said, frowning thoughtfully.

"I think it's quite apparent what happened here," Hamilton Burger said. "A scheme was cooked up for the purpose of confusing this witness. I feel that this is a matter which the Court should look into. I think it is a contempt of Court."

"I don't see how you make a contempt of Court out of it," Judge Hoyt said. "But it's quite possible the Bar Association might be interested."

Judge Hoyt glowered at Perry Mason.

"Why?" Perry Mason asked.

Judge Hoyt's face deepened into a frown. "You should know why," he said. "If your knowledge of legal ethics is so sketchy that you can't see why without my explanation, you had better study legal ethics."

"I've studied them," Mason said. "I am entitled to cross-examine a witness. I am entitled to do anything that is legitimate for the purpose of testing the recollection of the witness. If this witness had been absolutely positive that the woman he picked up out there was the defendant, and if the defendant had again engaged this cab on the evening of the third, he would then have recognized her instantly and said, 'Good evening, ma'am. I had you as a passenger earlier in the day.'"

"But she didn't engage the cab again," Hamilton Burger said. "Counsel was afraid to take that chance. That's the unfair part of it. He had some other women engage the cab and then give the receipt to this defendant."

"You're making that as an accusation?" Mason asked.

"Yes, I'm making it as an accusation."

"And you're willing to state to this Court that the defendant was not in the cab on the evening of the third—we're talking about legal ethics now, Mr. District Attorney; you're making a representation of fact to the Court."

"Well, now wait a minute," Hamilton Burger sputtered, "I only know what the witness said."

"And the witness said that he wasn't sure. Now are you are going to tell the Court *you* are sure?"

"You're not going to cross-examine me!" Hamilton Burger shouted.

"If you make statements of fact to the Court, I'm most certainly going to cross-examine you," Mason said.

"Come, come, gentlemen," Judge Hoyt said. "This is rapidly developing into a situation the Court doesn't like."

"Well," Mason said, "I'm not going to let myself be accused of unprofessional conduct. If *I* had been preparing this case for the prosecution, if *I* had been confronted with a taxicab receipt numbered trip nine-eighty-four, I certainly would have checked to see what trip nine-eighty-four was."

"Yes," Judge Hoyt said. "I think the district attorney

must admit that this entire situation has been predicated upon lax investigative work somewhere in the case. It is a peculiar situation that this receipt should have been introduced in evidence as the receipt for a particular trip."

"Well, it was the same amount and the same date and the same cab, and in possession of the defendant," Hamilton Burger blurted.

"Exactly," Judge Hoyt said. "And the Court feels that under the circumstances, it certainly would have been in order to have checked it to find out what trip it was."

Hamilton Burger started to say something, then apparently thought better of it.

Mason said, "If this witness had been telling the truth, if he could have made an absolute identification of the defendant, nothing that might have happened subsequently on the evening of the third could have confused him. If he permitted himself to become confused, it was because he wasn't as positive of his identification as the authorities tried to make him think he was when he picked the defendant out of the lineup the next morning."

"That, unfortunately, is now an inescapable conclusion," Judge Hoyt said. "Regardless of how it happened, Mr. Prosecutor, you must admit that the testimony of this witness has become hopelessly impaired. You would hardly be in a position to use this witness in front of a jury to make an absolute identification."

"I'll cross that bridge when I come to it," Hamilton Burger said angrily. "Right now, I'm interested in finding out how it happened that this trap was set. Your Honor must realize that if the defendant hadn't had a guilty conscience, she wouldn't have manipulated things so that there would have been this unforeseen development."

"I'm not too certain," Judge Hoyt said. "How do we know that this witness didn't confuse the faces of two people who got in his cab on the third of the month?"

"Well, of course," Hamilton Burger said angrily, "if that's going to be the Court's attitude——"

"The Court's attitude is determined from the testimony, Mr. Prosecutor," the judge interrupted coldly.

"Yes, Your Honor."

"Now, proceed."

Hamilton Burger appeared undecided.

"Of course," Judge Hoyt said, "in a preliminary examination you only need to show that a crime has been committed and that there is reasonable cause to believe the defendant has committed that crime. However, in the present state of the proof, the evidence is entirely circumstantial and the evidence which is before the Court is hopelessly contradictory."

Hamilton Burger said, "I can dismiss this proceeding without prejudice and I can then file another complaint."

"Or you can go before the grand jury and ask for an indictment and avoid a preliminary examination altogether," Judge Hoyt suggested.

"Of course," Hamilton Burger said, "that is exactly what counsel was trying to bring about. The more opportunities he has to cross-examine the prosecution's witnesses, the more opportunities he has for finding some minor inconsistency which can be distorted and magnified into something that is out of all proportion to its significance."

"Is there any proof that the defendant was riding in the automobile with the decedent when it was driven up to that house?" Judge Hoyt asked. "Were there any latent fingerprints of the defendant in the automobile?"

Hamilton Burger said shamefacedly, "Frankly, Your Honor, we didn't look. We felt that the positive identification of this cab driver, putting the defendant at the scene of the crime, was all we needed, particularly when we learned the weapon in the case had been sold to her husband. It wasn't until we started checking that we realized the signature on the firearms registration was that of another person, who had evidently been sent to pick up the gun for Mr. Harlan."

"Well, what do you want to do with this case?" Judge Hoyt asked.

"I'd like to have the defendant bound over," Hamilton Burger said tentatively.

Judge Hoyt shook his head. "Not unless you have some additional evidence."

"Well, I don't want the Court to turn the defendant loose," Burger said.

Judge Hoyt showed his exasperation. "I have been endeavoring to give you every consideration, Mr. Prosecutor. I appreciate your position, and the Court feels that there may have been some very ingenious device used here at least to confuse the identification. However, the fact remains that the identification *is* confused. Now, if you want to dismiss the case before the Court rules on it, go ahead and dismiss it."

"I move to dismiss this case," Hamilton Burger said.

"Very well, the case is dismissed; the defendant is discharged from custody."

"I'm going to ask the Court to order the defendant to remain in custody until I can get other proceedings."

Judge Hoyt shook his head. "You can have the defendant arrested on a warrant, if you wish. Or you can have her arrested on suspicion of murder while you are waiting for the grand jury to act. As far as the Court is concerned, once the proceedings are dismissed the defendant is discharged from custody."

"Very well, Your Honor," Hamilton Burger said.

"Court's adjourned," Judge Hoyt snapped.

As soon as the judge had arisen from the bench, the prosecutor marched out of the courtroom, his face livid with anger.

Perry Mason grinned at Sybil Harlan. "Well," he said, "that's the first round."

"What do I do now?" she asked.

"Wait here," Mason said. "You're going to be rear-rested."

"And I sit here and wait for that?"

"Sure."

"What about that taxi driver?"

Mason said, "By the time Hamilton Burger gets him in front of a jury, he'll have changed his story all around. But we'll have this transcript on which we can impeach him, and that will keep his testimony somewhat in line. After he's thought it over, he'll state that, giving the matter second thought, he feels that you probably were one of the two women who got in the taxicab later on in the evening and that you also were the one whom he took to the Union Station."

"What will you do if he says that?"

Mason grinned. "I'll ask him how it happened that when the matter was fresh in his mind he was so positive that you hadn't again entered the cab. I'll give him a bad time. Who signed for the gun that your husband bought?"

"I think it was his secretary."

"Well," Mason said, "they'll find out who signed his name. They'll serve a subpoena on her, put her on the stand, and have her identify her signature. They'll ask her what she did with the gun she received, and she'll be forced to say that she gave it to your husband."

"Then what?"

"By that time," Mason said, "we'll have tried to find out something else to do. In the meantime, I'm going to——"

Enright Harlan pushed open the gate that separated the space reserved for lawyers and came striding toward them.

Sybil Harlan gave him one brief glance and then, as she saw the expression on his face, stiffened as though bracing herself against the physical impact of a blow.

"I've just heard something, Sybil," he said.

"Well?"

"Mrs. Doxey, the daughter of George Lutts, told Roxy Claffin that *you* were the one who furnished Perry Mason with the money to buy a stock interest in the Sylvan Glade Development Company, so you could throw a monkey wrench in the machinery."

"Now, just a minute," Mason said. "Take it easy."

Harlan didn't even look at the lawyer but stood looking straight at his wife. "Is it true, Sybil?"

"Hold on a minute," Mason said. "We have a bunch of newspaper reporters back there. This is a hell of a time to start a family row."

"Will you deny it?" Enright Harlan asked.

Sybil met his eyes. "Do we have to discuss it now, Enny?"

"Yes."

"No, I won't deny it. It's true. She was trying to steal something very dear to me, and I decided I'd give *her* something to think of."

"You're doing Roxy a great wrong, Sybil. She can't control her emotions any more than anyone. Love comes and love goes. It isn't something you can turn on and off whenever you want to, like a water faucet. You don't have that much control of your emotions. But Roxy would never have done anything underhanded."

"Oh no, oh no, not that little minx! Of course not! Certainly not! All right, I retained Mr. Mason. *Now* what?"

"I'm sorry," Enright Harlan said coldly, and turned away.

"Wait a minute, Harlan," Mason said. "Come back here."

Harlan paused, looked over his shoulder.

"You don't want to do a trick like that," Mason told him. "You can't add that handicap to the load your wife's carrying. Newspaper reporters are watching you. If they see you turn away like this, they'll———"

"Let the whole world see me turn away," Harlan said and deliberately turned his back.

As he walked out of the courtroom, a couple of alert photographers, looking for a dramatic picture, snapped his angry features.

Mason moved around so that temporarily his body concealed Sybil Harlan's face. "Don't cry," he said. "Remember, we're playing poker. Chin up. Can you manage a smile?"

"Hell no," she said. "I can't keep from crying for over thirty seconds. Get that matron! Let me get out of here."

Mason caught Della Street's eye. "Go with her, Della. Get her out of here."

"What are you going to do?" Della Street asked.

"Divert the attention of those reporters," Mason said, striding after Enright Harlan.

Mason caught up with Harlan as the tight-lipped husband was waiting at the elevators.

"Harlan!" he called.

Harlan spun on his heel, looked coldly at Mason. "What is it this time?"

Mason, conscious of the reporters crowding him from behind, said, "You can't get away with it that easy."

"What do you mean?"

Mason said, "Your wife asked you a simple question. She's entitled to an answer. How did that gun get out of your possession and up at the scene of the murder?"

Enright Harlan, thrown entirely off balance, said, "What the . . . what the hell are you trying to do?"

"As your wife's lawyer, I'm trying to find out who killed George C. Lutts."

"Then you'd better ask the person who killed him!"

"This question I'm asking you. You can't keep walking out on it."

The elevator came to a stop. Enright Harlan hesitated for a moment, then shouldered his way into the crowded elevator without a word.

Mason turned back toward the courtroom. Newspaper reporters blocked his way. "What about the gun, Mr.

Mason? What were you insinuating? What's cooking? Are Harlan and his wife at odds?"

Mason said, "I'm trying to find out about certain evidence, that's all."

"What about the gun? Why did you ask Harlan that question?"

"Because the district attorney says it's his gun."

"Well," one of the reporters said, "his wife could have taken it."

"And so could Harlan," Mason said.

"Good Lord, he's standing back of his wife. You don't mean to insinuate that he——"

"He gave that gun to someone," Mason said. "I'd like to find out who it was," and pushed past the reporters. He met Della Street coming out of the courtroom, drew her to one side. "Everything under control?"

"Yes, she didn't cry until after she got out of the courtroom."

"Say anything?" Mason asked.

Della Street said, "She looked at me and said, 'That's what I get for underestimating an adversary. Let them kill me now.' She was white and shaking."

"All right," Mason told her, "now we know what the district attorney's case is and we can go to work."

11

∎

PERRY MASON PUSHED DOWN ON THE FOOT THROTTLE, sending his car whining up the steep grade. He brought it to a stop in front of the big three-storied house.

"You sit here, Della," he said. "Shut the motor off. I'll

fire two shots. Press the horn button once if you hear one shot, twice if you hear two shots.

"After that, turn on the radio. I'll fire two more shots. Give me the same signal."

Della Street nodded.

Mason took a skeleton key from his pocket.

"Will the police frown on this procedure?" Della Street asked.

"What procedure?"

"The breaking and entry part, the skeleton key."

Mason grinned. "I'm a stockholder in the company that owns the building. Even Hamilton Burger can't find a loophole in that."

"The police have finished searching the place?"

"Yes. They've been over it with a fine-toothed comb. They found one other bullet."

"They did? When?"

"Late last night. It was embedded in the wall on the south side and had been fired from the fatal gun."

"You didn't tell me."

"I didn't know it myself until this morning."

"Then there's only one other bullet to be accounted for?"

"Yes. The two bullets from the Peters' shells have now been found. The U.M.C. bullet is missing."

"Those are blank cartridges you're using?"

"That's right."

"Do they make the same amount of noise as the one with bullets?"

"I hope so," Mason said. "I don't dare to shoot any bullets to find out. We'll make a reasonable test."

"What do you want to prove?"

"Whether my client is lying."

"If she isn't?"

"So much the better."

"And if she is?"

"She's still my client," Mason said, and fitted his skeleton key to the lock in the door.

Mason climbed the first flight of stairs, looked around at the gloomy rooms, inhaled the musty air, then started up the second flight, paused midway up the flight to inspect the reddish-brown stain which had soaked into the wood, marking the place where the body of George C. Lutts had been resting when discovered by his startled son-in-law.

He climbed to the third floor, looked out of the window down the steep slope to the place where Roxy Claffin's house gleamed in the sunlight, a vision of white stucco, red-tiled roof, blue-tiled swimming pool, walled patio, green shrubbery and velvet lawns, the well-kept luxury of the place standing in sharp contrast to the contractor's unpainted board shack at the foot of the grade where the raw earth had been ripped away.

Mason stood with his back to the window. He raised a thirty-eight caliber revolver and pulled the trigger twice. The echoes of the explosion died away. From down below came the blast of an automobile horn. A second later there was another blast.

Mason waited for a full minute, then raised the gun and fired two more shots. This time there was no sound of the automobile horn.

Mason pushed the gun back in his pocket and descended the stairs.

"Okay?" Della Street asked.

"Okay," he said. "How plainly did you hear them?"

"I heard the two plainly. After that, nothing."

"Were you trying to listen for the second two?"

"When the radio was on, I tried to sit back, listening to the radio the way a person would."

"How loud did you have it on?"

"Pretty loud. Not blasting my eardrums out, but good and loud just the same."

"In other words, you were trying to give our client a break?"

"Well . . . I suppose I was."

"We can't do it that way," Mason said. "We have to know the real facts."

He got in beside Della Street, turned the radio on, adjusted the volume. "Leave it just like that, Della."

Again Mason climbed the stairs, waited a minute and fired two shots. This time there were two blasts from the horn below. They were short, as though Della Street had been reluctant to press the horn button.

Mason sighed, put the gun in his pocket and descended the stairs. He found Della Street sitting in the automobile, tears in her eyes.

Mason patted her shoulder. "Don't take it too hard, Della. I had to know . . . that's all."

"I like her, Chief."

"So do I, but we can't control the facts."

"Will the police make this experiment?"

"After she tells her story. You couldn't hear the shots when the radio was loud?"

"No."

"Would you have heard these last two if you hadn't been listening for them?"

She wiped her eyes. "I'd like to say no, Chief, but that won't help her. Yes, they came in very clearly.

"Of course," Della Street pointed out, "she may say she was listening to some program that was real noisy."

Mason nodded without enthusiasm. "I'm not going to put any words in her mouth, Della. I'm just going to ask her."

"The radio wasn't left turned on when you and Doxey drove up?"

"No. She says she shut it off when she went in the house."

"Where's the car now?" Della Street asked. "A lot might depend on what station the radio indicator was on."

"The police have the car. They're making a belated search for fingerprints."

"Finding any?"

"They're not telling."

"So what do we do now?"

"Now," Mason said, "I think we're ready to talk with Mrs. Doxey. I want to find out how it happened she told Mrs. Claffin about Sybil Harlan having retained me to throw a monkey wrench in the machinery."

"That was a mean thing to do," Della Street said, "right when Mrs. Harlan thought her husband was going to stand back of her, right when she thought Mrs. Claffin had been put in her place."

Mason nodded.

"Chief, suppose Mrs. Harlan is telling the truth. Someone must have been concealed in that house, waiting for Lutts. After all, you know, Lutts was a pretty smooth operator, and there undoubtedly were people who didn't like him."

"Let's look at the sheer mechanics of the thing," Mason said. "The murderer fired at least two shots; one of them went into Lutts's chest at a distance of about eighteen to twenty inches, the other one missed him and went into the wall. What would be the sequence of those shots?"

"What do you mean?"

Mason said, "After having shot Lutts in the heart at a distance of eighteen to twenty inches, the murderer would hardly have fired a second shot into the wall just for practice."

She nodded.

"Therefore," Mason said, "we have to assume the first shot was fired at Lutts and it missed him."

Again Della Street nodded.

"So," Mason said, "we try to reconstruct the conditions under which that first shot was fired. In all probability, Lutts had his back turned."

"Why do you say that?"

"I think it's logical. I don't think his murderer would have pulled a gun, aimed and fired, if Lutts had been standing facing the murderer."

"Well, he certainly was facing the murderer when the second shot was fired."

"Exactly," Mason said. "Which indicates that the first shot was fired when he had his back turned. Then that shot was a miss. Lutts must have whirled at the sound of the shot. He saw the murderer standing there, holding a gun. He could have done either one of two things. He could have tried to run away or he could have charged toward the murderer. Apparently he charged."

"How can you tell?"

"Either he charged toward the murderer or the murderer charged toward him," Mason said. "The first shot wouldn't have been a miss at twenty inches. Therefore, the distance between the murderer and the victim must have been shortened materially between the time the first shot was fired and the time the second shot was fired."

"That's right," Della Street said.

"So either Lutts was charging the murderer or the murderer was charging Lutts. Now then, at eighteen to twenty inches—and mind you, that's twenty inches from the end of the gun to the chest of the victim—Lutts would have been trying to do something to protect himself."

Mason took a tape measure from his pocket, said, "Get out, will you, Della? I want to try an experiment. Here, hold the gun."

"It's empty?"

"It's empty. It was only loaded with blanks in the first place."

Della Street took the gun.

"Point it at me."

She pointed the gun.

"Now stretch it out just as far as you can reach with your hand."

She pushed the gun out at arm's length. Mason took a steel tape measure from his pocket, measured off twenty inches.

"See what I mean?" he said. "At this distance, I'd be knocking the gun out of your hand."

"Unless I jerked my hand out of the way."

"That would be pretty hard to do with a gun. Now, hold the gun closer to you."

She crooked her elbow slightly.

"Closer," Mason said. "Hold the gun right up against your body. Lower it to your hip. Remember, the course of the fatal bullet was upward. The murderer shot from the hip."

She put the gun up against her hip. Mason measured off twenty inches from the gun to his chest.

"At this distance," he said, "I could break your jaw before you could pull the trigger."

"You might break my jaw and I might pull the trigger at the same time."

"That," Mason said, "is the thought I'm trying to explore."

"So what do we do now?"

"So now," Mason said, "we go talk with Mrs. Herbert Doxey. But first we telephone Paul Drake and find out which one of the possible suspects knew nothing about shooting a gun. Our murderer, whoever he was, must have missed that first shot at a distance of hardly more than ten feet."

12

∎

MASON STOPPED HIS CAR IN FRONT OF THE CALIFORNIA-type bungalow, opened the door of the car.

"Hold it," Della Street said. "I'm coming across to your side." She slid from the right side across under the steering wheel, with a tantalizing flash of shapely legs, and then was standing on the sidewalk, shaking her skirts down and placing her purse under her arm as she walked up to the door with Perry Mason.

Mason rang the doorbell.

The woman who answered it was red-haired, blue-eyed, about thirty, with high cheekbones and a mouth which, despite an attempt to change the lines with lipstick, remained a thin straight line.

"Good afternoon."

"Mrs. Doxey?"

"Yes."

"I'm Perry Mason."

"I thought you were. I've seen your picture."

"This is Miss Street, my secretary. May we come in for a moment?"

"Herbert isn't here."

"I wanted to talk with you."

"I'm rather upset these days, Mr. Mason. The——"

"I don't want to intrude on your grief," Mason said, "but I consider it rather important."

"It isn't only my grief, it's my housekeeping. I've let things go pretty much. Come in."

She led the way into a comfortable, spacious living room.

Mason looked around at the artistic furnishings appreciatively.

"It's big," she said. "Too big for just us two, now that Daddy is gone. I don't know what we'll do. He lived with us, you know."

"Yes, I know," Mason said.

"Sit down, please."

After they were seated Mason said, "I'll come directly to the point, Mrs. Doxey."

"That's what I like people to do."

"You and your father were very close?"

"In a way. We understood each other and respected each other. Daddy didn't confide very much in anyone."

"You knew that he had sold his stock in the Sylvan Glade Development Company?"

"I know it now."

"And you knew it on the third, the date that Mr. Lutts died?"

She hesitated for a moment, then said, "Yes, I knew it on the third."

"On the afternoon of the third?"

"On the evening of the third."

"When?"

"After he failed to show up for dinner—usually, he was very prompt. He wanted dinner at a certain hour— that was one of Daddy's peculiarities. People kept telephoning about stock."

"Do you have servants?"

"A servant who helps with housework—part time."

"And as a rule, dinner was right on time?"

"Right to the minute."

"So when he didn't show up you thought it was rather unusual?"

"It was very unusual. I may say it was unique. It was his custom either to be here or give us ample notice by telephone."

"So I take it, you discussed with your husband what might have been keeping him, when he didn't show up on the evening of the third."

"Yes."

"And it was then your husband told you about the transfer of stock?"

"Yes."

"And told you I had bought the stock?"

"Yes."

"Now then," Mason said, "your husband also told you that I was acting in a representative capacity?"

"He thought you were."

"And he told you the name of my client?"

"No, he didn't know."

"He didn't know?"

She shook her head.

"You asked him about it?"

"Of course. We speculated as to just who it might be. Herbert thought it might be either Cleve Rector or Ezekiel Elkins. He wouldn't have put it past either one of them to have manipulated things in that way, so that trouble could have been stirred up."

"I see," Mason said. "Eventually, you found out the identity of my client?"

"No, I don't know to this day who it was. I don't think any announcement has ever been made, has it?"

"But you've learned from your husband, informally and off the record, who that client is?"

She tightened her lips and shook her head.

"Do you know Mrs. Claffin?"

"I've met her."

"More than once?"

"Yes."

"Several times?"

"Three or four."

"Are you just on speaking terms, or are you close friends?"

"Just speaking terms."

Mason hesitated for a moment.

"Why are you asking me these things, Mr. Mason?"

"Because I'm trying to clarify a matter which may be of some importance."

She remained silent.

"Did you at any time speculate with Mrs. Claffin as to the identity of my client?"

"No."

"Did you discuss with Mrs. Claffin the fact that I had bought stock in the company?"

"No, I haven't seen her since you bought the stock."

Mason exchanged glances with Della Street. "Well, thank you," he said. "I was just trying to find out something about Mrs. Claffin and her attitude."

"I'm afraid I can't help you at all, Mr. Mason."

She was obviously waiting for him to take his departure. Abruptly, the front door opened, a cheery voice sang out, "Hello, honeybunch."

Mrs. Doxey got up. "We have company, Herbert."

"I saw a car parked out front—didn't know whether it was someone who had parked or—— Why, hello, Mr. Mason. What are *you* doing here? And Miss Street. It's a pleasure."

Mason said, "I was trying to find out something about what had happened after the directors' meeting on the third."

Doxey lost much of his cordiality. "My wife doesn't know anything about the business."

"So she was telling me. Now, Mr. Lutts evidently had a shrewd suspicion as to who my client was when I put across that stock deal."

"He did. He *knew* who it was, but he didn't tell me. I've already explained that."

"When was the last time you saw him?"

"That afternoon—after the directors' meeting. We went over to the restaurant and had a couple of hamburgers. You know all that, Mason. I've told you all this."

"Did he discuss my buying that stock with you?"

"We didn't talk about anything else—what did you think we'd be talking about?"

"And at that time he made some speculation as to the identity of my client?"

"Of course. That was what interested us. That was the sixty-four dollar question, but there weren't any answers. I was inclined to think it was Elkins. Daddy Lutts thought it had to be an outsider. Then some idea came to him, and Daddy Lutts went to make a phone call. He learned something he didn't see fit to pass on to me."

"Do you know Mrs. Claffin?"

"Of course, I know Mrs. Claffin."

"You've met her several times?"

"What the hell is this—some sort of a cross-examination? I know her, yes. What's that got to do with it?"

"Did you ever talk with her about my buying the stock?"

"I haven't seen her for—Enny Harlan is her business agent, and nearly all my dealings with her were through him."

"How about telephone conversations?"

"Sure, I've had telephone conversations with Harlan."

"Any speculation with him as to who my client might be?"

"Some on his part, none on mine. He tried to pump me for information, and I told him I didn't have any."

"In other words," Mason said, "you haven't told anyone that I was representing any particular party."

"I don't like the idea of you coming in here and asking my wife a lot of questions and then asking me a lot of questions," Doxey said.

"You're the secretary of the company," Mason told him. "I'm a stockholder. I have a right to know."

"You don't want to know because you're a stockholder in the company. You want to know because you're representing Mrs. Harlan in a murder case."

"All right. But the fact still remains that you're the secretary of a company in which I'm a stockholder."

"All right, so what."

"I want to know if you communicated any ideas you might have had concerning the identity of my client to Enright Harlan or to Mrs. Claffin?"

"The answer to that is no. Now, I take it that's all you wanted to find out."

"That's all," Mason said.

Mrs. Doxey said, "Herbert, Mr. Mason has been very nice and very considerate. There's no need to be nasty about it."

"I'm running this," Doxey said.

"All right," Mason told him. "Thank you very much."

"Don't mention it," Doxey said sarcastically, and escorted them to the door.

"After all," Della Street asked Mason when they were back in the car, driving to the office, "does it make any great difference?"

"It may."

"Why?"

"I don't know yet, but Doxey certainly changed his attitude."

"Yes. You've made an enemy out of him now, Chief."

"That's right. That's what interests me. Why did he blow up?"

"He just didn't like the idea of being questioned. Just because Enright Harlan says Mrs. Claffin got the information from some person doesn't mean that that's where she *really* got it."

Mason parked his car. He and Della took the elevator and stopped in at Drake's office before going down the corridor to Mason's office.

"Hi, Paul," Mason said. "How was La Jolla?"

"Oh, fine," Drake said sarcastically. "I was down there for all of fifteen minutes, I guess, and then I got your message to come back."

"Well," Mason told him, "it turned out that the case I had down there wasn't terribly important after all."

"Yes," Drake said dryly, "I read about it. The taxicab driver blew up on the witness stand and couldn't identify anyone, so there was really no need of my going in the first place."

"I didn't say that," Mason told him. "The case you were sent down to La Jolla to work on had nothing to do with the taxi driver."

"Oh, I know, I know," Drake said. "Just one of those coincidences. Isn't it funny how they'll trap you, Perry? It wouldn't be any trouble at all to reach an entirely erroneous conclusion in a matter of that sort, just judging from circumstantial evidence."

"Never mind all that," Mason told him. "What have

you all found out about the people on that list I gave you, Paul?"

"Well," Drake said, "at four-thirty on the afternoon of the third, Herbert Doxey was at home with his wife. He'd been there since shortly before four o'clock. He was taking a sun bath in a screen enclosure in the back yard. He's got a sunburned back to prove it, too. Enright Harlan and Roxy Claffin were together."

"You're sure?"

"Sure."

"How do you know?"

"Well, they were out at Roxy's house. Roxy answered the telephone. She was talking on the phone a little before four o'clock and she was talking again at four-fifteen. Enright Harlan got there a little before four-thirty. They had an appointment for a little after five o'clock with an attorney named Arthur Nebitt Hagan, and they left Roxy's place shortly after four-thirty.

"Now then, you come to Neffs, and, believe it or not, Neffs was at the Sunbelt Detective Agency, hiring a detective to shadow certain people. It was his theory that your client had to be one of half a dozen possible individuals, and he wanted to find out who.

"Cleve Rector was closeted with Jim Bantry of the Bantry Construction and Paving Company."

"At four-thirty?" Mason asked.

"Well, there we run into a little trouble. Apparently, he left Bantry at around four o'clock. He says that he stopped in at a bar for a cocktail and then went to his office, getting there around five o'clock."

"You can't verify his story as to where he was between four and five o'clock?" Mason asked.

"Well, we *know* he was at the contractors at four and we *know* he was at his office at five, and we *know* the driving time between the two is about twenty-five minutes. He couldn't have gotten into very much mischief in that time. Of course, when you come right down to it, Perry, we don't have the type of evidence that would give him an alibi."

"*I* don't want to give him an alibi," Mason said. "Let him furnish his own alibi. I just want to know how much evidence he can bring to bear."

"Well, apparently that's it. He gave the name of a bar where he stopped in for a cocktail. The guy who was tending bar at the time was busy. Rector's picture doesn't mean a damn thing to him. Rector may have been there, or he may not as far as the bartender is concerned."

"All right," Mason said, "that leaves Ezekiel Elkins. What about him?"

"Now then," Drake said, "I've been saving that choice tidbit until the last. There is something very, very mysterious about Ezekiel Elkins. He's not talking."

"Not with anybody?"

"Not with any of *my* men. We've used all of the known tricks on him, and he's not talking. Incidentally, Mr. Elkins has a nice black eye."

"Where did he get it?" Mason asked. "Did he run into a door in the dark of the night?"

"He ran into somebody's fist in broad daylight."

"Who *is* Elkins talking to—anyone?"

"He's had a chance to talk."

"To whom?"

"To the district attorney."

"You don't know whether he talked or not?"

"No, naturally the district attorney isn't going to tell me."

"What does the district attorney tell the newspaper reporters?"

"That he had several witnesses in who could explain matters somewhat, and Elkins was among them. He didn't say whether Elkins talked or what they talked about. Just smiled and let it go at that."

"Well, that's a thought," Mason said.

"With the finding of that second bullet," Drake

pointed out, "it turns out that the gun must have been fired at least twice inside the house up there, and the third empty shell indicates that it may have been fired three times. Now what had it been fired *at?*"

"I wish I could tell you that," Mason said.

"Did your client hear the shots?" Drake asked.

"What makes you think my client was anywhere around there?" Mason asked.

"Your client could help one hell of a lot if she would co-operate. It would shorten the investigation."

"How come, Paul?"

"She could tell us *exactly* when the murder was committed. The autopsy surgeon can place the time within twenty minutes—and twenty minutes is twenty minutes."

Mason nodded.

"The other thing your client could do is tell how many shots were fired and how those shots were spaced. In other words, whether there was one shot and then quite an interval and then another shot. Whether two shots came close together. Or even, perhaps, if there was a third shot fired."

"But what in the world would my client have been doing out there . . . how did she get out there and——?"

"Now wait a minute," Drake said. "Don't blow a gasket over this thing, Perry. I'm simply asking you. I'd like very much to have that information. It would simplify my investigative work."

Mason said, "Paul, no one has proven that my client was out there—yet. But *if* my client *had* been out there, she would have been sitting in Lutts's car, listening to the radio, and the radio would have been playing so loud that she couldn't have heard the shot."

"Shots," Drake corrected, "plural."

"All right, plural—shots."

"Della Street and I have been conducting experiments out there at the scene of the murder," Mason said. "Anyone who might have been in Lutts' car, waiting for him to come downstairs, was bound to have heard the two shots that were fired unless the radio in the car was on."

"Was the radio on when you and Doxey went out there and Doxey discovered the body?"

"No."

"Who had the car keys?" Drake asked.

"To Lutts' car?"

"Yes."

"Why, he did, of course."

Drake shook his head. "They weren't in his pockets when the body was searched."

"The devil!" Mason exclaimed.

"Makes a difference?" Drake asked, his eyes searching the lawyer's face.

"Perhaps. What would the murderer have wanted with car keys?"

"He may have wanted to borrow the car."

"And the police didn't search the car for fingerprints?"

"Not then. They're doing it now. Here are some pictures of the car, for what they're worth."

Drake pulled out some eight-by-ten glossy photographs. Mason studied them.

"That's just the way the car was found?"

"That's right."

Mason studied the ignition switch.

"What's wrong?" Drake asked.

Mason said, "Call up the agency that sells this car. See if it's possible to turn on the radio when the ignition is locked and the key removed."

"Oh, oh!" Drake exclaimed.

"Get busy," Mason told him.

Drake put through the call.

"Don't give your name," Mason warned. "Tell them you're a customer. Give them any kind of a stall."

Drake nodded, motioned Mason to silence, said, "Hello. . . . On your last year's model car, is it possible to turn on the radio when the ignition is locked . . . ? Yeah, my neighbor thinks my kid got in his garage, turned on the radio and ran the battery down. . . . Oh, yes, I see. You're sure . . . ? That's true of all last year's models . . . ? Okay, thanks."

Drake hung up the phone. His eyes avoided the lawyer's. "When the ignition is in the locked position, Perry, there isn't any way you can turn on the radio. The car was especially designed that way because of complaints that night attendants in public garages would run the battery down by letting the radio run all night."

"Well," Mason said, "that's that. Come on, Della, let's go."

13

∎

JUDGE SEDGWICK LOOKED AT PERRY MASON. "THE peremptory challenge is with the defendant."

"The defendant passes," Mason said.

Judge Sedgwick glanced over at the prosecutor's table, where Hamilton Burger, the district attorney, was sitting beside Marvin Pierson, conceded to be one of the most brilliant of the trial deputies in the district attorney's office. "The peremptory is with the people."

"The people pass."

"Very well," Judge Sedgwick said, "the jury will stand and be sworn to well and truly try the issues in the case of the People of the State of California versus Sybil Harlan."

The jurors arose and held up their hands—five women and seven men, solemn-faced as befitted jurors who are about to decide issues which will involve the life of a fellow mortal.

"Do you wish to proceed with your opening argument, Mr. Burger?" Judge Sedgwick asked.

Hamilton Burger could not refrain from one triumphant glance at Perry Mason. He was about to explode a bombshell which would leave the defense floundering and helpless. The greatest pains had been taken to preserve secrecy in the matter, and the district attorney had every reason to believe that what he had to say would come as a terrific surprise to the defense.

Hamilton Burger walked up and stood in front of the jury.

"Ladies and gentlemen," he said, "I'm going to make perhaps the briefest opening argument that I have ever made. We expect to prove to you, through witnesses, that Sybil Harlan, who is married to Enright Harlan and who is very much in love with her husband, felt that an attachment might be developing between one Mrs. Claffin and Enright Harlan. She knew that Mrs. Claffin was working with her husband, Enright, on a real estate development. She, therefore, retained Perry Mason, her present attorney, to provide a series of business complications which would introduce an element of discord into what she feared might become a romance.

"From a map which will presently be introduced, you will see that the scene where the murder was committed was an old house, a former mansion situated high on a hill which was about to be removed to make way for a modern subdivision development. The defendant secured a skeleton key, which enabled her to open the door of that building. She had a pair of binoculars, and she made it a habit to sit up in that building, looking down on the adjoining property which belonged to Mrs. Claffin.

"The defendant's husband was quite a sportsman and a collector of guns. He had no fewer than twenty-eight rifles, seven shotguns and seven revolvers."

Hamilton Burger glanced triumphantly at Mason. "We expect to show from the garage attendant who serviced the defendant's car on the day of the murder that on the day in question there was a pair of binoculars and a revolver in the glove compartment of her car. We expect to show that shortly before the murder, the decedent, George Lutts, met the defendant just as the defendant emerged from a beauty shop. We don't know whether by appointment, or, if so, who made the appointment. We do propose to show you that they met, that the defendant got in Mr. Lutts's car and that Lutts then drove her to the parking lot where her car was parked. We propose to show by the parking attendant that at that time the defendant opened the glove compartment of her car and took out the gun, that she put the gun in her handbag and then joined the decedent on what was to prove to be his last ride.

"We will next show you the defendant, pale, nervous, evidently suffering from shock, walking and running to the highway that leads from the country club, which, as you will presently see from the map, runs within a relatively short distance of the scene of the murder. The defendant stopped a taxicab and had the taxi driver take her to the Union Station.

"At the Union Station, the defendant transferred cabs. She picked up another cab, and, mark this well, ladies and gentlemen of the jury, because it is highly important —she had this cab *take her to her residence*. We don't know what she did there. We do know what she had an opportunity to do there. She then had the taxi, which had been waiting in front of her house, drive to the parking lot where her car had been located. At that time, she entered her car and did something to the door of the glove compartment.

"After that, the defendant telephoned someone, then returned to the taxi and had the taxi driver take her to the building where Perry Mason, her present attorney, has his office.

"We expect to show that George C. Lutts was killed by a thirty-eight revolver, that that revolver was one which came from the collection of Enright Harlan.

"On the strength of that evidence, ladies and gentlemen of the jury, we are going to ask for a verdict of first-degree murder. I am not going to make any recommendations as to what you should do in connection with assessing the death penalty. That is a matter which is entirely within the discretion of the jury, and this office does not want to adopt any position. You have the discretion in the event you find the defendant guilty to recommend that she be punished by imprisonment for life. We leave that matter entirely in your hands."

Hamilton Burger turned and walked back to his counsel table, giving one swift, triumphant glance in Mason's direction as he passed the table.

"Does the defense wish to make an opening statement now or later?" Judge Sedgwick asked.

Mason said, "Your Honor, may we have a brief ten-minute recess while I give the matter consideration? Certain statements made by the district attorney relate to matters with which I am not personally familiar."

"We object," Hamilton Burger said. "Counsel has had every opportunity to confer with his client. The testimony which was given by witnesses before the grand jury has been delivered to him."

"But, Your Honor," Mason said, "many of the matters stated in the district attorney's opening statement were not presented to the grand jury."

"Naturally," Hamilton Burger said, "I didn't have to present my whole case at that time and, Your Honor, in order to show my good faith, I may say that some of these witnesses were discovered after the indictment."

"The Court will grant a ten-minute recess," Judge Sedgwick announced.

Mason turned to Sybil Harlan. "All right," he said in a whisper, "can he prove that?"

Her lips were quivering as she tried to whisper. "I didn't think anyone saw me."

"You lied to me?" Mason asked.

"I tried to . . . tried to make things look a little better. As soon as I knew that he had been shot, I knew that having a weapon in my handbag——"

"I know," Mason said wearily. "You thought you'd fool me a little and that that would make me a little more diligent in my defense. You did go to the Union Station, then take a taxicab and go to your house?"

She nodded. "But only to change my shoes and stockings."

"And then telephoned me from the parking lot?"

Again she nodded. "I put the gun back in the glove compartment. Someone must have seen what I was doing and jimmied open the glove compartment and took out the gun while I was at your office."

"That was *after* Lutts had been killed?"

"Of course."

"Then how did it happen the fatal bullet came from that gun?"

"It couldn't have, Mr. Mason. Either someone's lying or someone switched the bullets after they were placed in the district attorney's office."

"Don't be silly," Mason told her. "You get me to try this case on that theory and you'll be in the gas chamber."

She met his eyes. "What other theory is there, Mr. Mason?"

Mason studied her. "I'm damned if I know," he admitted.

"It's all we have, the *only* chance we have. Please do as I ask you," she said.

Mason watched her thoughtfully. "You're not the type that likes to lie," he said. "All of this is foreign to your nature. Now *why* did you lie? Was it because you killed George Lutts?"

"No."

"Why?"

She hesitated for a moment, then poured forth the thoughts that were on her mind. "Mr. Mason, I never felt so downright cheap in all my life. I did lie to you.

I lied to you because . . . well, when I got home to change my shoes and stockings, Ruth Marvel came over. She's my closest friend. Her house adjoins mine, and when she saw me drive up in the cab, she came running over to see what was wrong. She knew I had taken my car with me when I left.

"Well, I confided in Ruth. I gave her the sketch, and Ruth, who is really very clever and who has excellent judgment, told me that since I hadn't reported the thing to the police when it happened, I couldn't possibly afford to do it then.

"I told her I was going to see you, and she said that was fine, but that a lawyer worked better on a case when he was enthusiastic about it. She said my first line of defense was to hope that no one knew I had been out there with Lutts, that police would find some clue pointing to the real murderer and that I'd never even be questioned, much less suspected.

"Then she said that if I *should* happen to be dragged into it, and they could prove I was out there with Lutts, the only other thing for me to do was to show that I had been in fear for my life.

"She told me to remember to tell you and to tell everybody else that I had heard the murderer walking around upstairs, that I had seen the hand and the gun——"

"You didn't actually see or hear him?" Mason asked.

She shook her head.

"What *did* you see?"

"Nothing. I was listening to the radio down in the car. I didn't even hear the shots. That's the truth, Mr. Mason. The first thing I knew was that I went in there and he was dead. Of course, the murderer must have been in there at the time, and if I'd gone up the stairs far enough, he'd either have shot me or knocked me out and dashed out of the house. Apparently, Lutts was the only one he was after. When he heard me coming, instead of coming toward me, he must have retreated.

He didn't want me to see him. I had enough presence of mind to realize that. If I'd seen his face, then he'd have had to kill me, too. So I ran."

"What about the car keys?" Mason asked. "How could you have been playing the radio if——"

"The keys were in the car, Mr. Mason. And I really and truly did have the radio turned on."

"Loud?"

"Pretty loud."

"Experiments show it would have to have been very loud for you not to have heard the shots."

"Well, it was loud enough so I didn't hear the shots, I can tell you that."

"But police didn't find the keys to the car," Mason said. "They——"

"That's where I made my big mistake, Mr. Mason."

"You made a lot of big mistakes," Mason said grimly. "What about those ignition keys?"

"It's very seldom that I ride in a car with someone else. I'm usually driving. So when I get out of a car, I automatically take the ignition keys with me, and that's what I did when I decided to go up and see what was happening in the house. I switched off the radio, took the ignition keys, went up the stairs, found Mr. Lutts dead, turned and ran screaming down the hill. It wasn't until I got home that I remembered about the keys."

"Then what did you do with them?" Mason asked.

"That's one thing, Mr. Mason, they're never going to trip me on. I hid those keys where they'll never, never, never find them."

"Does Ruth Marvel know where they are?"

"No. No one knows. And no one ever will know."

Mason sighed. "Can't you see what you've done? If you had told me this story, I could have given you some intelligent advice. You lied to me, and now you're out on a limb. Moreover, you made the mistake of talking to Ruth Marvel."

"No. It was all right to tell Ruth," she said. "We can trust Ruth. She'd never breathe a word."

"How do you know?" Mason asked. "Suppose the district attorney should subpoena her. If you had been talking to me, you would have been talking to your lawyer. The communication would have been confidential and privileged. Anything you told Ruth Marvel isn't privileged. If the district attorney gets wind of it and puts her on the stand, she either has to tell what you told her or become an accessory after the fact."

"But how in the world would he ever know——"

"He might get a lead," Mason said, "because you got Ruth Marvel to go in that taxicab with you when you went out the second time. The way Hamilton Burger is preparing this case, I wouldn't be too surprised if he hasn't had detectives scouting the neighborhood and then letting the taxi driver— What's the matter?" Mason asked, as he saw the expression on her face.

"He *did* ask Ruth Marvel to come to his office," Sybil Harlan said in a panic. "He asked her some perfectly innocuous questions, and she was feeling very pleased with herself at the way she had handled herself, but . . . but——"

Mason said grimly, "If your friend, Ruth Marvel, had had a little more experience and a little less conceit, she wouldn't have been feeling so smart. Now we're in one hell of a fix."

The bailiff called out, "Jury! Jury! Jury! Jury!"

The jurors filed into court, glancing curiously at Mason and the white-faced defendant.

Judge Sedgwick emerged from chambers and took his place on the bench.

Mason heaved a deep sigh and swung his chair around so as to face the witness stand.

■

14

HAMILTON BURGER PUT ON HIS CASE WITH THE DEADLY, well-rehearsed precision of a lawyer who has carefully blueprinted every possible development.

He introduced a map of the premises. He introduced the testimony of the police officers who had been summoned when the body was discovered. The ballistic expert told of the characteristics of the fatal bullet and the test bullets and stated that beyond question, the fatal bullet had been fired from the revolver that had been found on the side of the steep hill.

The taxi driver, who had picked Mrs. Harlan up at the Union Station, had driven her to her house, then to the parking lot, and from there to the building where Mason had his office, made a positive identification.

By the time of the noon recess, the district attorney had laid all the statistical groundwork of the corpus delicti. By afternoon he was ready to put on his array of witnesses who would clinch the case against the defendant.

Veteran courthouse attachés, who were following the trial with interest, realized that Jerome Keddie, the taxi driver whose testimony Mason had riddled at the time of the preliminary hearing, was being saved until such time as the prosecution had forged such a deadly chain of evidence that the failure of Keddie to make an absolute identification would be a minor matter.

After the noon adjournment, Hamilton Burger arose impressively. "Call Jacques Lamont to the stand."

Lamont came forward, was sworn, gave his name and

address, said that his occupation was that of a parking lot attendant.

"Are you acquainted with the defendant in this case?"

"By sight, yes."

"In what way?"

"There is a beauty parlor about half a block down the street from my parking lot. She patronizes this beauty parlor regularly and leaves her car in my parking lot."

"Directing your attention to the third day of June of this year, did you see the defendant?"

"I did."

"At what time?"

"At about two-thirty."

"And what happened?"

"She parked her car in the parking lot."

"Did you see her again?"

"Yes, sir."

"When?"

"At about four o'clock, a little before four, I guess."

"What did she do, if anything?"

"She entered the parking lot. She was looking around, apparently looking for me and——"

"Never mind your conclusions. Just state what happened."

"Well, she looked around. When she didn't see anybody, she went directly to her car. She opened the glove compartment."

"Where were you at the time?"

"As it happened, I had just been moving a car to let my assistant bring out a car which had been parked behind it. I was backing up, so that I was sitting in a car directly parallel with the defendant's car."

"How close were you to the glove compartment of the defendant's car?"

"Seven or eight feet."

"What did you see the defendant do, if anything?"

"She opened the glove compartment, took out a pack of cigarettes and a gun."

"What do you mean by a gun?"

"It was a blued steel revolver."

"I'm going to ask you to look at plaintiff's Exhibit D in this case, and ask if you can identify it as the gun."

"Well, I can't say it was *that* gun. But I can say that the gun she put in her purse looked just like it. It was about the same size and appearance."

"Very well. Then what happened?"

"She walked out of the parking lot and entered a car that was waiting by the entrance, a car that was being driven by a man."

"Did you get a good look at that man?"

"No, sir, I did not."

"You couldn't identify him if you saw him again?"

"No, sir, all I know is that it was a man who was driving a car, a blue two-tone sedan. I didn't notice the make."

"Then what happened?"

"The defendant went away in that car."

"When did you next see the defendant?"

"Later on, on the afternoon of the third, around five-forty-five."

"And what did she do, if anything?"

"She drove up in a taxicab."

"Where were you at the time?"

"I had been down at the far end of the parking lot with a car. I was walking back."

"What did the defendant do, if anything?"

"She walked directly to her car."

"And what did you do?"

"I thought she was going to take it out, so I——"

"Never mind what you thought. What did you do?"

"I walked rapidly toward the car, so that if she was wanting to pay the parking fees and take it out, I'd be handy."

"What did you see her do, if anything?"

"I saw her open the glove compartment of her car."

"What did she do?"

"She was doing something at the glove compartment."

"Could you see what she was doing?"

"Sort of fumbling."

"Then what?"

"Then she made a telephone call at the phone booth, and walked back to the taxicab which had been kept waiting."

"When did you next see her?"

"It was about half an hour later."

"What did she do then?"

"She came and turned in her check, paid the parking fees, and picked up her car."

Hamilton Burger turned triumphantly to Perry Mason. "Cross-examine," he said.

Mason glanced at the clock, yawned, said, "No questions."

"What?" Hamilton Burger shouted, surprised.

"No questions," Mason repeated.

Hamilton Burger fought back his surprise; then, with the air of a man bringing a difficult task to a triumphant conclusion, said, "Jamison Bell Gibbs, take the stand."

Gibbs gave his name, age, occupation and address to the court reporter, then turned expectantly to Hamilton Burger.

"You say your occupation is operating a service station?"

"Yes, sir."

"Are you acquainted with the defendant?"

"Very well, yes, sir."

"Do you, from time to time, service her automobile?"

"Yes, sir."

"When was the last time you serviced her automobile?"

"On the third of June of this year quite early in the morning."

"Who brought the automobile into your station for service?"

"The defendant."

"What did she tell you?"

"She told me she was in a hurry, that she wanted a rush lubricating job and the oil changed in the crank-case."

"What did you do?"

"I serviced the car, gave it a complete lube job, checked the tires and the battery."

"Did she ask you to do anything else?"

"She didn't, no, sir. However, I did clean out the front of the car. I noticed it was a little dirty. Quite a bit of dust had been tracked in, and I took out the floor mats and cleaned it."

"And then what?"

"I left a note containing the charges for the service, which is what I always do."

"What did you do with that note?"

"I slipped it in the edge of the glove compartment."

"What happened?"

"The latch on the glove compartment wasn't entirely closed, and the paper slipped through, down to the bottom. I was afraid she wouldn't see it, so I pressed the catch that opens the glove compartment and picked up the paper."

"What did you see, if anything?"

Mason glanced at the jurors and saw that they were leaning forward with rapt interest.

"I noticed there was a gun in the glove compartment."

"Anything else?"

"Some binoculars . . . that is, I assume they were bin-oculars. They were in the case."

"What was the relative position of the gun and the binocular case?"

"The gun was to the front of the glove compartment."

"Nearest your hand as you opened the glove compartment?"

"Yes."

"And where were the binoculars?"

"In the back part of the glove compartment."

"Now, what did you do with reference to that gun?"

"Well," the witness said, "sometimes things get stolen out of glove compartments and——"

"Never mind that," Hamilton Burger interrupted sharply. "I'm asking you to tell exactly what you did. You can discuss the reasons for what you did when you are asked the proper questions on cross-examination. I am only asking you to tell this jury what you did."

"I took the gun out and handled it."

"Are you familiar with revolvers?"

"Oh, yes. I'm a gun lover."

"Have you ever fired a gun?"

"Yes, indeed, many times."

"I hand you this revolver which has been introduced in evidence and ask you if you have ever seen it before."

"Yes, sir."

"Where?"

"In the glove compartment of the defendant's car."

"The same gun?"

"Well, of course, I didn't take down the number on the gun, but it was the same make, model and style."

"Cross-examine," Hamilton Burger snapped triumphantly.

"No questions," Mason said casually.

"Your Honor," Hamilton Burger said, "my next witness is a hostile witness. I have her under subpoena and am going to have to put her on the stand out of order because of various reasons, which I do not think are necessary to go into at this time. I may also state, if the Court please, that her testimony at this time will perhaps have no apparent connection with the case. However, I can assure the Court that it will be connected up, that it is important, and I ask permission of the Court to call this hostile witness out of order at this time."

"Very well," Judge Sedgwick ruled, "you may call the witness. If there are objections to the questions, the Court will rule on these objections as they come up."

"Mrs. Ruth Marvel," Hamilton Burger said.

"Oh, good Lord!" Sybil Harlan exclaimed in a despairing whisper.

"Take it easy," Mason warned under his breath. "Remember now, a poker face! The jurors are watching you."

Mason glanced at the clock, settled back in his chair as though all of these dramatic witnesses the district attorney was bringing forward were, after all, testifying to no more than routine preliminary matters.

Ruth Marvel had evidently been crying and was apparently angry. She permitted herself to be sworn, gave her name, address, took the witness stand, avoided Sybil Harlan's eyes and glared angrily at the district attorney.

"You have been a friend of the defendant for some time?" Hamilton Burger asked suavely.

"Yes," the witness snapped.

"You knew her on the third of June of this year?"

"Yes."

"You saw her on that date?"

"Yes. Several times."

"What was the last time you saw her?"

"I don't know the exact time. In the evening."

"The early evening?"

"Yes."

"What did you do at that time?"

"I went with her to look at some property."

"Where?"

"I don't remember."

"What kind of property?"

"Real estate."

"More than one parcel?"

"I don't remember."

"Did she tell you she was interested in property?"

"She asked me to go with her."

"Did she tell you she was interested in property?"

"She asked me to go with her."

"Did she tell you she was interested in property?"

"She told me to tell the taxi driver we were to look at property."

"Now then, Mrs. Marvel," Hamilton Burger said, "you're testifying in a murder case. You're under oath. There are severe penalties for perjury. There are severe penalties for becoming an accessory after the fact. I am going to ask you if the defendant made a statement to you as to the reason, the real reason, she wanted to engage that taxi."

"Now just a moment, Your Honor," Mason said. "I don't like to object to routine questions of these preliminary witnesses——"

"Preliminary witnesses!" Hamilton Burger shouted, his face livid with rage.

Mason glanced at him in some apparent surprise.

Hamilton Burger started to say something, then caught the judge's eye and lapsed into silence.

"Proceed, Mr. Mason," the judge said.

"In this case, however," Mason said, "counsel is cross-examining his own witness. He is taking leading questions. He is threatening the witness. Moreover, the testimony seems to be incompetent, irrelevant and immaterial."

"May I be heard?" Hamilton Burger asked.

Judge Sedgwick nodded.

"If the Court please," Hamilton Burger said, "this witness will, I believe, if she is forced to, testify to a most damaging admission made by the defendant. She is friendly with the defendant; she is hostile to me; she has never told me what her testimony would be. I only know by inference and from what she has told other people. The Court has my assurance, professionally, that this is the case."

"The objection will be overruled," Judge Sedgwick announced. "However, I will entertain a motion to strike out this testimony should it not prove pertinent or be materially different from that outlined by the district attorney in his statement."

"You will answer the question, Mrs. Marvel."

"She said she wanted to engage a particular cab."

"Did she say why?"

"She . . . she said——"

"Yes, yes, go on," Hamilton Burger prompted.

"She said that it was a cab she had ridden in earlier in the day."

"And did she tell you that she didn't want the cab driver to recognize her?"

"Something like that."

"Go on," Hamilton Burger said. "What did she tell you?"

Ruth Marvel started to cry.

"I must insist on an answer," Hamilton Burger said.

"She said that her lawyer had told her to get this cab, to have me ride around with her, and pay him off when the meter got to two dollars and ninety-five-cents."

"Would you know the cab driver if you saw him again?"

Ruth Marvel nodded mutely.

"Will Mr. Jerome C. Keddie stand up?" Hamilton Burger asked.

Keddie, the cab driver, stood up.

"Is that the man?" Hamilton Burger asked.

"Yes," Ruth Marvel said, in an answer that was almost indistinguishable.

"Cross-examine," Hamilton Burger snapped triumphantly.

Mason smiled reassuringly at the witness. "Mrs. Marvel, there's no reason for you to be upset about any of your testimony. Didn't the defendant simply tell you that she was acting under my advice, that she thought a certain taxicab driver was going to identify her and that she wanted to test his memory to see whether he really knew who she was?"

"Now, I object to that," Hamilton Burger said.

"Counsel is leading a witness who is very friendly to his side of the case and———"

"How do you know she's friendly?" Mason said. "She certainly testified for you readily enough and without reservation. This is cross-examination, and I have a right to cross-examine the witness."

"Objection overruled," Judge Sedgwick said.

"Isn't that substantially what happened?" Mason asked sympathetically.

"Yes," she said.

"Well, don't feel bad," Mason told her, "simply because the prosecution called you to testify as its witness when one of your friends is on trial. The defendant told you that under my instructions she was going to test the recollection of a possible witness, didn't she?"

"That's right," Ruth Marvel said.

"And you got in the taxicab that was being driven by this gentleman, this Jerome C. Keddie who has just stood up?"

"Yes, sir."

"And Mr. Keddie didn't recognize her, did he? In any event, he gave no sign of recognition that you could see?"

"No, sir."

Mason smiled and said, "That's all. That's all the defendant was trying to accomplish. There's no secret about it."

"There isn't now!" Hamilton Burger shouted. "Now that your scheme has backfired!"

"Backfired?" Mason asked, as though Burger had taken leave of his senses.

"That will do," Judge Sedgwick ruled. "There will be no personal exchanges between counsel. Mr. Prosecutor, your remark was uncalled for. The witness is excused."

"Now," Hamilton Burger said, "I'll call Jerome C. Keddie to the stand."

Keddie came forward and was sworn.

"Did you see the defendant on or about the third day of June of this year?" Hamilton Burger asked.

"Yes, sir."

"Where?" Hamilton Burger asked.

"I was coming back from the country club and——"

"Do you see this map on the blackboard?"

"Yes."

"Can you point to the place where you saw the defendant?"

"Yes, sir."

"Please do so."

The witness approached the map. "It was right here," he said. "And when I first saw her she was running up the street. Then she stopped and walked for a way, getting her breath. Then she started running again. Then she walked. Then she saw me and waved her arm."

"Return to the witness stand, please," Hamilton Burger said. "Then what happened?"

"She got in the cab with me and was all breathless. She seemed very much excited and disturbed. I asked her where she wanted to go. She couldn't tell me at first. Then she told me to take her to the Union Station."

"And you took her there?"

"Yes, sir."

"What time was this?"

"I picked her up a little before five o'clock. Around a quarter to five, I guess."

"And what time did you get to the Union Station?"

"A little after five o'clock."

"On the third of June?"

"Yes, sir."

"Cross-examine," Hamilton Burger said.

Mason smiled affably. "When did you next see the defendant, Mr. Keddie?"

"I don't know."

"You don't know?" Mason asked in simulated surprise.

"No, sir. I know that I saw her the next day in a lineup, and I may have seen her again that evening, but I just can't be sure. You see, we have so many passengers and sometimes we don't look back when——"

"Now just a moment," Mason said. "Never mind making an argument. Just answer the question."

"Your Honor, I submit that's part of his answer," Hamilton Burger said. "A witness always has a right to explain his answer. I submit the witness be allowed to finish."

"I think it would be better for you to bring these matters out on redirect examination," Judge Sedgwick ruled. "You'll have ample opportunity to bring out the complete situation on redirect examination."

"Very well," Hamilton Burger said, yielding with poor grace.

"Now, when you testified on the preliminary examination," Mason said, "you were very positive that you hadn't seen the defendant from the time you picked her up on the afternoon of June third until you saw her in the lineup on June fourth, isn't that right?"

"Yes, sir."

"That's all," Mason said.

"Were you mistaken at the time of the preliminary examination?" Hamilton Burger asked.

"I was confused."

"Were you mistaken?"

"Yes, sir, I was."

"That's all."

"Just a minute," Mason said. "You say you were mistaken, Mr. Keddie?"

"Yes, sir."

"Do you mean by that that you swore to something that wasn't so?"

"Oh, Your Honor," Hamilton Burger said, "I object to that as not proper cross-examination. That's an attempt to browbeat the witness."

"I'm not browbeating the witness," Mason said. "I'm

just asking him if he swore to something that wasn't so."

"It was an honest mistake," Hamilton Burger said.

"Are *you* now trying to testify," Mason asked, "as to the state of mind of this witness?"

"I'm telling the Court the facts."

"I want the witness to tell the facts," Mason said.

"The objection is overruled," Judge Sedgwick said.

"You testified to something that wasn't so?" Mason asked.

"Yes, sir, I was mistaken. I was confused."

"You aren't confused now?"

"No, sir."

"How did you happen to recognize your mistake?"

"Why, the district attorney found the person who had rented the cab. He pointed her out to me and told me she was a friend of the——"

"Just testify to what you know of your own knowledge," Hamilton Burger said. "Don't testify to hearsay."

"No, no, go right ahead," Mason said to the witness. "Tell me what Hamilton Burger told you."

Judge Sedgwick smiled.

"Your Honor, that's improper. That's hearsay evidence," Burger protested. "What I may have said to the witness is entirely outside of the issues."

"He's giving his reasons, Your Honor," Mason said in a conversational tone of voice which was in sharp contrast to Hamilton Burger's excited tones.

"Go ahead," Judge Sedgwick said, smiling. "Answer the question."

"Go ahead," Mason told the witness. "You were saying that Hamilton Burger told you— What did he tell you?"

"Well, he told me that he'd had detectives trace down all of the close friends of the defendant to see if they could find the person who had been in the cab with her, and he pointed out this witness who has just been on the stand and told me she was the one, and then I recognized her."

Mason smiled. "The district attorney pointed her out to you?"

"Yes, sir."

"Where did he point her out to you?"

"In his office."

"Did she see you at that time?"

"No, sir. I was in another room. It was a room that had one of those trick mirrors—it was a window on my side but a mirror on her side."

"The district attorney put you in that room?"

"Yes, sir."

"And then put Mrs. Marvel on the other side of this trick mirror?"

"Yes, sir."

"And then the district attorney came into the room and pointed out Mrs. Marvel to you and told you she was the one?"

"Yes, sir."

"So that made you feel that you had testified erroneously at the preliminary hearing?"

"Yes, sir."

"And sworn to something that wasn't so?"

"Yes, sir."

"At the preliminary hearing, before you had had the benefit of the advice of the district attorney, you said you had never seen the defendant again until you saw her in the lineup on the fourth, isn't that right?"

"Yes, sir."

"Well," Mason said affably, "you're to be congratulated on having the district attorney take such pains with you. If it hadn't been for his interference, you'd have testified to the same thing now that you testified to at the time of the preliminary examination, wouldn't you?"

"I suppose so. Yes."

"So your testimony today has been inspired by statements made to you by the district attorney?"

"Well, I guess so, yes."

"Thank you," Mason said. "That's all."

Hamilton Burger, angry and exasperated, said, "Very well, that's all. I have no further questions. I'll call Stephen Ardmore to the stand."

Ardmore came forward, was sworn, testified that he was a detective and had been a detective on the third of June of the present year.

"Did you have occasion to examine the house occupied by the defendant and her husband, Enright Harlan?"

"Yes, sir."

"When was that examination made?"

"On the fourth of June of this year."

"Did you have occasion to examine certain wearing apparel belonging to the defendant?"

"I did."

"I call your attention to a ceratin pair of gloves and ask you if you examined those gloves?"

"I did."

"What did you find, if anything?"

"When I placed those gloves under a vacuum cleaner in which there was a filter to trap any dust recovered from those gloves, I found certain foreign substances in the filter paper."

"Did you identify some of those foreign substances?"

"Yes, I identified one of them."

"And what was it?"

"Several granules of sugar."

"Sugar?" Hamilton Burger asked, smiling at the jury.

"Yes, sir."

"You mean common household sugar?"

"Yes, sir."

"So then what did you do?"

"So then I went to the house occupied by the defendant and her husband and examined the various sugar containers."

"And what did you find, if anything?"

"In the bottom of a sugar bowl I found a set of car keys."

"Did you indeed?" Hamilton Burger said. "Did you mark them for identification?"

"I did."

"I hand you a set of keys and call your attention to the mark etched in the keys and ask you if that is the set of keys that you found?"

"Yes, sir, a set of two keys."

"Did you subsequently determine what locks those keys fit?"

"Yes, sir, I did."

"What locks were they?"

"This one is the key to the ignition of the automobile driven by George C. Lutts on the day of his death, and this is the key to the trunk of that automobile."

"You tried them to make certain they worked?"

"Yes, sir."

"Cross-examine," Hamilton Burger said.

Mason grinned. "You don't know who put those keys in the sugar bowl, do you, Mr. Ardmore?"

"I only know that there was sugar on the gloves of the defendant."

"Answer the question. You don't know who put those keys in the sugar bowl?"

"No, sir."

"And prior to the time you discovered those keys, you had been searching the house?"

"Yes, sir."

"Other police officers had been searching the house?"

"Yes, sir."

"The husband was living in the house?"

"Yes, sir."

"Some witnesses had been interrogated in the house?"

"Some, yes, sir."

"Why didn't you look in the sugar bowl before all these other persons had an opportunity to go through the house, planting evidence wherever they wanted?"

"You can't do everything at once, Mr. Mason."

"Then why didn't you shut up the house until after you had searched it?"

"Well, we . . . we didn't know what we were going to find."

"So you feel you should know what you're going to find before you take any steps to see that evidence isn't planted?"

"I don't think this evidence was planted."

"I'm not asking you what you think," Mason said. "I'm asking you why you didn't look in that sugar bowl before anyone had an opportunity to plant something there."

"Because I didn't know there was anything in the sugar bowl."

"And," Mason said, "you didn't search the gloves, the wearing apparel, or even look under the fingernails of any other person in that house to see if you could find any sugar?"

"Well, no, sir."

"This woman's husband was there all the time. Didn't you examine his fingers to see if you could find traces of sugar under the nails?"

"No, sir."

"That's all," Mason said.

"No further questions," Hamilton Burger said.

Hamilton Burger called Janice Condon to the stand. She testified that she had been employed as Enright Harlan's secretary for a period of some three years, covering the time when the revolver which had been introduced in evidence had been purchased. She had been instructed by her employer to go to the gun store and pick up the gun, which had previously been ordered by Harlan, and to sign his name to the register of firearms; that she knew it was irregular and that the dealer knew it was irregular, but Harlan was a very good customer and the dealer had conveniently turned his back while she was signing Harlan's name and had winked at the irregularity.

"Cross-examine," Hamilton Burger said to Perry Mason.

"No questions," Mason said casually. "We would have stipulated to the testimony of this witness. There was no necessity of calling her."

"You could have said so earlier," Hamilton Burger snapped.

"You didn't ask me," Mason retorted, smiling.

"That will do," Judge Sedgwick said. "Proceed with your case, Mr. District Attorney."

Hamilton Burger said, "Your Honor, I note that it is after four o'clock. I have one more witness. I may state that I have been taken entirely by surprise in this case. We started getting the jury yesterday afternoon. This morning we had the jury by ten-thirty. I had expected that it would take me at least three days to put on my case. I call to the Court's attention that so far there have been very few questions asked on cross-examination, there have been almost no objections to evidence on the part of the defense. This has made for a very unusual situation. I find that I am running far ahead of schedule. I think it would be in order to request an adjournment at this time."

Judge Sedgwick, obviously completely puzzled by Mason's tactics, looked down at the lawyer.

Mason smiled and said, "Well, Your Honor, we've made remarkable headway, and I frankly confess that I see no reason to object to evidence which I think is pertinent and have no desire to cross-examine witnesses who are obviously telling the truth. It seems to me, therefore, that counsel can put on his last remaining witness and then the people can, in all probability, rest their case by the time we usually adjourn."

"No, Your Honor," Hamilton Burger said. "This witness will undoubtedly be subjected to a long and grueling cross-examination. He is a surprise witness and——"

"And therefore," Mason interrupted, "the prosecution obviously would like to take advantage of a surprise attack. The defendant insists that we proceed in the ordinary course of events and that this witness be called now. We resist any motion for an adjournment at this time."

Judge Sedgwick said, "I think the defense position is well taken, Mr. Prosecutor. You may call your witness."

With poor grace, Hamilton Burger said, "Ezekiel Elkins."

Ezekiel Elkins came forward and took the witness stand. He gave his name, age, occupation, and settled back with tight-lipped determination.

"You are a director of the Sylvan Glade Development Company and a stockholder in that company?"

"Yes, sir."

"George C. Lutts, the decedent, was also a stockholder and a director?" Hamilton Burger asked.

"Yes, sir."

"Were there any unusual developments in connection with your directors' meeting on the third of June of this year?"

"There certainly were."

"I will state to Court and counsel," Hamilton Burger said, "that I am going to connect up these matters."

"No objection," Mason said. "Go right ahead."

"Describe what happened at the directors' meeting," Hamilton Burger said.

Elkins gave a brief picture of what had happened at the meeting.

"Now then, what did you do after the meeting?" Hamilton Burger asked.

"I thought that George Lutts was slipping one over and——"

"Never mind what you thought," Burger interrupted sharply. "I am asking you what you *did*."

"Well, I decided to follow George Lutts because I thought he might be in——"

"Never mind what you thought. You followed George Lutts, did you?"

"Yes."

"Where did he go?"

"Well, he went out to lunch with Doxey, his son-in-law and secretary of the company, and then he got in his car and drove to the Acme Coiffure and Beauty Salon."

"And then what?"

"He parked his car and waited."

"For about how long?"

"Oh, I'd say for two or three minutes."

"Where were you?"

"About half a block behind."

"Then what happened?"

"Then the defendant came out of the beauty parlor, and George Lutts opened his car door and called to her."

"And what did she do?"

"She got in the car with him."

"Then what?"

"Then they talked for a little while."

"And then what?"

"And then Lutts drove down about half a block to this parking lot, where the defendant had her car."

"And then what?"

"Then the defendant got out and went up to where her car was parked——"

"Now, just a minute," Hamilton Burger said. "Do you know, of your own knowledge, that it was her car?"

"No, sir, I don't."

"Then, just tell what you know of your own knowledge, please."

"Well, she went to a car. She opened the glove compartment, and I don't know what she did."

"You could see her open the glove compartment?"

"Well, I saw her hands up there on the dash, about where the glove compartment was."

"And then what?"

"Then she got back out of the car and closed the

door and walked back out to where Lutts was sitting in his car."

"And then what?"

"Then she got in the car with Lutts and they drove away."

"What did you do?"

"I followed along until I got to a point where I realized they were going up to the Sylvan Glade Property and——"

"Never mind what you realized. Just how far did you follow them?"

"Well, I followed them out to within about half a mile of where the road turns off to the Sylvan Glade Property."

"Then what did you do?" Hamilton Burger asked.

The witness seemed embarrassed.

"Go on," Hamilton Burger said.

"Well, I was concentrating on following the car in front of me and I . . . well, I cut in on another car."

"And then what happened?"

"I cut in in front of him, and he speeded up and got over on my left side and ran me off the road, so I had to stop."

"Then what?"

"Then there was an altercation."

"What do you mean by an altercation?"

"I wanted to hurry on, so I could follow Lutts and the defendant, and this man became abusive and I was in a hurry and impatient and lost my temper and . . . well, I said some things and he said some things and——"

"Go on," Hamilton Burger said.

"And he poked me in the eye," Elkins admitted.

"And then what?"

"Well, then several cars stopped and . . . and I took a swing back at him, and he hit me in the stomach, and . . . well, I got sick. I had the wind knocked out of me."

"And then what?"

"Then he got in his car and drove away."

"And left you standing there?"

"Yes. But I wasn't standing—I was all doubled up."

"So then what did you do?"

"I turned around and went home."

"And when did you next see Mr. Lutts?"

"I saw his body at the funeral."

"You may inquire," Hamilton Burger said.

Mason looked at the clock and smiled at the Court. "If the Court please, it has *now* reached the hour of adjournment."

Judge Sedgwick, recognizing Mason's tactics, smiled back at him and said, "So it has. It is now time for the Court to adjourn."

"If the Court please," Hamilton Burger said, "it seems to me that if counsel has a brief cross-examination, it would be possible to rest the prosecution's case and——"

"You are assuming that the cross-examination will be brief," Judge Sedgwick said. "The Court cannot make such assumption. This is the conventional hour of adjournment, Mr. District Attorney, and the Court will take a recess until tomorrow morning."

15

PERRY MASON, DELLA STREET AND PAUL DRAKE gathered in a gloomy session in the lawyer's private office.

"Gosh, Perry," Paul Drake said, "shouldn't you have

tried to break down some of the identification there? Couldn't you have cross-examined and——"

"Sure, I could have," Mason said. "But that's not the way to try this case. Jurors are pretty smart, Paul. You start trying to keep things out of evidence that everyone knows is the truth, and pretty quick the jurors get the idea that you're afraid of the truth.

"Now you can see what happened in this case. Hamilton Burger has been laying for me. He's smarting under the sting of prior defeats. He's made up his mind that this is one case that's going to be so thoroughly prepared, so thoroughly checked that there won't be the faintest opportunity of anything going wrong. He was hoping, of course, that I'd keep batting my head against a brick wall with a lot of cross-examination and objections. I might have gained a technical point or two, but I'd have lost the sympathy of the jury.

"This is one case where all the facts are so carefully dovetailed that there can't be any question. Of course, my client tells me that the gun she put back in the glove compartment hadn't been fired, that it was the same gun she took out of the glove compartment, that she went home in the taxicab to change her shoes and stockings, since they had become so bedraggled and soiled from walking down from the hill that she was ashamed to be seen in them. That *may* be true. She's lied to me before. She'd doubtless lie again. A desperate woman will nearly always try to color the facts so that they will be in her favor."

"If I were a lawyer," Drake said, "I wouldn't represent a client who lied to me."

"Then you wouldn't have very many clients," Mason told him, "particularly in criminal cases. I don't know why it is, but it's not once in fifty times that you'll find a client who tells you the *entire* truth. Nearly all of them, no matter how innocent they may be and how honest they may be, will try to sugar-coat the facts so that they become more favorable."

"What are you going to do?" Drake asked.

"I'm afraid I'm going to stake everything on Ezekiel Elkins' black eye," Mason said. "If I can cross-examine him and make that black eye look significant, I can, perhaps, brand him as the murderer of George Lutts. Otherwise, I'm going to have to put the defendant on the stand, and when I put her on the stand, Hamilton Burger is going to crucify her."

"There's no alternative?"

"Not that I can see at the present time," Mason said.

"Well, I can tell you this, Perry. I haven't been able to prove that Elkins was in any kind of an automobile accident and I haven't been able to prove that he wasn't."

Mason said, "The advantage of trying a case the way I'm trying this one is that the jurors become quite sympathetic. They feel that you're not going to waste their time and the Court's time. They'll feel that whenever I start in on a stern cross-examination now, I will have some mighty good reason for it, and they'll follow every question I ask with rapt attention. This is my strategy. It has to be. By passing off all of these other witnesses as being merely preliminary, the mere fact that I start tearing into Elkins on cross-examination is going to impress that jury tremendously."

"Then you're planning to put the defendant on the stand?"

"That depends on whether I get anywhere with Elkins," Mason said. "If I can build a good suspicion in the minds of the jury, I *may* be able to get by without putting the defendant on the stand. But the chances of that are only one out of a hundred."

"I'd hate to be in your shoes," Paul Drake said. "This is one case I don't like."

"I don't like it myself," Mason admitted. "But if you're a card player you frequently pick up hands that you don't like. Just because you get a poor hand is no reason you should throw down your cards in disgust and not even try. You have to make the best out of every case you handle. What did you find out about marksmanship, Paul?"

"What do you mean?"

"About the various parties concerned—how much experience they have had in handling guns."

"Well," Drake said, opening a notebook, "if you want a list of the persons who would probably have missed George Lutts at ten feet, I can give them to you on the fingers of one hand."

"Who?"

"Elkins, for one. He's never fired a gun in his life. Your client, for another. She says she closes her eyes whenever she pulls the trigger. That's what she told one of her friends. And if you want to consider Roxy Claffin as a suspect, she's a lousy shot—at least, she's supposed to be. Among other things, Enright Harlan was supposed to be teaching her how to shoot. Apparently, she wasn't doing too well.

"Now, on the other side you have Regerson B. Neffs who claims to be a good pistol shot, or at least he was in his younger days. You have Enright Harlan, who is a *most* expert pistol shot. You have Herbert Doxey, who won a bunch of medals for pistol shooting. And you have Cleve Rector, who describes himself as a fairly good shot."

Mason started pacing the floor. "How the devil did Lutts know that I had been retained by Mrs. Harlan, Paul?"

Drake shrugged his shoulders and said, "That's one of the mysteries in the case. Apparently, he got it through his banking connections. When he went out to lunch with Doxey, he certainly didn't have any idea. That is, he didn't when he first sat down to lunch. But then he got some sudden inspiration and went to the telephone booth there in the restaurant and put through a call to someone, presumably some chap in the bank.

Evidently, they traced the check you had placed in your account."

"I don't like that," Mason said. "That would mean the violation of the banking code."

"I know. But those things do happen."

Again Mason started pacing the floor."

"Chief," Della Street said solicitously, "I can see that you're going to be up all night, pacing the floor, trying to get this thing straightened out."

Mason, his face granite hard, said, "Well, we have some pieces of the jigsaw puzzle. Some of them fit and some of them don't fit. I'm going to keep trying to shuffle them around until I find some combination which makes them fit.

"What results are you getting from your shadows, Paul? What is Roxy Claffin doing?"

"Gloating, mostly. She's sitting on top of the world, with Enright Harlan like a sheep being led to the slaughter. She may be planning on subleasing her house. She's started cleaning it out. She was out in her garage today, took all the old junk down to the dump and threw it away."

Mason's eyes narrowed. "What sort of junk?"

"Old empty paint cans, a broken trunk, a stool, some old inner tubes, some torn canvas sacks, and a box of battered up old scrap iron and stuff."

"Where is all that?" Mason asked.

"Down on the dump, out there. It's nothing. My man got a look at it when she loaded it, and then after she'd left he went out and inspected it."

"Get that junk," Mason said, "all of it. Where's your man?"

"He's off duty now. I can get him and——"

Mason said, "Dammit, Paul, in a case of this sort, don't ever consider anything insignificant. Get that junk and get it in here just as fast as you can."

Drake looked at his watch and sighed. "Okay," he said.

"And those inner tubes. What's wrong with them?"

"Evidently, Perry, she was just cleaning out the garage. She threw a bunch of stuff in——"

"I want that stuff, Paul. Get your men on the job. I want all of it."

"You'll have your office filled up with a whole garageful of junk," Drake said wearily.

"That," Mason told him, "is exactly what I want. You get that stuff and bring it here. Della and I will go grab a bite to eat. We'll meet you here after . . . let's see, nine o'clock."

"Tonight?"

"Sure, tonight," Mason said impatiently. "What the hell did you think? Tomorrow morning?"

"I didn't know," Drake said.

"Well, you know now," Mason told him. "Come on, Della."

Two hours later, Mason, Della Street and Paul Drake faced a crestfallen detective across Mason's desk.

"What do you mean you can't find 'em?" Mason asked.

Blanton, the detective, said, "That's what I mean, Mr. Mason. They're not there."

"You must have got the wrong place," Mason told him.

"No, I didn't. I know right were she put them."

"How do you know?"

"The same way I know anything. The same way I know where your office is."

"What dump was this?"

"Well, it's a dump out there about three miles beyond her place, out where there's an old barranca they're filling in. It isn't used for a city dump, but the people who live around there throw stuff in it. It's evidently been used for quite a while."

"What sort of stuff?"

"Oh, tin cans, boxes . . . all kinds of junk."

"Exactly what did Mrs. Claffin do?"

"Well, it was about seven-thirty this morning, about

. . . well, about half an hour, I guess, after she got up. She opened up her garage, and I could see she was doing stuff on the inside, so I moved my car around to where I could look in with my binoculars."

"And what did you see?"

"Saw her loading things into this car."

"Where was she putting the things?"

"In the rear storage compartment."

"How good a view did you have?"

"Not too good at the time . . . real good later on."

"When did you get this good look?"

"At the dump, after she'd left. I followed along, taking care that she didn't realize that she was being spotted. Then when she drove out to the dump, I just went on past."

"And then what?"

"Well, I went down the road . . . well, nearly a mile, I guess. I parked the car and looked through my binoculars. I saw her throwing this stuff on the dump and then she turned around and drove back to the house. I was supposed to be following her, but I thought I'd better take a look at this stuff on the dump, so I detoured back to the dump where I could see the stuff."

"You got a good look at it there?"

"Sure, I got a good look. That's what I'm trying to tell you, Mr. Mason. I went out to the exact spot on the dump and checked the stuff close."

"Exactly what was it?"

"Well, there were some old inner tubes, there were some boards that had been on some sort of a packing case, there was a coil of old wire, and there was some scrap iron. There was a stool, a pretty good stool, some torn canvas sacks."

"Tell me about the torn canvas sacks."

"They had been pretty good sacks at one time, the money sacks that a bank uses for currency. They'd been sewn up and then ripped open along the sides. That is, they'd been cut open. And there was a box of old junk. There was scrap iron on the bottom."

"What kind of scrap iron?"

"Bolts and nuts. All kinds of scrap. I remember there was a piece of iron rail in there and some sort of an iron wheel and . . . oh, maybe a couple of hundred pounds of junk."

"She couldn't have lifted a box of that kind into the trunk," Mason said.

"That's what I'm trying to tell you, Mr. Mason. She just used the box to haul out all of this old scrap iron from the garage. She must have put the box in the back storage compartment of the car, and then chucked this scrap iron in it, and then after she got out to the dump, she just used one of the boards to pry this box out and dumped it and went away.

"She drove away as soon as she dumped it. I'm sorry, I guess I overlooked a bet, Mr. Mason. I made a note of it in my report, but I was supposed to follow her, so I didn't dare take too much time prowling around on the dump. I went right back and picked her up at the house."

"She drove directly back to her house?"

"That's right. I spotted her car, and then kept an eye on her and stayed with her until she went to court. I come on at four o'clock in the morning and work until noon, and then my relief takes over. I made out a report and described this junk and the old inner tubes and things."

"The significant part of the whole business is that they're gone now," Mason said.

"Well, that may not be so significant, Mr. Mason. The iron in that box was worth something. You know, she didn't need to take that stuff down there. She could have called a junk peddler, and he'd at least have been willing to haul it away for the iron and stuff that was there. And it was a pretty good stool. Some of that stuff probably could have been used—the stool and some of those old bolts and nuts."

"But," Mason said, "the old inner tubes are missing, everything is missing."

"Every blessed thing she took out there is missing," Blanton admitted.

"Well," Mason said, "there's nothing we can do about it at the present time, except try to figure out *why* it's missing."

"I'm sorry," Blanton said, "I don't see how I could have played it any different. I was just shadowing her and——"

"It's all right," Mason said. "You should have telephoned Drake right away. When there's anything unusual—Paul, put a couple more men on Mrs. Claffin. I want to find out everything she does. I want to know everyone she sees, and if anything she does is the least bit significant, I want to be notified immediately. No matter what's happening, get word to me immediately. Have word relayed to Della, and she can bring it to me in the courtroom. No matter what I'm doing, I want to know."

Drake nodded. "I'll get busy on it right away."

Mason turned to Della Street. "Okay," he said wearily, "you may as well go home, Della. Tomorrow could be the most disastrous day in my legal career."

Drake and Blanton left the office. Della Street went to the outer office, adjusted the switchboard, returned, and turned out the desk light. Then she walked up to the lawyer, looked up at his troubled eyes.

"It isn't your fault, Chief," she said. "If Mrs. Harlan hadn't done all of that elaborate window dressing before she called you, she——"

"I know," Mason said, "but . . . well, I have the responsibility."

"And I suppose you're going to stay here and pace the floor, wrestling with this thing?"

"I'm not going to waste time sleeping while this thing's unsolved, Della."

"You can't do any good just beating your head against a brick wall."

"Perhaps I can find a way to detour around the wall," Mason said. *"Why* did that junk disappear?"

Della Street said, "I'm going to stay if you stay."

"No, Della, you go get some sleep."

She came close to him. "You may get some ideas you'll want to have written up."

Mason circled her with his arm. "Bless you, Della. You worry as much about this as I do."

"If she's guilty, you can't help that," Della Street said.

"I know," Mason said, holding her closer to him. "What a comfort you are with your steadfast faith and loyalty, Della."

"You know you have that, Chief," she told him, "always."

Mason bent and kissed her.

Her arm circled his neck. "Oh, Chief, I wish——"

She broke off as Mason's form suddenly became rigid. "What is it, Chief? What's the matter?"

"I've just thought of something," Mason said. "That junk that disappeared. Hang it, Della! That's significant."

Della Street's voice was wistful. "And I take it," she said, "the client comes first."

Mason patted her shoulder, then abruptly strode over to his desk. "Of course the client comes first, Della. That's what a lawyer's for. Della, sit in that chair. Let me ask you some questions."

Mason's voice was sharp with excitement.

"Here, Della, take a notebook. Make a list of questions. Let's start analyzing this case. When a chemist starts analyzing an unknown substance, he tries to find out the basic ingredients that are in it by applying various tests. In other words, he asks the substance questions. Why don't we start asking this case questions?"

Della Street said with some asperity, "I suppose if

you were getting married, and just as the wedding march was starting you got an idea about a case, you'd be off for the courtroom. Go ahead, Chief, I've got my pencil all ready. What are the questions?"

"The disappearing junk," Mason said. "Why did it disappear?"

Della Street's pencil made swift shorthand notations in the notebook.

Mason started excitedly pacing the floor.

"That disappearance is the most significant clue in the whole case. That's the break we've been waiting for. Why did that junk disappear?" Mason asked.

"Well," Della said, "of course, it couldn't have got up and walked away under its own power."

"Exactly," Mason said. "And by that same token, Roxy Claffin didn't go back and pick it up."

"How do we know?"

"We know," Mason said, "because Roxy Claffin was being shadowed. Don't you see what that disappearance means, Della?"

She started to say something, checked herself, sat watching Mason as he excitedly paced the floor.

"Here are some more questions, Della. Make a note of these. Three shots were fired from the fatal revolver. Two bullets have been found. The third bullet has not been found. In what is the third bullet embedded? And why is the third empty cartridge, the one which contained the bullet that is missing, of a different brand from the other shells in the gun?

"Now here's another question: Lutts got the information that connected my purchase of the stock in the Sylvan Glade Development Company with Sybil Harlan through a bank leak, but where did Enright Harlan get that information? *He* says Roxy got it from Mrs. Doxey. Mrs. Doxey denies that."

Mason said excitedly, "Type out that list of questions, Della. Let me have it. We'll start considering *all* the various answers which will fit in with the facts. Della, we're on the track of something!"

His excitement reached Della Street. She jerked the cover off her typewriter, ratcheted in a sheet of paper and her fingers started flying over the keys.

Mason, his face showing intense concentration, continued pacing the floor.

Suddenly the lawyer reached for the telephone, dialed Paul Drake and said, "Paul, get a four-wheeled truck of the kind used by bellboys to transport baggage. Take the wheels off, remove all oil from the axles and put on some rosin or something so they'll squeak to high heaven.

"Pile some boards, a stool and a couple of hundred pounds of scrap iron on it, cover the whole thing with a cloth and be prepared to wheel it into court tomorrow when I give you a signal. Never mind why. Just get the stuff together."

And Mason was smiling as he hung up the telephone.

16

∎

JUDGE SEDGWICK FROWNED WITH OBVIOUS DISTASTE as he surveyed the jammed courtroom.

One of the newspaper columnists had made an analysis of Perry Mason's strategy in the Case of the People versus Sybil Harlan, and that analysis had been so interesting, so deadly accurate that it attracted sensation-hungry spectators as honey attracts flies.

The columnist had pointed out that Perry Mason undoubtedly had some ace up his sleeve, but also pointed out that the lawyer couldn't be certain whether or not the district attorney would be able to trump his ace. Mason, therefore, in order to emphasize the one play that he had, was deliberately underplaying the rest of the case.

If the lawyer had been completely without any high cards of his own, the columnist pointed out, he would necessarily have had to go into court objecting to this question and that question, moving to strike out answers as not being responsive, engaging in all of the technicalities of a person putting up a last-ditch legal fight.

The columnist went on to point out that the house had been used as a veritable shooting gallery. The police had conducted experiments, the district attorney had conducted experiments, and there even were rumors that Perry Mason, as attorney for the defense, presumably checking some aspect of the case, had purchased a box of blank cartridges. There was, of course, no direct evidence as to what he had done with them, but readers could put two and two together.

The defense attorney's act-in-the-hole was probably no part of his own case but would depend upon some masterly cross-examination of a witness for the prosecution. The last witness for the prosecution was Ezekiel Elkins, and Mason had shrewdly jockeyed the district attorney into such a position that Elkins had concluded his testimony on direct examination just as court had adjourned, so that Perry Mason would be able to start his spectacular cross-examination in the morning.

There was, of course, the columnist pointed out, the possibility that Mason intended to recall one of the prosecution's witnesses for further cross-examination, a strategy which had been followed quite frequently by the defense attorney. But in view of the fact that he had made virtually no objections and offered virtually no cross-examination, the possibility that he would recall a witness was, in the opinion of veteran courthouse attachés, rather unlikely.

In any event, it was quite probable that the morning session of the court would be jam packed with fireworks.

The Court went through the usual preliminary incidents, calling court to order, having the attorneys stipulate that the jurors were all present, that the defendant was in court. Then Judge Sedgwick glanced at the crowded courtroom. "The Court wishes to remind the spectators," he said, "that this is a court of justice. It is not a theater. The Court will tolerate no disturbances, no indication of public feeling in this matter. The Court will clear the courtroom if there is any violation of decorum.

"Now then, Mr. Mason, you may proceed with the cross-examination of the witness, Ezekiel Elkins. Mr. Elkins, you will please resume your position on the stand."

Elkins settled down in the witness chair, cleared his throat, folded his hands and looked at Mason with calm, cold eyes. He had, of course, read the papers, knew what to expect, and gave every outward indication of being prepared for it.

Mason arose to cross-examine the witness.

"You are, or were, in a sense, a business partner of the decedent, George C. Lutts?"

"No."

"You were on the board of directors of the Sylvan Glade Development Company?"

"Yes."

"You still are?"

"Yes."

"You attended the meeting of the directors on the third of June of this year?"

"Yes."

"At that meeting Mr. Lutts announced that he had sold his holdings in the corporation?"

"Yes."

"There had been an agreement among the directors that if anyone should desire to dispose of his holdings in the company, he would first give the other directors an opportunity to buy the stock?"

"Yes."

"That agreement had not been reduced to writing?"

"No."

"You resented the fact that Mr. Lutts had sold his stock in violation of that agreement?"

"No."

"Didn't you say at the directors' meeting that you thought it was a breach of the agreement?"

"Yes."

"But you didn't resent it?"

"No."

Mason smiled at the witness. "You finished giving your direct testimony yesterday, Mr. Elkins."

"Yes."

"Where were you last night?"

"Oh, Your Honor," Hamilton Burger said, "this is not proper cross-examination. It's incompetent, irrelevant and immaterial. It's an attempt to pry into the private affairs of the witness."

"Sustained," Judge Sedgwick snapped.

"Were you closeted with the district attorney for more than two hours last night?" Mason asked.

Sedgwick glanced at the district attorney.

"Your Honor, Your Honor," Hamilton Burger said, "it's incompetent, irrelevant and immaterial. It's not proper cross-examination. If counsel is interested, I will admit that I talked with Mr. Elkins last night. He had already given his direct testimony, and I wanted certain matters cleared up. There's nothing illegal about a district attorney talking with his own witness."

Mason said, "I submit, Your Honor, that the objection by the district attorney was not made in good faith but was simply a framework which enabled him to make the statement he did for the purpose of influencing the jury."

"I resent that," Hamilton Burger said.

"The objection is overruled. The witness will answer

the question. Counsel will refrain from personalities," Judge Sedgwick said.

"What was the question?" the witness asked.

The court reporter read the question, "Were you closeted with the district attorney for more than two hours last night?"

"No," Elkins said.

Mason smiled, "You mean you weren't with him for as long as two hours?"

"No."

"You were with him for two hours?"

"Yes."

"More than that?"

"Yes."

"As much as three hours?"

"Yes."

"More than three hours?"

"No."

Then Mason said, now sure of his ground, "What did you mean by saying that you weren't closeted with the district attorney last night?"

"We weren't in a closet," Elkins said.

A ripple of laughter in the courtroom was silenced by the frowning of the judge.

"I see," Mason said. "Now, at the session with the district attorney which took place in his office rather than in a closet, you discussed your cross-examination and what you would say on the witness stand."

The witness fidgeted.

Hamilton Burger, on his feet, said, "I certainly discussed his position as a witness and told him that he could expect a most grueling, desperate, last-ditch——"

"That will do, Mr. District Attorney. Sit down," Judge Sedgwick said. "The witness is being interrogated, not the district attorney."

"Yes, Your Honor."

"We talked about many things," Elkins said.

"And isn't it a fact," Mason went on, "that your answers of 'yes' and 'no' to my questions are because the district attorney warned you, in substance, that you might get into trouble if you volunteered any information or gave full answers; didn't he say to you in effect that the way to confuse Perry Mason would be to listen to the questions with the utmost care and then answer them in the fewest possible words—answer yes or no wherever it was possible to do so?"

Elkins, for the first time, lowered his eyes. He cleared his throat, glanced at the district attorney.

Judge Sedgwick was also looking at the district attorney.

Hamilton Burger started to get to his feet, then changed his mind and remained seated.

"Can't you answer that question?" Mason asked.

"Well, he did say something like that," Elkins admitted.

"So," Mason said, "this policy of yours of answering questions in the fewest possible words was suggested to you by the district attorney at a conference last night?"

"I can answer questions any way I want to."

"Certainly," Mason said, "certainly. But I am pointing out to you that this pattern of answering questions in the fewest possible words was suggested to you by the district attorney last night."

"We discussed it, yes."

"I am pointing out to you," Mason said, "that this pattern of answering questions in the fewest possible words was suggested to you by the district attorney last night, was it not?"

"Yes."

"And the district attorney told you that that would be the most sure way to confuse me in my cross-examination, didn't he?"

"He said that it would be the best defense I had."

"Best *defense?*" Mason said.

"Yes."

"What do you have to defend yourself against?" Mason asked.

"I have to support my testimony."

"In other words, having told a story you're going to stand by it?"

"It was the truth."

"So, you and the district attorney conspired last night to try and confuse me, so that you could support, at all costs, the story you had told."

"Oh, Your Honor," Hamilton Burger said, "I should not be forced to sit through this. I have been rebuked by the Court for one of my objections, but I must insist that this use of the word 'conspired' is a definite distortion. I submit that this question has already been asked and answered in effect, that it is argumentative and not proper cross-examination. Counsel has made his point, and now he is arguing with the witness."

"Sustained," Judge Sedgwick said. "I think you have covered this phase of the case, Mr. Mason. Let's get on with the cross-examination."

"Very well, Your Honor," Mason said. He turned to the witness. "Now, you felt after you left that directors' meeting that there was some move afoot in connection with the Sylvan Glade Development Company about which Lutts had information that you didn't, isn't that right, Mr. Elkins?"

"Quite naturally. I knew that if Lutts had received an offer at anywhere near the book value of the stock, he would have communicated with the others . . . so, I surmised . . . I will answer your question by simply saying yes."

Mason said, "Now, Mr. Elkins, you and I will get along a lot better if you follow your own inclination, rather than remembering what the district attorney told you—to answer in as few words as possible."

Hamilton Burger said, "I submit, Your Honor, that the witness has a right to answer the questions in any way he sees fit."

"I am asking for legitimate information, Your Honor," Mason said, "information to which the jury is entitled and to which my client is entitled. I am perfectly willing to agree that the witness may answer the questions any way he wants to, just so he answers the questions truthfully and completely. But I am pointing out to the witness that if he follows the habit of answering yes and no and answering in the fewest possible words, he is going to be on the stand a far longer time, and, in view of the circumstances and in view of the admission of the witness that these tactics were worked out in the district attorney's office for the purpose of confusing me, I insist that I be given an opportunity to conduct a most searching cross-examination."

"You don't need to make statements of that sort to the Court, Mr. Mason," Judge Sedgwick said. "No one is seeking to curtail your cross-examination. I may state that the Court understands the situation here and is going to give you the widest latitude in connection with your cross-examination. Now go ahead and cross-examine the witness."

"And," Mason said, turning to Elkins, "you felt that the reason Lutts had not given the other directors the opportunity to buy his stock at the price he had been offered was that that price was so large he wanted to accept the offer before it could be withdrawn. That's substantially what you thought?"

"Yes."

"If there had been any such peculiar development in connection with the stock of the company, you wanted to get in on it, isn't that right?"

"Yes."

"You decided to shadow Mr. Lutts?"

"I've already stated that."

"You made some considerable effort to see that your shadowing was unnoticed?"

"Yes."

"Specifically, what did you do?"

"Just what your question insinuated. I did everything I could to remain inconspicuous."

"You stayed in the office of the company while Mr. Lutts was in there?"

"Mr. Lutts was in his private office. I stayed in the office of the company, yes."

"Could you see into Lutts' office?"

"Well, there was a frosted glass partition. I could see vague silhouettes."

"And then what?"

"Then Regerson Neffs, another director in the company, entered the office and remained with Mr. Lutts for a while."

"And then what?"

"Then Mr. Neffs went out."

"And what were you doing during this time?"

"I pretended to be writing some memo on the stationery of the corporation."

"That was just a blind?"

"Yes."

"So you could keep an eye on Mr. Lutts?"

"Yes."

"And what happened after Mr. Neffs went out?"

"Mr. Lutts went into the office of his son-in-law, Herbert Doxey, who is the secretary of the corporation. He was holding some papers in his hand. As soon as he saw me sitting in that outer office, he hurriedly moved his hands so as to conceal the papers."

"And that gave you an idea that he might have been holding a duly endorsed certificate of stock?"

"Yes."

"In other words, he was buying stock from Neffs, is that right?"

"That's what I surmised."

"So then what did you do?"

"I thought perhaps I had aroused his suspicions. I went out to my car and parked it where I could see the entrance to the office."

"And you waited there until Lutts came out?"

"Yes."

"He came out with Doxey?"

"About three-five. They drove to a restaurant not too far away, where we sometimes eat, and I could see from the way Lutts ordered and ate that he was in very much of a hurry."

"What else did you notice?"

"While there, he placed a telephone call."

"Made it or received it?"

"Placed it. He went to the telephone booth. He was there for some time; then he came back."

"Do you know how many calls he made?"

"One."

"Do you know whom he called?"

"No. I could see his hand when he dialed the number, but I couldn't see what number it was."

"You're certain that he made only the one call?"

"Yes."

"You were watching him all the time?"

"Yes."

"He received no call?"

"No."

"What happened after he had completed his call?"

"He bolted his lunch in very much of a hurry."

"Then what?"

"Then Mr. Lutts came out, apparently gave Doxey some last-minute instructions and got in his car."

"And you followed?"

"I followed."

"And went where?"

"I followed him to the beauty shop, where I waited until Mrs. Harlan, the defendant in this case, came out."

Mason stood for a moment, regarding the witness in frowning concentration. "You then followed Lutts and the defendant out to a place near the turn-off to the property of the Sylvan Glade Development Company?"

"Yes, sir. First, of course, there was that stop at the parking lot which I have testified to."

"And then you had this altercation and turned back?"

"Yes."

"So then you had one eye swollen and you had lost track of Lutts and the defendant. You thought you knew where they were going, so you turned around and went back home?"

"Not directly home."

"You made a stop?"

"Yes."

"Where?"

"I stopped at a butcher shop and got a beefsteak to put on my eye," the witness said.

There was a ripple of laughter in the courtroom, and Judge Sedgwick indulgently joined in the levity to the extent of smiling, after which, however, he held up his hand, signifying that he wanted complete silence in the courtroom.

"All right," Mason said, "you got a beefsteak for your eye, and then you went home."

"Yes."

"Then what did you do?"

"I remained quiet. I found that I had become rather unnerved and angry. I have trouble with my blood pressure. I took medicine the doctor had prescribed for me, which has a tendency to quiet me and, I believe, lower my blood pressure. I remained home during the evening."

"You didn't try to do any more business in connection with picking up stock?"

"No."

"I submit," Mason said, "that you gave up rather easily, Mr. Elkins. You started out with a grim determination to find out what was back of all of this activity in the Sylvan Glade Development Company stock, and then suddenly you seemed to lose all interest in the matter."

"I had a good punch in the eye," Elkins said. "I suddenly realized that my health was worth more than a few dollars. I felt that I would go to work the next day, when I felt better."

"Go to work in what way?"

"I intended to call on Mr. Doxey and ask to inspect the stock ledger. I intended to find out how many shares of stock Lutts had bought from Neffs and intended to force some sort of a showdown."

"Neffs had been generally opposed to your policies in the company?"

"Quite frequently. We didn't get along."

"Is it true that Lutts was rather belligerent in his reactions?"

"Objected to as incompetent, irrelevant and immaterial, and not proper cross-examination, calling for a conclusion of the witness," Hamilton Burger said.

"I think I'll permit that question," Judge Sedgwick said. "The objection is overruled."

"Well, he was always inclined to start a counteroffensive in case anyone tramped on his toes."

"Exactly," Mason said. "So, in case someone had fired a shot at him and had missed, the natural reaction for George Lutts would have been to turn and charge his assailant."

"Your Honor," Hamilton Burger protested, "I object to that question on the ground that it's not proper cross-examination, that it's argumentative, that it calls for a conclusion of the witness, that it invades the province of the jury and——"

"You don't need to go any further," Judge Sedgwick said. "The objection is sustained. This question is clearly objectionable, Mr. Mason."

"I am trying to establish a certain fact," Mason said, "and——"

"The Court knows quite well what you're trying to establish," Judge Sedgwick said. "You're entitled to cross-examine this witness, and when you argue the case to the jury, you are entitled to engage in any reasonable surmise. But you can't use this witness as a sounding board against which to make a premature argument to the jury. Now, go ahead."

Mason said, "In view of the Court's ruling, I feel that I have explored this phase of the matter as far as I can go."

"I think you have, too," Judge Sedgwick said. "However, I'm not going to preclude you from framing questions."

"Now this mysterious affair that you had with the motorist out there when you got your black eye, did you——?"

"I object to characterizing this as a mysterious affair," Hamilton Burger said. "Counsel can frame his questions so that he leaves out all of this argumentative material——"

"Objection overruled," Judge Sedgwick said. "If counsel wishes to refer to it as a mysterious affair, he has that right. The witness can explain the situation, if he wishes. Go ahead, Mr. Mason. I believe you were interrupted by the objection."

"This mysterious accident that you had," Mason continued, "you don't know with whom you had the altercation?"

"There was nothing mysterious about it; it was just a roadside altercation."

"You didn't get the man's name?"

"No."

"You didn't get the license number of his car?"

"No."

"Why not?"

"I didn't choose to report it."

"What kind of a car was he driving?"

"A big car."

"Do you know the make?"

"No."

Mason announced suddenly, "I have no further questions on cross-examination."

Judge Sedgwick glanced up in quick surprise.

Hamilton Burger heaved a sigh of relief. "That, Your Honor, is the people's case," he said. "The prosecution rests."

"The defense will proceed," Judge Sedgwick announced.

"Yes, Your Honor," Mason said.

"Call your first witness," Judge Sedgwick said. "Or do you wish to make an opening statement at this time?"

"No, Your Honor," Mason said, "I'll waive my opening statement. As my first witness I'll call——" He looked around the courtroom——"Enright Harlan."

Hamilton Burger's face showed unmistakable surprise.

"Come forward and take the stand, Mr. Harlan," Judge Sedgwick directed.

Enright Harlan came forward, held up his right hand and was sworn.

"Your name is Enright A. Harlan? You are the husband of the defendant in this case?"

"Yes, sir."

"You have your residence at 609 Lamison Avenue in this city?"

"Yes, sir."

"You are a sportsman, an outdoor man, a hunter?"

"I do quite a bit of hunting and fishing."

"You are in the real estate business?"

"Yes."

"As a realtor, you sold Mrs. Roxy Claffin certain property to the north of the Sylvan Glade Development Company?"

"Just a moment," Hamilton Burger said. "I object, Your Honor. This is incompetent, irrelevant and immaterial."

"It is merely preliminary," Mason said.

"If the Court please," Hamilton Burger protested, "here is a witness whom I couldn't call. The law specifically provides that in a case of this sort, the husband cannot be a witness against his wife, unless the wife consents. Counsel for the defense is, therefore, in a position to call this very, very friendly witness. I therefore insist that the examination be conducted within the strict limits laid down by the law."

Judge Sedgwick ruled, "The question, quite obviously, is preliminary, so the witness may answer it."

"Yes," Enright Harlan said, "I did some work for Mrs. Claffin."

"When did you first meet Mrs. Claffin?"

"About . . . about eight or ten months ago."

"How did you meet her?"

"She looked me up."

"You weren't introduced to her by any members of the board of directors of the Sylvan Glade Development Company?"

"No," Harlan said, smiling faintly. "The situation was the other way around. She introduced me to one of the directors—Herbert Doxey."

"Did you meet any of the other directors through her?"

"No."

"You have a collection of revolvers?"

"I had seven revolvers, yes."

"How many do you have now?"

"I have the full quota of revolvers, with the exception of the one taken by the police. It is in evidence as the fatal weapon in this case."

"So that you have six revolvers left?"

"That's right."

"You heard the testimony about the revolver which has been introduced in evidence and which is described as the fatal weapon?"

"Yes."

"Is that your gun?"

"Mr. Mason," the witness said, "this is putting me in a very uncomfortable position. I don't want to testify against my wife in this matter, and I——"

"Nevertheless," Mason said, "whether it's a disagreeable task or not, I'm asking you to answer the questions."

"Well . . . I . . . yes, it's my gun. I sent my secretary to pick it up when I bought it, which is why the name on the gun register is not in my handwriting."

"Now then," Mason said, "you got to know Mrs. Claffin quite well in connection with your business deals?"

"What do you mean by that?"

"You saw a good deal of her?"

"She had some real estate matters and——"

"Answer the question. You saw a good deal of her?"

"I was there quite a bit, yes."

"She was living there alone in a house to the north of the Sylvan Glade Development Company's holdings?"

"Yes."

"Rather a nice house?"

"Yes."

"Did you," Mason asked, "at any time discuss with her the question of her personal safety, living out in an isolated district that way?"

"Objected to as incompetent, irrelevant and immaterial, calling for hearsay testimony," Hamilton Burger said.

"Sustained," Judge Sedgwick ruled.

"Did you ever take it upon yourself to give her lessons in shooting a revolver?"

"Yes."

"What revolver did you use?"

"It was one of mine."

"Out of your collection?"

"Yes."

"Did you," Mason asked, "ever give Roxy Claffin a revolver from your collection for her personal protection?"

"Objected to as incompetent, irrelevant and immaterial," Burger said.

"Overruled," Judge Sedgwick said, his voice showing sudden interest.

"Answer the question," Mason said.

"I . . . well, as a matter of fact, I did."

"When?"

"I would say about . . . oh, sometime in April."

"Some two months prior to the murder?"

"Something like that."

"She still has the weapon?"

"No, she returned it to me."

"When?"

"Objected to as incompetent, irrelevant and immaterial," Hamilton Burger said.

Judge Sedgwick looked at Mason, looked at the district attorney. Suddenly, at something he saw in Mason's face, the judge settled back in his swivel chair and said, "The objection is overruled. Answer the question."

Harlan said, "She returned the weapon to me on May thirtieth. She said she was more afraid of the gun than of prowlers, that she was such a poor shot she couldn't hit a man anyway."

"That was on May thirtieth?"

"Yes."

"What did you do with that weapon?"

"I put it back in my collection of weapons."

"When?"

"That afternoon."

"What kind of a weapon was it?"

"A Smith and Wesson revolver."

"Similar to the People's exhibit in this case?"

"The same type of weapon. I buy revolvers in pairs, so that I can do target shooting with a friend and we will both have the same type of weapon."

"Do you keep your weapons insured?"

"We have an over-all comprehensive policy, covering breakage, theft, loss."

"Do you keep a record showing the numbers of your various guns?"

"Objected to as incompetent, irrelevant and immaterial," Marvin Pierson, the trial deputy, said. "It is, if the Court please, completely extraneous, entirely removed from the subject matter of this case."

"Objection overruled."

"Yes, I keep a list of numbers."

"Do you have that list with you?"

"No, of course not."

Mason turned and caught the eye of Paul Drake. The lawyer signaled the detective.

Mason stood for a long moment facing Enright Harlan. "Where do you keep your firearms, Mr. Harlan?" he asked.

"My rifles and shotguns are kept in a series of gun cabinets with glass doors. My shotguns——"

"How about your revolvers?"

"They are kept in a concealed, locked container."

"A *locked* container?"

"Yes. It's a specially constructed compartment."

"That container or compartment is always kept locked?"

"Yes, sir. I am very particular about that. I have a very high-grade lock on it. It is one which I am assured cannot be picked. There are only two keys to that lock. I have always been apprehensive lest some burglar break into the house, steal my revolvers, and use them in a career of crime. These revolvers are therefore kept in a locked wall compartment, concealed behind a sliding panel."

"There are two keys to that receptacle?"

"Yes."

"You have one?"

"Yes."

"Who has the other?"

"Now just a moment," Judge Sedgwick said, interrupting the witness. "Don't answer that question, Mr. Harlan. Mr. Mason."

"Yes, Your Honor."

"A peculiar situation has developed in this case."

"Yes, Your Honor."

"As the district attorney has pointed out, the prosecution has no power to call this witness. He cannot be examined for or against the defendant in this case without the permission of the wife."

"I am familiar with the law, Your Honor."

"Therefore, it would seem that certain evidence which might be directly adverse to the defendant in this case can only be brought out through this witness, and that you are the only one having the power to bring it out."

"Yes, Your Honor."

"But you are charged with representing the interests of the defendant. The Court does not want to see the interests of the defendant jeopardized. The Court points out to you your professional responsibility in this matter."

"Yes, Your Honor."

"Under those circumstances, do you still insist upon an answer to this question?"

"I do, Your Honor."

"It is most unusual," Judge Sedgwick said.

"It is an unusual case, Your Honor."

Judge Sedgwick's lips tightened. "The Court is without power to prevent this situation if—Mrs. Harlan."

Sybil Harlan looked up.

"Do you object to having your husband called as a witness in this case?" Judge Sedgwick asked.

"Not if Mr. Mason says that is the thing to do."

Judge Sedgwick sighed. "Very well, the witness will answer the question."

"Who had the other key?" Mason asked.

"My wife."

Judge Sedgwick frowned, started to say something, checked himself.

"So that the only two persons who could possibly have access to that receptacle where the revolvers are kept are you and your wife?"

"That's right."

The swinging doors of the courtroom were pulled aside. Wheels creaked, as Paul Drake and an assistant, pushing a four-wheeled hand truck with loudly squeaking wheels, entered the courtroom.

"What is this?" Judge Sedgwick asked.

"If the Court please," Mason said, "I must beg the indulgence of the Court, but as a part of my case it is necessary for me to introduce in evidence some material that has been discarded by one of the . . . well, it is very heavy material. This was the only way I could bring it to Court. I am sorry it is necessary to interrupt proceedings at this time——"

"You should have waited until the Court takes its recess," Judge Sedgwick said. "This is a disturbance we cannot tolerate."

"But," Mason said, "I need this evidence as a part of my case."

"Well——" Judge Sedgwick raised his eyes, looked across the room at Paul Drake. "You there—with that truck!"

"Yes, Your Honor," Paul Drake said.

"Wait there until counsel finishes the examination of this witness, and then the Court will take a brief recess.

"Now, go ahead, Mr. Mason. We cannot stand such interruptions . . . and it seems to me you could have secured a more silent truck."

"Yes, Your Honor."

"Proceed with the examination of this witness."

Mason turned to the witness. "I want you to check your remaining revolvers with the list of numbers, and I want you to produce that list of numbers."

"Oh, Your Honor," Hamilton Burger said, "this is entirely beside the point."

"If the Court please," Mason said, "I intend to connect this up. I will assure the Court that this is a very vital part of my defense. I want this witness to get the list of numbers on those revolvers and to check the revolvers. I want a complete inventory."

"I don't see why, Mr. Mason," Judge Sedgwick said. "According to the testimony which you yourself have now introduced, that weapon is now definitely brought home to the possession of this witness, the husband of the defendant. I fail to see what can be ascertained by finding out anything about the other remaining weapons."

Mason said, "I might wish to prove, at least by inference, that someone else had access to that locked receptacle."

Judge Sedgwick stroked his chin. "Well, of course, that is a different matter."

He turned to the witness. "How long will it take you to go to your house, get the list of numbers, open that receptacle and check the weapons that are in it?"

"I would say probably forty-five minutes to an hour. It will take about that to get out there, open the place, find the list, check the numbers and get back to court."

"I want the witness to do that," Mason said.

"You have some other witness you can put on while that is being done?" Judge Sedgwick asked.

"Unfortunately, Your Honor, I do not. I am going to ask the Court to take an adjournment until one-thirty this afternoon. I feel that we are entitled to this because this case is running well ahead of schedule, and I think that in large part this has been due to my desire to cooperate with the Court and counsel in getting the facts before the Court."

Judge Sedgwick shook his head. "I appreciate counsel's co-operation. However, the Court cannot take such a long recess. The Court will adjourn until eleven-thirty. I feel that Mr. Harlan can get out there and back in that time. The Court will ask one of the officers to provide Mr. Harlan with police transportation. This may expedite matters somewhat. You will get out there, get that list, and get back just as soon as possible, Mr. Harlan. Court will take a recess until eleven-thirty."

Spectators started filing from the courtroom. Mason stood up, signaled Paul Drake and received in return an affirmative signal. Then Drake and his assistant started pushing the heavily loaded four-wheeled truck down the aisle of the courtroom, while astonished spectators regarded the cloth-covered load with curiosity.

Mason turned to Sybil Harlan.

"All right," he said. "We've made our gamble. We've put all of our chips on the turn of a card. By eleven-thirty you'll either hit the jackpot or you'll be headed for the gas chamber or for life imprisonment."

Mason moved over to hold the swinging gate in the bar open for the passage of the squeaking truck. As the two men pushed the heavy truck through, the lawyer moved up alongside Drake.

"Everything's covered?" he asked.

"Everything's covered. If any one of those persons on that list you gave me leaves the courtroom, he'll be followed by detectives who are too skillful to lose a trail—at least, when a man's in a hurry."

"He'll be in a hurry," Mason said.

"Can you tell me what you're trying to do, Perry?"

Mason grinned. "I'm laying a trap for a nervous accomplice."

17

.

AT ELEVEN-TEN PAUL DRAKE PUSHED A MEMO INTO MA-
son's hand. The note read, "Herbert Doxey drove like
mad to his house, opened the garage door, unlocked the
door of a closet in his garage, then emerged and is now
driving back this way at a leisurely pace."

Promptly at eleven-thirty Judge Sedgwick reconvened
court.

"Is it stipulated that the defendant is in court and
that the jurors are all present, gentlemen?" he asked.

"So stipulated," Mason said.

"You were examining Enright Harlan, Mr. Mason."

"Unfortunately, he has not returned as yet," Mason
said. "I——"

"Then proceed with some other witness," Judge Sedgwick said. "You can put Mr. Harlan on the stand as
soon as he comes in."

"Very well," Mason said. "I will call Herbert Doxey
to the stand."

Doxey came forward and was sworn.

"You are the son-in-law of the decedent?" Mason
asked.

"That is right," Doxey said in a low voice.

"You are acquainted with the property of the Sylvan
Glade Development Company?"

"Yes, sir."

"And with that of Mrs. Roxy Claffin which adjoins
the Sylvan Glade property to the north?"

"Yes, sir."

"How long have you known Mrs. Claffin, by the way?" Mason asked.

The witness hesitated.

Mason looked up, simulating surprise at the witness's hesitance. "Can't you answer that?"

"I . . . I'm trying to think."

Hamilton Burger, suddenly observing the expression on the witness's face, jumped to his feet. "I object to the question. It is incompetent, irrelevent and immaterial."

"It is preliminary, Your Honor," Mason said.

Hamilton Burger became vociferous. "It doesn't make any difference, Your Honor. It is completely incompetent, irrelevant and immaterial. This has no bearing whatsoever on the issues in this case. This is——"

"The objection is sustained," Judge Sedgwick snapped. "The Court considers that question highly improper, Mr. Mason."

"I might assure the Court that it is——"

"The Court desires no argument whatever on that question."

"Very well," Mason said, turning to the witness. "You knew that Roxy Claffin had taken certain articles from her garage and put them on a dump heap yesterday morning?"

"Just a moment, just a moment," Hamilton Burger shouted. "The same objection, Your Honor. An attempt to cross-examine his own witness. Incompetent, irrelevant——"

"Sustained," Judge Sedgwick snapped.

Mason turned to look at the door of the courtroom. "It appears, Your Honor, that Enright Harlan has now returned to court. In accordance with the understanding of the Court, I would like to withdraw this witness from the stand and return Mr. Harlan to the stand."

"Very well," Judge Sedgwick snapped. "This witness

will be temporarily excused. Mr. Harlan, you will come forward and take the stand."

Harlan came forward, apparently rather reluctantly. He sat in the witness chair and glanced at Mason with a puzzled frown.

Mason said, "Now, you have been out to your house during the recess of the court, Mr. Harlan?"

"Yes, sir."

"You unlocked the concealed compartment where you keep your revolvers?"

"Yes, sir."

Mason glanced at the clock on the wall of the courtroom. "You found that lock in perfect working order?"

"Yes, sir."

"Was there any evidence that the receptacle had been tampered with?"

"No external evidence, no."

"That receptacle is concealed behind a sliding panel in the wall?"

"Yes, sir."

"You say there was no external evidence that the receptacle had been tampered with?" Mason said. "Was there any internal evidence?"

"Well—" The witness hesitated, then said, "In a way, yes. There is something I can't understand."

"You had a list of the numbers of the revolvers that are in your possession?" Mason asked.

"Yes, sir."

"And you were accompanied by an officer?"

"Yes, sir."

"And you checked the numbers of those guns against the list?"

"Yes, sir."

"Were they all there?"

"Yes, sir. But . . . but one of the weapons in there isn't mine."

"It isn't?" Mason asked, as though the answer surprised him.

"No."

"And what weapon is this?"

"This is a Smith and Wesson, thirty-eight caliber revolver with a five-inch barrel, and . . . well, it was . . . it was just like mine, but it has a number on it that isn't on my list."

"Do you have any idea how that weapon got into your collection?"

"No, sir, I don't. I thought . . . well, I thought that everything was all right, and now I suddenly find I have an extra revolver in my collection—and that one of *my* revolvers is missing."

"Now then," Mason said, "I want you to listen to this question carefully. Could that weapon which you found in there have been the weapon which Mrs. Roxy Claffin gave you on May thirtieth?"

"Yes, it *could* have been."

"In other words, on May thirtieth you took the weapon which Mrs. Claffin gave you and, as I understand it, you went to your house, you slid back the panel which concealed the metal receptacle, you unlocked that receptacle and put the weapon inside, did you not?"

"Yes."

"And at that time, what can you say with reference to the number of weapons that you had?"

"They checked."

"But you didn't check the numbers on the weapons with the list that you had?"

"No, sir. There was no reason to do so."

"In other words, your weapon collection checked out numerically until the discovery of the so-called fatal weapon?"

"That's right—with the understanding, of course, that my wife had one weapon in her glove compartment. She had told me she was taking one."

"Thank you," Mason said. "That's all."

Judge Sedgwick said, "The Court notices that it has

reached the hour for the noon adjournment. The Court will take a recess until two o'clock this afternoon."

Mason beckoned to Paul Drake, said, "Paul, we're going to have to get out of here without meeting any reporters. We can head for the judge's chambers, hurry down the corridor, hit the stairs to the lower floor, and catch the elevator there. Let's go! You have one of your men guarding that bunch of junk on the truck?"

"I have a good man there," Drake said. "No one's going to take a look under that cloth until you say so."

"That's fine," Mason told him. "Let's go. Come on, Della."

They hurried through the door as though going to the judge's chambers, then detoured to an exit door, sprinted down the corridor, down a flight of stairs and took an elevator.

Mason got his car and said, "The first thing to do is to get out to Herbert Doxey's place before Doxey realizes what's up."

"Just what is up?" Drake asked.

"We'll darn soon find out," Mason said. "But you can see what happened. The third shell in the murder weapon is the one that is significant."

"The bullet that went with that third shell never has been located," Drake said.

"That's the significant part of it," Mason told him. "There wasn't any bullet."

"What do you mean?"

"Wait and see," Mason said.

The lawyer piloted the car skillfully through traffic, arrived at Doxey's house. The three of them ran up the walk and pressed the bell button. Mrs. Doxey came to the door, regarded them in surprise.

"We want to look in your garage for a moment, Mrs. Doxey," Mason said.

"Why . . . where's Herbert?"

"We left him up at court. He was in conference and——"

"Why, if it's all right with him, it's all right with me," she said. "Help yourself."

"Thank you," Mason said, and led the way out to the garage.

He went at once to the closet in the back of the garage. "Do you have the key for this?" he asked Mrs. Doxey as he tried the door.

"I have a key in with my extra household keys. We haven't been keeping it locked lately. Herbert had this designed so we could keep his tools in a safe place. People got to stealing his tools and——"

"Yes, yes, I know," Mason interrupted impatiently, "but we want to get in there right away."

"Well, I'll run and get my key," she promised.

She entered the house, was back within less than a minute with a key. Mason unlocked the door, then took the key out of the lock and handed it to her. "Thank you very much, Mrs. Doxey," he said.

For a moment she remained with them out of curiosity, then said, "Well, if you'll excuse me, I've got lunch ready to put on the table. I expect Herbert at any moment."

Mason turned on a light in the closet. "There you are, Paul," he said. "There's the disappearing junk."

"But what the deuce is it?" Drake asked.

"Don't you see?" Mason asked. "Those boards were part of a carefully constructed shooting stand. The box of scrap iron was used to hold it steady at the bottom. Those canvas sacks which have been ripped open were filled with sand. Here, look at them. You can see some of the sand still clinging to the inside. A magnifying glass will show it very plainly.

"Did you ever see an expert marksman testing a gun from a rest, Paul? He sits on a stool and holds his arm along a shelf, where sandbags furnish a brace for his arm. He rests his hand holding the gun on a sandbag which has been partially filled with sand, she he can scoop out a place for the gun and his hand. He takes careful aim from this position and squeezes the trigger.

"That shooting stand had been carefully planted in the contractor's shack. There is a knothole in the shack, and a gun could have been lined up so the bullet went through that knothole, sped directly to the house up on the hill and into Lutts' chest. That accounts for the upward course of the bullet."

Drake looked at the lawyer with complete bewilderment. "You're crazy, Perry."

"Why am I crazy?"

"The powder pattern shows that the fatal bullet was fired from a distance of eighteen to twenty inches. Furthermore, Roxy Claffin has an ironclad alibi and Doxey has an alibi. He was out taking a sun bath and——"

"In an enclosure that was concealed by a canvas curtain," Mason said.

"But he has a sunburned back to prove it. He was out too long and— Gosh, Perry, one of my men got a look at his back. It was really red and irritated."

Mason grinned at Paul Drake and said, "It was a slick scheme, Paul, but we're going to tear it to pieces."

"Well, I'd like to know how," Drake said.

"Be in court this afternoon and you'll find out," Mason told him.

13

■

Judge Sedgwick called court to order and looked at Perry Mason with a peculiarly speculative expression. "Mr. Harlan was on the stand," he said.

"I have no further questions of Mr. Harlan," Mason said.

"Cross-examination?" Judge Sedgwick asked Hamilton Burger.

The district attorney was quite frankly puzzled. "Not at this time," he said. "I may want to recall him later for a question or two, if I may do that, Your Honor."

"No objection, no objection in the least," Mason said affably. "Now, I believe that Herbert Doxey was on the stand. Will Mr. Doxey come forward, please?"

There was silence.

"Call Mr. Doxey. Herbert Doxey," Judge Sedgwick said.

The voice of the bailiff boomed through the courtroom. A loud-speaker in the corridor blared out, *"Herbert Doxey."*

"Apparently, he hasn't returned from lunch yet," Mason said casually. "Oh well, we'll call Mrs. Roxy Calffin."

"Mrs. Claffin, come forward," the bailiff intoned.

Roxy Claffin jumped to her feet. "Why . . . why . . . I don't know anything. I——"

"Come forward and be sworn," Mason said.

She came forward reluctantly, a beautiful woman with

a peaches-and-cream complexion which was now suddenly dead white with panic.

"Hold up your right hand and be sworn," the judge said.

Her hand was shaking visibly as she held it up.

"Now, sit down in that witness chair," Mason said, "and tell us about the load of junk you took out to the dump yesterday morning, Mrs. Claffin."

"I object. That's incompetent, irrelevant and immaterial," Hamilton Burger said.

Mason said, "I'll connect it up, Your Honor."

"I think you'd better lay your foundation then, Mr. Mason. The Court believes the objection should be sustained at this time."

"Very well," Mason said.

Mason turned to the witness. "You knew, did you not, that Herbert Doxey had been using the unpainted contractor's shack on your property for the purpose of doing some work?"

"Why . . . he had a right to. He was the secretary of the company that was cooperating with me in———"

"Please answer the question," Mason said. "You knew he was doing some work out in that shack?"

"Yes. He said he wanted to put in some tables for drafting and doing some confidential work there. He asked me to say nothing about it to anyone."

"Now then, Enright Harlan loaned you a revolver?"
"Yes."

"What happened to that revolver?"

"I returned it to him, just as he said, on the thirtieth day of May."

"*Why* did you return it?"

"I was afraid to have the gun around. I'm a very poor shot and . . . well, guns terrify me."

"Had you ever shown that gun to Herbert Doxey?"

"Why, yes. Mr. Doxey knew that I was shooting with Mr. Harlan. He had been a crack shot, and he wanted to give me some instruction."

"Did he ever handle that weapon?"

"You mean the one that Mr. Harlan gave me?"

"Yes."

"Why, yes, I believe he did."

"Under such circumstances that he could have substituted weapons, so that the weapon you returned to Mr. Harlan on May thirtieth could have been a weapon substituted by Mr. Doxey?"

"Your Honor," Hamilton Burger said, "that question is objected to as incompetent, irrelevant and immaterial, no proper foundation laid, argumentative, and assuming a fact not in evidence. There is no evidence whatever that anyone substituted weapons."

Judge Sedgwick was watching the witness's face with steady concentration. "The Court wants to hear this evidence, Mr. District Attorney," he said.

"But, Your Honor, if the Court please, the jury is present and——"

"The objection is overruled. Sit down."

"Answer the question," Mason said.

"Yes," Roxy Claffin said in a low voice. "I . . . I guess there *could* have been a substitution. It *was* possible."

"You *knew* there had been a substitution, didn't you?" Mason asked.

"Oh, Your Honor," Hamilton Burger said, "counsel is now seeking to cross-examine his own witness and . . . well, if the Court please, this whole inquiry is now going far, far afield."

"It may be the field we want to be in," Judge Sedgwick said sternly. "Let's follow up this line of questioning a little more.

"Mrs. Claffin."

"Yes, Judge."

"Call me 'Your Honor.' "

"Yes, Your Honor."

"Did you know that the revolver which you returned

to Mr. Harlan on May thirtieth had been substituted?"

"I . . . I don't think I have to answer that question."

"I think you do," Judge Sedgwick said. "You will be in contempt of Court unless you answer, or unless you adopt the position that the answer would tend to incriminate you. Was that revolver which you returned on May thirtieth substituted or not?"

The witness suddenly began to cry.

"Answer the question," Judge Sedgwick said.

"Yes," she said, "it was a substituted gun that I returned."

"You knew it was substituted?" Judge Sedgwick asked.

"Yes."

"Who told you?"

"Herbert Doxey knew that I . . . that I . . . well, that I wouldn't be too upset if anything should happen to Mrs. Harlan, and he told me that all I had to do was follow his instructions and that I could have Enright Harlan all to myself."

For a long moment there was silence in the courtroom and then suddenly there was a ripple of voices from the spectators.

Judge Sedgwick banged angrily with his gavel. "Silence in the courtroom!" he shouted. "Mr. Mason, proceed with your examination."

Mason said, "Did you know Doxey was planning to kill his father-in-law?"

With tears streaming down her cheeks, Roxy Claffin shook her head. "Not then."

"But you knew afterwards?"

"I . . . no, I didn't *know*."

"You knew that Herbert Doxey was in that contractor's shack when you and Enright Harlan left to see your lawyer?"

"Yes." The voice was almost a whisper.

"Afterwards, you realized what must have happened and you were afraid you would be implicated, so you went to the contractor's shack and cleared it out."

"Not that," she said. "Mr. Doxey cleared it out and put the things in my garage, and then when I thought the coast was clear, I took them down to deposit them on the dump."

"And told Mr. Doxey what you had done?"

"Yes."

Mason smiled affably at Hamilton Burger. "Go ahead and cross-examine, Mr. Burger. This is your witness."

Hamilton Burger was looking at the witness with an expression of dazed surprise on his face. "I . . . I . . . I think I should . . . Your Honor, I'd like to have a recess."

Judge Sedgwick nodded. "The Court would, too. The Court is going to take a thirty-minute recess. During that time the jury will remember the admonition of the Court. You will not form or express any opinion concerning this case, nor permit yourself to be addressed by anyone concerning the case, nor will you discuss it among yourselves. Court will reconvene in thirty minutes."

Judge Sedgwick got up and stalked into his chambers. Behind him the courtroom was bedlam.

"Come on," Mason said to Della Street. "Let's get away from this and into the witness room. We're on the homestretch now, and it's all downhill," and Mason grinned reassuringly at the bewildered Sybil Harlan.

19

■

Mason, Della Street, Sybil Harlan, Paul Drake and a policewoman sat in the witness room to one side of the courtroom.

"Will you kindly tell me what this is all about?" Drake asked. "How could the powder pattern have shown that the gun was held within eighteen or twenty inches of Lutts' chest if he had been shot by Doxey down there in that contractor's shack?"

Mason grinned. "That's the third cartridge, Paul."

"What do you mean 'the third cartridge?' "

"The U.M.C. That cartridge was a blank. The bullet had been extracted and the powder held in place with a chalk paste, which would disintegrate when the gun was fired. Doxey wanted it to appear that Lutts had been killed by someone standing at close range, so he went back after the murder and fired the blank cartridge at the body from a distance of twenty inches.

"He had intended to lure Lutts out to the house and kill him at a time when it appeared he had an unshakable alibi, and then Mrs. Harlan entered the picture, and it was a heaven-sent opportunity for Doxey."

"How do you mean?"

Mason said, "Remember, Doxey had spent some time out there in that contractor's shack, safely concealed. He could look through the knothole and see the window up there in the house on the hill. But no one could see him. Only Roxy Claffin knew that he was there, and she wasn't telling anyone for obvious reasons.

"So Doxey knew that Sybil Harlan was keeping the premises under regular survey. He knew that if he could make it appear that Lutts had been killed with a gun carried by Sybil Harlan, he would have committed the perfect crime and Mrs. Harlan would be the one who would have to take the rap.

"Doubtless, at first, he simply intended to show that Mrs. Harlan had been going out to the house pretty regularly, and then finding Lutts killed with the gun she had been carrying would present a case of circumstantial evidence she could never refute and——"

"What about the gun?" Drake said. "I still don't get it."

"That," Mason said, "was simple. Enright Harlan gave Roxy Claffin a gun. Doxey took that gun. He purchased one just like it and gave it to Roxy, with instructions to return it to Harlan. It was exactly the same make, model, size and caliber as the one Enright Harlan had loaned to Roxy Claffin. Naturally, Harlan had no reason to compare numbers. He certainly thought it was the same weapon he had given her. So he took it and put it back in his collection and thought his guns were all accounted for. He was willing to swear the gun he loaned Roxy had been returned. Actually, the gun that he had given Roxy Claffin was then in the possession of Herbert Doxey.

"Doxey knew that Mrs. Harlan was carrying one of her husband's guns in her glove compartment. He also knew from Lutts that she was at the beauty parlor that day. He had only to kill Lutts with one of Harlan's guns, leave it where he knew it would be discovered at the proper time, then dash up to the parking lot, watch his opportunity to get into Mrs. Harlan's car, jimmy open her glove compartment, take the gun, and that's all there was to it. He had committed the perfect crime.

"Then Roxy Claffin got concerned about having things in her garage which she knew were telltale evidence. So she took the stuff out and threw it on the dump. She told Herbert Doxey what she had done, and Doxey became panic-stricken. He was afraid that someone might find the sandbags which had been cut open and the sand dumped out, the boards from the shooting stand and the stool. He was terribly afraid someone might put two and two together, particularly if that someone had ever done any shooting from a sandbag rest.

"So Doxey slipped out and picked up all that stuff and took it to his own garage. That was where he gave us the break we wanted. His accomplice had been too nervous, and Doxey, trying to cover up, made a fatal slip.

"However, if he hadn't done this, we would have learned the true facts anyway."

"How?"

"Elkins really gave the whole show away. Lutts was dying to learn the identity of my client. He went out to lunch with Doxey. During lunch he learned who had retained me."

"From the bank," Drake said.

Mason shook his head. "He had no chance to contact the bank."

"Of course he did, Perry. He made a phone call, don't you remember?"

"*One* phone call," Mason said.

"Well, that was enough," Drake retorted, his voice showing an impatience at what appeared to be Mason's stupidity.

"Only *one* phone call," Mason said, "and that was to Enright Harlan's house. Remember, the maid told Mrs. Harlan that Lutts had called and she told Lutts he could reach Mrs. Harlan at the beauty shop. Elkins swears there was only *one* call. He's positive of that."

"Then, how the devil *did* he find out?" Drake asked.

"Don't you see, Paul? It's the key clue. Doxey told him."

"Doxey!"

"That's right. Doxey had been watching the house on

the hill. He knew of Sybil's interest. He put two and two together when I entered the picture. He knew who had retained me. He communicated his knowledge to Lutts at lunch, and told him my client must have discovered something on the grounds or in the house which changed the value of the property. He probably suggested that Lutts make her go out there with him and show him just what it was. Doxey did this because he wanted Lutts to go out there to the house. He'd tried to lure Lutts out there by sending him an anonymous letter calculated to send Lutts running out to his death.

"But then I entered the picture and it gave Doxey a wonderful opportunity. He stopped by home to establish an alibi, then dashed out to the contractor's shack while Lutts was calling for Mrs. Harlan at the beauty shop.

"Doxey was the only one who could have told Lutts who my client was. The very fact he told us that Lutts found out through a banking leak shows he was lying.

"Doxey's alibi is a badly sunburned back. He could have gotten that lying in his curtain-enclosed sun bath, or he could have gotten it after he murdered his father-in-law by the brief use of a quartz lamp."

"I'll be damned!" Drake said. "But if Doxey missed that first shot, how did it happen that——"

"He didn't miss that first shot," Mason said. "That bullet had been fired two or three days before the murder, when Doxey was testing the gun and his accuracy. He fired one shot, which went through the window and into the wall. That was all the assurance he needed that he was in form and could count on picking Lutts off with one shot.

"It only remained for him to get Lutts out there at a time when Sybil was there or had been there. He hoped the anonymous letter would accomplish it; but when I entered the picture, he considered it a heaven-sent opportunity. Lutts had told me he was going to have his books audited. I'm sorry to say, the significance of that didn't dawn on me until a short time ago. Undoubtedly, Herbert Doxey had been manipulating the books of the corporation and he knew that his father-in-law was getting suspicious."

"Where's Doxey now, Perry?"

"Panic-stricken, trying to make an escape and thereby clinching the case against him."

The door of the room was abruptly pushed open. Enright Harlan came striding in. Sybil arose from her chair.

"Sybil!" Enright said, and took her in his arms, patting her shoulder.

"Oh, Enny," she said, "it's been terrible! Thank you so much for standing by me."

Enright Harlan looked guilty. "Hang it, Sybil," he said, "I lost my head. I . . . I did things I shouldn't. I——"

Sybil Harlan straightened. "Why, what are you talking about, Enny? I told you I understood you were making a play for that Claffin woman, in order to get her business. I knew that she was the vain type that demanded lots of attention and flattery. Why you did *just* right, Enny. You *had* to make a living for the firm of Harlan and Harlan."

"You forgive me?" he asked.

Her laugh was clear. "Why, Enny, there's nothing to forgive! Don't be silly. Let's not even talk about it."

There was a knock at the door. The bailiff said, "Judge Sedgwick wants the parties in court. Mrs. Claffin has made a complete confession. The police are searching for Herbert Doxey, and the judge wants to instruct the jury to return a verdict of not guilty in the case against Mrs. Harlan."

Sybil linked her arm through that of her husband. "Come on, Enny. Let's get this over with. Forget about the past."

Perry Mason, Della Street and Paul Drake remained behind for a moment.

"Well, I'll be darned," Drake said, as the others went

out through the door. "The way she handled that—and all the time she looked so damn demure, so utterly innocent!"

"Women," Mason said, "are at their most deadly dangerous when they look like that."

Della Street glanced up at Perry Mason. "Come on, Chief," she said solicitously. "You've had a sleepless night. Get this case over with and then go and get some rest."

Drake, looking at Della Street's face, said, "Darned if you aren't looking demure and innocent yourself, Della!"

The glance she flashed Drake held nothing of gratitude.

How to do <u>almost</u> everything

What are the latest time and money-saving shortcuts for painting, papering, and varnishing floors, walls, ceilings, furniture? (See pages 102-111 of HOW TO DO *Almost* EVERYTHING.) What are the mini-recipes and the new ways to make food—from appetizers through desserts—exciting and delicious? (See pages 165-283.) How-to-do-it ideas like these have made Bert Bacharach, father of the celebrated composer (Burt), one of the most popular columnists in America.

This remarkable new book, HOW TO DO *Almost* EVERYTHING, is a fact-filled collection of Bert Bacharach's practical aids, containing thousands of tips and hints—for keeping house, gardening, cooking, driving, working, traveling, caring for children. It will answer hundreds of your questions, briefly and lucidly.

How to do <u>almost</u> everything

is chock-full of useful information—information on almost everything you can think of, arranged by subject in short, easy-to-read tidbits, with an alphabetical index to help you find your way around —and written with the famed Bacharach touch.

SEND FOR YOUR FREE EXAMINATION COPY TODAY

We invite you to mail the coupon below. A copy of HOW TO DO *Almost* EVERYTHING will be sent to you at once. If at the end of ten days you do not feel that this book is one you will treasure, you may return it and owe nothing. Otherwise, we will bill you $6.95, plus postage and handling. At all bookstores, or write to Simon and Schuster, Dept. S-52, 630 Fifth Ave., New York, N.Y. 10020.

SIMON AND SCHUSTER, Dept. S-52
630 Fifth Ave., New York, N.Y. 10020

Please send me a copy of HOW TO DO *ALMOST* EVERYTHING. If after examining it for 10 days, I am not completely delighted, I may return the book and owe nothing. Otherwise, you will bill me for $6.95 plus mailing costs.

Name..

Address...

City:............................State........Zip........

☐ *SAVE!* Enclose $6.95 now and we pay postage. Same 10-day privilege with full refund guaranteed. (N. Y. residents please add applicable sales tax.)

P 66/2

VOLUME TWO
(Over 1,000,000 copies of Volume one sold)

THE WAY THINGS WORK

**From aerosols to video tape
recording. 1,057 two-color drawings.
Clear, concise explanations.**

How do aerosols work? (See page 20 of THE WAY THINGS WORK, VOLUME TWO.) How is foam plastic made? (See page 52.) How can the performance of your automobile's engine be improved? (See page 260.) How does the color get into TV? (See page 288.) What is inertial navigation? (See page 374.) How do safety bindings on skis protect you? (See page 444.) What are the different methods of video tape recording? (See page 560.)

This remarkable book will answer hundreds of your questions (and the "hows" and "whys" your children ask) about theories and their practical application in machines that, seen or unseen, are part of our everyday lives.

Now you can know *The Way Things Work*

Here are concise, carefully detailed descriptions of the principles and the working parts of musical instruments, industrial metallurgy, ballistics, wing geometry, ship stabilizing, automotive engineering, computers, generators—in short, of hundreds of things small and large, simple and complex, that make you wonder, "How does it work?"

And those who *didn't* read Volume One will surely want to take advantage of our offer to obtain *both* of these invaluable reference books that explain the marvels of technology that daily fill our world.

The books that satisfy the curiosity most of us feel when we push a button, or throw a switch, or turn a knob on any one of the hundreds of appliances and machines that surround us with their mysteries.

Send for your free examination copy today

We invite you to mail the coupon. A copy of Volume Two of THE WAY THINGS WORK will be sent to you at once. If at the end of ten days you do not feel that this book is one you will treasure, you may return it and owe nothing. Otherwise, we will bill you for $9.95 plus mailing costs. At all bookstores, or write to Simon and Schuster, Dept. S-54, 630 Fifth Avenue, New York, N.Y. 10020.

**SIMON AND SCHUSTER, Dept. S-54
630 Fifth Avenue, New York, N.Y. 10020**

☐ Send me a copy of *Volume Two* of THE WAY THINGS WORK. If after examining it for 10 days I am not completely delighted, I may return the book and owe nothing. Otherwise, you will bill me for $9.95 plus mailing costs.

☐ Send me for 10 days' free examination, a copy of *Volume One*, at $9.95 plus mailing costs. Same return privilege.

Name...

Address...

City...State........................Zip...................

☐ SAVE. Enclose payment now and publisher pays mailing costs. Same 10-day return privilege with full refund guaranteed. (New York residents please add applicable sales tax.)

P 67/2

How to raise a brighter child

These new methods, based on the theories of famous physicians, educators and behavioral scientists, are simple and fun—and they can increase your child's I. Q. by 20 points or more! Start using them as early as possible—even right after birth!

Imagine a 21-month-old with a reading vocabulary of 160 words...a boy of four who enjoys teaching himself major number principles...a girl not yet four who reads at the third grade level! None of these children was born a genius. Yet, through the early learning concepts described in this remarkable new book—HOW TO RAISE A BRIGHTER CHILD—all are being helped to develop above-average intelligence and a joyous love of learning.

Now you can give your little pre-schooler the same happy advantages...and they may well last throughout your child's life. For according to recent research, a child's I. Q. level is not permanently fixed at birth. It can be raised—or lowered by 20 points or even more in the precious years before six, by the way you rear your child at home.

Take the book now for a 30-day FREE trial

Send now for your copy of HOW TO RAISE A BRIGHTER CHILD. When it arrives, turn to the section that applies to your child *right now*, at this particular stage in his life. Apply some of the early learning techniques it shows you how to use. Then if not convinced this one book can make a world of difference in your child's mental development, return it within 30 days and owe nothing. If you decide to keep the book, it is yours for only $5.95 plus a small mailing charge. Take advantage of this opportunity! See your bookseller or mail the coupon today.

Joan Beck is known by millions of readers who follow her syndicated column, "You And Your Child." A graduate of Northwestern University, holding Bachelor's and Master's degrees, she has received several academic and professional awards and honors. She is married to Ernest W. Beck, a medical illustrator. They have two children, aged 15 and 12.